THE   GENTLEMEN SETTLERS

THE
GENTLEMEN SETTLERS

A Romance of Colonial Australia

PAMELA BLAXLAND

Angus & Robertson · Publishers

For Gar

First published in 1975 by
ANGUS AND ROBERTSON (PUBLISHERS) PTY LTD
102 Glover Street, Cremorne, Sydney
2 Fisher Street, London
159 Boon Keng Road, Singapore
PO Box 1072, Makati MCC, Rizal, Philippines
107 Elizabeth Street, Melbourne
222 East Terrace, Adelaide
167 Queen Street, Brisbane

ISBN 0 207 95637 5

Registered in Australia for transmission by post as a book

Printed in Great Britain by
Butler & Tanner Ltd, Frome and London

The name 'Australia' is purposely not used in this story, since it did not come to be generally accepted until about 1817, some three years after the explorer Flinders had published his *Voyage to Terra Australis*. Prior to this, the western part of Australia was usually known as New Holland, and the eastern section as New South Wales. That the name was gradually coming into use, however, is shown by the fact that John and Harriott named their first daughter to be born after their arrival 'Louisa Australia'.

Similarly, at the beginning of the nineteenth century, Tasmania was known as Van Diemen's Land, and Mauritius as Ile de France.

I would like to thank all the many people who have helped me in the research and writing of this book, and particularly Bruce and Robin Wilson and Mrs Joan Hodgson.

AUTHOR'S NOTE

In the cloisters of Canterbury Cathedral, England, a fourteen-year-old Scholar of King's School one day played truant, and carved the outline of his foot on one of the long stone benches. Inside that outline he laboriously chipped out in neat capitals his name and the year: 'J. BLAXLAND / 1788'. They are still visible today, standing out clearly among the many other hiero-glyphics and initials which have defaced the cloister over the years.

On the other side of the world, in the Blue Mountains of New South Wales, Australia, there stands Mount Blaxland, named after one of the pioneer-explorers who first found a way across the mountains in 1813 to the fruitful land beyond. His journey, as described in his journal, is part of Australian history. This is the tale of the connection between the footprint and the mountain, and what led Gregory and more particularly his elder brother John Blaxland to risk their fate and their fortune and sail out to New South Wales with their families to settle in what was then a remote little convict settlement, but was destined to become one of the great nations of the world today.

The descendants of the 'gentlemen-settlers from Kent' – those 'troublesome Blaxland brothers', as Governor Bligh called them – are now to be found both sides of the world. In Kent, the family home at Fordwich still stands, and the tiny village of Newington nestles amongst the hopfields and cherry orchards as it did over a century and a half ago. In New South Wales, in another Newington, the stately mansion John built is now a State Hospital and Home.

PART I

If we survey, with critical acumen, the whole surface
of England, there is no portion of its territory more
abundant, or more calculated to captivate the eye,
than the county of Kent.

        –W. H. IRELAND, *Topography of England*, 1828

Chapter 1

He was cantering over the wooden bridge leading into Fordwich village when he saw them – a small group of boys and
girls laughing and shouting in the meadow down by the river.
Boredom rather than necessity had made him ride fast over the
dusty roads from Sittingbourne; now both he and his mare were
hot and sweating. All he wanted at that moment was to satisfy
his thirst at the George and Dragon before reaching his
mother's house. But the noise distracted him, and there was
something horribly familiar about the black tail-jackets and
white cravats of the two boys in the centre of the group.

He pulled up his horse abruptly, and turned her head down
the track to the river. Dismounting, he tossed the reins over
the gatepost and leant over the crossbar to have a closer look.
Now he could see why they were all clapping their hands and
laughing. The two boys had rigged up a mock guillotine from
willow branches, plaited reeds and rotting boat planks they had
dragged from the river.

'Come on, it's only a game,' they were urging. 'You're half
French anyway; who better to play the Queen?'

'But I don't want to die, I want to live!' Even from a distance
he could see that the girl stood her ground firmly, tossing back
the long dark hair below her frilled lace cap and staring obsti-
nately at her would-be executioners. 'Let someone else act poor
Marie Antoinette, for I won't do it!'

The other children pulled forward another girl who had been
standing apart, silently watching them all. She was bare-
headed, but in the straggling golden curls she had twisted a
wreath of cowslips.

1

'Come on, Bennett, you'll do! Why, she's even got a crown on already! If the French girl won't join in we'll have you instead. *You*'ve no cause to go putting on grand airs. We all know your mother was put on the ducking stool. You're only the witch's daughter!'

'Witch's daughter, witch's daughter, Bennett-the-witch's daughter!' The taunting chant was taken up by all the children, and the sound made the startled martins fly up from the willows bordering the river. They swooped into the blue sky above them, then disappeared behind the sharp outline of the village church spire the other side the meadow.

The onlooker had seen enough. With a muttered oath of impatience he vaulted over the gate and strode through the long damp grass. The circle of village children scattered as quickly as the darting birds at the sight of the broad-shouldered young man pushing his way between them. He gave the wobbling edifice a well-aimed kick and seized one of the two boys angrily by the shoulders.

'Gregory! What tomfool game is this you think you're playing? What are you doing at home today, anyway? I'd expected to hear from Mother you were working hard at your studies at Canterbury. In my day a King's Scholar had more worthwhile things to do than frighten the wits out of village girls, I can assure you! You're sixteen – you should be ashamed of yourself!'

Behind his older brother's back the culprit, a sturdy, well-built boy with thick, curly hair, pulled a face. 'It's Ascension half-holiday, John. Have a heart!' He gave an exaggerated sigh of despair. 'Lord! Can't you remember how boring school was? This morning we've had Matins in the Cathedral – back to school for dull old speeches all in Latin from Livy – we've only got this afternoon left to enjoy ourselves! This was just a game, anyway – Tom and I thought it up during old Naylor's dreary sermon.'

John Blaxland cuffed both boys and frowned down upon his irrepressibly cheerful brother. Of course he remembered nine years back to when he was a King's Scholar. And if the masters' efforts to turn him into a good classics scholar had not succeeded, they were even less likely to do so with Gregory, who needed an outdoor life, not one bounded by school walls and musty volumes.

'Well, you can take that gruesome toy to pieces, anyway, he said curtly. 'There's enough real tragedy going on across the Channel without you boys making a game of it. No matter how many heads fall it seems the madman Robespierre won't be satisfied!'

2

He turned, suddenly remembering the two girls, who were silently watching him. He had thought of both as children, but on closer inspection he realized that the dark-haired one was older than he had thought. Though not tall, she had a well-developed figure; and there was something about the composed, half-amused way she was studying him that he found momentarily unnerving. The other girl he guessed at little more than twelve or thirteen, skinny as a young colt, with bare ankles and feet protruding from the grass-soaked hem of her outgrown gown. From her expressive small face, wide blue eyes gazed at him as if he was some latter-day saint who had saved her from the dragon.

'Where do you two live?' he demanded with scant courtesy. 'Isn't it time you busied yourselves at home instead of play-acting with my fool of a young brother? Your mothers probably need you.'

'They haven't got mothers, either of them,' Gregory remarked cheerfully. 'Bennett helps down at Lewis's farm and Harriott's just arrived to stay with us.' He moved closer to his brother and added in a confiding whisper, 'You know how Mother's always getting hold of some lame duck or other! This one's just arrived from India, believe it or not – her father was a French Count who once knew the Bankses, or something.'

Momentarily disconcerted that he had taken them both for village girls, John ordered Gregory and his friend to escort the older girl home to the Manor House and told the younger one to follow him. It would only take a couple of minutes more to ride round by Lewis's farm. 'Come on, child,' he called impatiently over his shoulder as he walked back across the meadow. 'If you hurry I'll give you a ride behind me.'

Obediently the girl called Bennett picked up her bedraggled skirt and ran after him, still clutching her cowslips. When she reached his horse, she suddenly hesitated.

'You're not afraid, are you?' he asked, surprised.

'Afraid? No, sir, I'm not afraid of nothing!' she replied with spirit. 'I was just looking at you and your horse – such a fine creature.'

'Yes – well – let's get going then.'

He was amused, somewhat taken aback, by the ambiguity of her admiration. He put his large hands round her slight waist and swung her up behind him in the saddle. She clung to him tightly, her sharp elbows needling into the sides of his leather jerkin as they rode off towards the village. She was only a child, but he found the sensation oddly comforting.

*   *   *

3

The Manor House – the Blaxland family home – was at the top of Fordwich High Street. When John arrived some twenty minutes later the family were already at table, the dark-haired girl seated with them. He was glad she was there – with a stranger in their midst he should be spared the inevitable reproaches that it was five months since he had last come to see them. Then it had been Christmas, soon after the death of his young wife in childbirth, and the visit had been a failure. The bells of Great Harry at Canterbury Cathedral, ringing out their Christmas message as he rode past, stressed his loneliness: what joy could there be for him in the birth of the Christ Child when his own beautiful, gay Sarah and infant son lay buried under a new marble slab at Newington?

His family had all tried, too obviously, to comfort him. His mother, arms outstretched and over-loving; his grandmother and aunt, tearful and hovering; Bess, his sister, usually so understanding, silent and solemn; Christopher, his elder brother, irritatingly pontifical; and Gregory, probably to cover up his feelings, more extrovert than usual, whistling carols unceasingly. Had his father been still alive it might have been different. The bluff, genial man who had been eight times Mayor of Fordwich before his early death in 1780 would have known instinctively that John wanted to be left in peace. John had gone home to Newington after a couple of days in ill humour with the lot of them.

This time, to his relief, the atmosphere was quite different. The family were all talking animatedly and his mother, as always when supervising servants and the serving of food, greeted him with affectionate preoccupation.

'John dear!' She kissed him fondly, then motioned him to the empty place beside her. (Twenty-four-year-old Christopher, thickset and self-important, was in John's old place at the head of the big oak table.)

'Gregory told us you were on your way' his mother continued, 'how glad we are to have you! You'll forgive us for not waiting, but the roast ducks were spoiling. Oh, you've already met Harriott de Marquet, I believe?' The girl, who was laughing with Gregory, looked up at her name and inclined her head gravely to John as he sat down. 'Now, as soon as everyone is served you must tell us your news, John, and how life is at Newington.'

Fortunately, John knew this really meant that his mother was herself anxious to talk, which she accordingly did, leaving John to enjoy his food in peace. She had been so pleased when her dear friend Lady Banks had asked her if she could do this small

4

service for her and take the young girl into their family for a time, she told him in a loud whisper. Harriott was only sixteen; such a charming girl, and such a sad history! Her father had been an officer in the bodyguard of Louis XVI when the troubles began, so he left France and was fortunately able to establish himself as a wealthy merchant in India. In Calcutta he had met and married Harriott's mother, the daughter of an English Colonel who was an aide to Warren Hastings, the Governor-General. Harriott had been born at the Governor-General's white marble palace, and should have had such a brilliant future; but then her mother died and her father decided it was best she be sent back to Europe.

Puzzled, John asked what all this had to do with the Bankses. Mrs Blaxland paused dramatically; she was obviously enjoying her story and pleased to have an interested listener. 'Ah! Well – her father had originally thought of a French convent, but of course by the time she had made the long journey home from India that was out of the question. Fortunately Mr Hastings had recommended her to the care of Sir Joseph and Lady Banks, who have been kindness itself to the poor child, who couldn't possibly go to her French relations. So that is why she is here,' Mrs Blaxland concluded triumphantly, with a sidelong glance at Harriott. 'It is *so* pleasing to feel we can do something for her.'

While his mother was talking John noticed the girl herself sitting quietly, speaking to the others every now and then in a soft voice that still carried traces of a French accent. He was about to make some remark to her when Gregory suddenly swore loudly and leaped up from the table.

'Christopher, what's that damned cur of yours got in his mouth?' He rushed across the dining room to a large hound that lay stretched out by the doorway peacefully chewing the remains of what looked like an old piece of cloth or leather. With a cry of genuine anguish, the boy bent down, prised open the dog's reluctant jaws, and extricated the remains of its meal.

'It's my kangaroo skin! My piece of dried skin Sir Joseph Banks gave me when I was small all those years ago – that he brought back when he went with Captain Cook to New South Wales!' Gregory's face was scarlet with emotion as he held up reverently the mangled, chewed object. 'It's something I'll never have again,' he said, near to tears. 'It was precious – from that strange animal across the world – and now your damnable, great cur has stolen it from my room, Chris. Why can't you look after him? I'll murder him, and I'd like to murder you!'

5

'Gregory!'

Mrs Blaxland's voice rose vainly in the uproar. Gregory rushed at the dog to hit him, the animal moved out of the way and in doing so caught its feet in the fringed border of the table runner, dragging it down. In a moment everything was confusion – screams, spilt pitchers, overturned dishes, barking dog, and maids scurrying off for buckets and cloths. Over and above it all Mrs Blaxland could be heard saying despairingly, as Gregory ran out, 'Can't that boy ever come home without upsetting the household?'

An hour later, after hunting everywhere, John found his youngest brother disconsolately throwing pebbles into the river that ran at the bottom of the walled back garden.

The Stour was silting up now, with emerald strands of weed streaming like wet hair just below the surface; and at the water's edge sleek drakes and mallards were preening themselves in the warm sunshine.

In earlier times sailing luggers had come from as far away as northern France, bringing stone from Caen to build Canterbury's great cathedral. Now the crane on the wall of the Town Hall adjacent to the Manor House was little used, nor was the ducking stool; only the small dungeon under the Town Hall occasionally gave some poor wretch of a trout-poacher time for thoughtful repentance.

'I suppose you've come to say I ought to be in there,' Gregory greeted John rebelliously, nodding towards the nearby dungeon. 'You're against me, like everybody else in this family!'

Expressing his dislike of Gregory's recent boorish behaviour, John finally got the boy to confess his real grievance.

'It's just that they won't let me *do* anything, John. What use am I, kicking my heels term after boring term at Canterbury – when all I want is to be a farmer, or a soldier like you were, or, best of all, go off exploring distant lands!' He turned to his brother, his round boy's face with its eager eyes alight with enthusiasm. 'That must have been something, John, when you think of it – to be one of the first Englishman ever to set foot on those far-off shores – even if all they've done with New South Wales since is to make it a penal settlement!'

John's eyes suddenly crinkled into a smile, and he squeezed the boy's arm understandably. 'You know, it could be worse, your present life, despite old Naylor. You've got a lot to be proud of, living here. Dad used to say to me when I was young, that no Kentish village has seen more history than Fordwich, and we're part of it. After all, the Blaxlands have lived in various parts of Kent for centuries –'

'I know, I know,' Gregory interrupted impatiently. He began chanting, parrot-fashion, 'In the year 597 an early John Blaxland was at the baptism of Ethelbert, King of Kent, the first English Christian King, and afterwards they say he gave Saint Augustine land at Canterbury to build his abbey. Then another John Blaxland went off to the Crusades, and yet another was captain of the guard to the Virgin Queen, and she gave him more land. . . .' He broke off, grinning, and disrespectfully punched his elder brother. 'Why, it's you that should be proud, John, not I. They were all your namesakes! I haven't got to live up to them, thank God. None of them was a Gregory!'

Chapter 2

The knowledge that his family needed him helped to shake John out of his lethargy. After his Ascension Day visit he settled the immediate problem of his difficult youngest brother by arranging for him to spend part of the summer holidays with relations on their farm at Graveney. But any peace of mind this should have brought to Fordwich Manor was dispelled when news leaked back that, instead of helping with the haymaking, Gregory had talked his cousins into making daily trips to the nearby fishing port of Whitstable. There they were discovered gleefully hunting for smugglers and French spies among the hardworking oyster fishermen, and generally making themselves thorough nuisances.

'So now,' Bess wrote despairingly to John, 'on top of all else poor Mother is constantly worrying that Gregory may be snatched up by the press gangs and carried off to sea!' John raised an amused eyebrow: surely even his doting mother knew her youngest son had plenty of native cunning. And from what he knew of Gregory, and the boy's love of adventure, he might not mind even that. 'You will not be surprised to hear that Harriott de Marquet is still with us,' Bess had added a casual postscript, 'and with this wretched war lasting a year and a half already, it looks as if she may be here for some time yet.'

Not only his mother's protégée but the 'wretched war' also looked as if it had come to stay. That was not really so unusual; it was the sixth time in the century that England and France had been at war. But this time there was a difference: this time France was also in the middle of a revolution. Even the most insular inhabitant of south-east Kent was beginning to realize that the hair-raising tales recounted by the numerous *emigrés* arriving at Dover and Ramsgate were actually happening in a country little more than twenty miles away. If anarchy could grip France, what was to prevent its sweeping across that narrow stretch of water to England?

''Tis a bad thing, that Terror over there,' one of John's cattledrovers at Newington pronounced knowledgeably, as they were looking at some new calves together one warm summer day. 'They kill their King and Queen – and now more and more heads are falling. What think ye of it all, sir?'

John had no answer, nor could he do much to ease the growing concern of his labourers. Prices were rising alarmingly, more and more common land was being enclosed, thus depriving the countryman of one of his longest-standing privileges. And now a food shortage was threatening. John spent long hours at Newington in the fields with his men, urging them to load the heavy bales on to the carts while the weather held good. In the orchards their wives stood with looped-up skirts while their children climbed up to gather the rosy apples for their mothers' baskets. John had a cheerful word of encouragement for each one: it had never been more imperative than in this year of 1794 to get the harvest safely in.

One September day when he was down at the barn supervising grain storage, a servant ran in to say his brother had arrived at the Hall. Wiping his earthy hands on his breeches and cursing at the interruption, John turned to see Christopher, immaculate in a new broadcloth jacket, standing in the barn doorway and eyeing John's sweat-stained shirt and muddy jacket with disfavour. 'Well, John! Everyone at Fordwich thought it was time we had news of you?'

John inquired after the family; then, feeling some brotherly gesture was required, reluctantly invited Christopher to eat with him. Time was too precious to bring any of his servants in from the fields to prepare a meal at the Hall, so he suggested they go over to the Rose at Sittingbourne. There, after an ample dish of boiled mutton and turnips washed down by wine, Christopher, considerably mollified, got down to the purpose of his visit. Was the war news making John think of taking up his commission again?

John threw back his head and roared with laughter. How obvious Christopher was, sitting there so smugly and carefully flicking invisible crumbs off his light fawn breeches!

'No, thank you!' He paused to refill both their glasses. 'Three years in the Duke of York's Cavalry was enough for me! I'm a farmer, Chris, not a soldier. I can do more good raising cattle and growing corn here than ever I could chasing the French or Austrians out of Flanders. Anyway, if I re-enlisted, Dundas would probably have me shipped out on one of his damfool expeditions to the West Indies, where I'd die of yellow fever within a week. No, Chris, you can't get rid of me as easily as that!'

His manner was jesting, but his laugh held a touch of rancour. How could Christopher understand what Army life today was really like? The rank and file enlisting only for the drink, their uniforms shabby, and half the poor devils without **boots. Billy Pitt wasn't** much better than Christopher in

9

comprehending what real warfare meant. And now that he'd made his drinking companion, Dundas, Secretary of State for War, what hope was there for improvement? The man only did what the City merchants told him to; and rumours were going round that he was even planning to sell regimental rank in return for recruits.

Christopher shifted uncomfortably in his chair. 'John, don't be a fool! You've quite misunderstood me, why should I want you to go off?' He changed the subject hastily, asking John if he would like their sister to come to stay for a few weeks after Michaelmas. 'She'd like to come,' he added hastily, seeing John start to remonstrate, 'and Mother said she could be spared. Perhaps she could bring Harriott too; it would make a change for her from Fordwich. . . .'

'Getting fed up with all your women, Chris?' John grinned. 'Well, I suppose they can come if they wish, but I'll have no time to entertain them,' he said off-handedly.

After Christopher had left, John regretted he had agreed so unthinkingly to the visit. What did he want with chattering females who would come interfering in his way of life or upsetting his memories? He had got used now to life on his own at Newington. Sarah had loved the place passionately. He often thought of how she used to run her hands lovingly over the smoke-darkened oak beams that stood out in stark contrast to the whitewashed walls. She had thought Newington Hall the most beautiful house in the world, especially in the springtime, when the mellow brick house walls were almost submerged in the sea of fragile white cherry blossom that surrounded the entire village. She had wanted nothing better than to raise their children there and farm their lands.

It was on a hazy October day, when the autumn hedgerows were bright with scarlet rosehips and blackberries, that the Blaxland family carriage came lumbering along the narrow lanes to Newington, and deposited its two occupants at the Hall.

Disentangling himself from his sister's fond embrace, and the thick folds of her brown travelling cloak, John noticed Harriott standing behind her, carefully checking their baskets and boxes with a servant, and then looking around her eagerly.

'I had thought Newington Hall would be in the centre of the village, like Fordwich, Mr Blaxland,' she smiled as she gave him her hand in greeting. 'I had not expected it would be in the middle of all these orchards. It is very beautiful.'

John was struck afresh by the low-pitched voice with its

10

attractive foreign inflexion. There was something quite appealing about the girl, he thought. Not exactly pretty, but with an unusual quality, a certain distinction; extremely slight compared with Bess, and the long yellow fitted coat with its brown velvet edgings enhanced her youthful looks.

'I hope you will not find it dull here, so deep in the country, mademoiselle,' he said.

'Of course not, how can any fresh place be dull?' She followed him into the hall, and he was suddenly aware of how empty the great fireplace looked without the stone pitchers of bulrushes and beech-leaves that Sarah had always arranged there before the start of winter fires.

'I will get one of the maids to show you to your rooms,' he said. But at that moment Bess returned from the kitchen, where she had been instructing the cook to warm the pies she and Harriott had brought. Talking volubly about the shortcomings she had already noticed in the house, she led the way upstairs, beckoning Harriott to follow.

The girl obeyed meekly enough, but John was amused by the way she stopped halfway up the stairs, and turned back to look at him.

'I think you should know, Mr Blaxland, I prefer that you do not address me as "mademoiselle".' She held herself very straight as she looked down, but in spite of her dignity he had the uncomfortable feeling she was laughing at him. 'It is problem enough having a French surname in your country with this war, without that extra encumbrance!'

In spite of John's fears, the visit brought its compensations. It was good to be greeted at the end of the day by succulent smells of roast pheasant or new-boiled fowl and leeks instead of the indifferent meals his maids had been giving him.

'My Bess, what changes you have made!' he said appreciatively to his sister several days later, coming in from the yard at sundown.

'Yes, it's a start.' Bess gazed around complacently, wiping her hands on her voluminous blue apron. 'We got the kitchen maids to put down new rush matting – the other was positively stinking. You'd better get one of your men to bring in some of those big logs and stack them ready for the winter; when the nights get cooler you'll need them.' She glanced across at Harriott, who was putting some plates on the dresser, and added in a lower voice, 'How we're going to keep that child warm later I can't imagine, she'll hate our Kentish winters –' then broke off in horror as she caught sight of her brother's muddy boots. 'John, just look at the mess you've brought in

11

with you – I'll wager half the farmyard has come with you, and how you stink! Go out and take them off, and wash your hands under the pump before you come back to this clean kitchen!'

John's humour was not improved when he suddenly realized Harriott was obviously finding Bess's reprimand highly diverting.

'Lord, woman, how you fuss!' he growled, tugging off the offending boots and throwing them outside. 'A little morsel of cow-dung and you act as though I should be put in the stocks at Fordwich. Whose house is this, anyway, and whose kitchen?'

He regretted his words the minute he'd said them. Poor Bess – sharing the housewifely duties at Fordwich Manor with mother, grandmother and aunt could not be exactly easy. She was twenty-six already, and no man had asked for her, so there was no house of which she was truly mistress, nor ever likely to be.

In clumsy masculine fashion he tried to take the hurt from her kindly, plain face. She was right, of course: in the past year he had ceased to trouble. Now he would go and clean himself up and put on his best jacket for their benefit – so long as the moths hadn't invaded the closet! Then they'd light new candles and open a bottle of French brandy somebody had 'found' for him at a Romney Marsh inn. His knowing wink made Harriott suddenly laugh, and even Bess began to smile.

'Very well then,' she said. 'We'll eat in ten minutes – but I don't doubt the food will stick in my throat if it's washed down with smuggled brandy!'

During those first warm weeks of October, as Bess and Harriott set his house in order, John spent time with his tenant-farmers and bailiffs, discussing the best future use of his valuable land. Cattle or grain? Hops or apples? Crops or fallow? The war, and constantly rising food prices, made these decisions vital. Now that he was losing more and more labourers to the militia, there would be more work than ever for the men that were left.

As the days shortened he had his cattle herded down to the marshy reaches at Luddenham by the Swale estuary. This left the grazing meadows farther inland available to be ploughed up for winter sowing. When he heard whispers of criticism in the district he answered brusquely that, if the war was not ended next year, it was grain that would provide bread to fill men's bellies, not buttercups. To make the land serve double purpose he had sheep brought over from one of his Romney

Marsh farms. Nobody could protest at the luxury of apple and cherry trees if good wool and mutton were grazing underneath!

At the end of the month the weather began to change. A strong gale stripped the trees of the last of their golden glory. An unexpected sharp frost made Bess tap the barometer anxiously, and say that she and Harriott ought to be getting back to Fordwich.

The three of them were sitting by the big log-fire in the hall after their evening meal. Bess was threading peeled apple rings on to strings for drying, and Harriott was kneeling by the hearth putting chestnuts to roast among the hot ashes.

'But have we done all we can for your brother, Bess?' Harriott sat back on her heels and looked up sharply. The firelight shining on her sleek dark head and long russet gown had brought a sudden glow to her cheeks. Was it imagination or did her voice sound disappointed?

John bent forward with the long iron tongs to help her retrieve a smoking chestnut. 'You've done more than enough, both of you.' His voice was unusually gentle. 'If the French arrived and laid siege to Newington tomorrow, I could live here for ten years without starving, I wager! No, Bess is right. The winter's almost upon us. I don't want you both finding yourselves snowed up here and mother at Fordwich going frantic. We'll start to make arrangements tomorrow.'

They left on a lowering November morning, when thin skeins of dying bonfire smoke drifted up between the leafless trees and the countryside was starkly bare. Bess had kissed him cheerfully with the air of one whose mission has been accomplished, but Harriott, pinched and pink-nosed from the cold, managed no more than a bleak, watery smile when it was time to say goodbye.

John was annoyed to find he missed them after they had gone. The house seemed lonely without Bess's continual fussing, and he missed the feeling of Harriott's large dark eyes upon him. He felt no better in the days that followed. It rained incessantly. By early December the streams were overflowing and the fields had become seas of mud that washed away much of the newly sown grain upon which such high hopes had been set. Cooped up in the Hall, without even the normal winter pleasures of hunting or shooting, John's mood changed from frustration to angry despair.

When he was able to ride out, he seemed invariably to pass a handful of his former farm labourers in assorted uniforms squelching up and down in the mud with patriotic fervour; one or two of their officers drilling them looked at him with a certain insolence that was something quite new. He wondered why until a friend of his bachelor days came over from Canterbury and appealed to him to train a newly formed unit of local volunteers, and looked at him as if he were a traitor when he politely refused.

The war news did nothing to cheer him. The British Army in the Low Countries was valiantly fighting a losing battle. Her Austrian allies were behind the Rhine, the French had already reached Cologne, and Prussia and Spain were quietly negotiating a separate peace.

''Tis not only the French, 'tis the typhus that is our redcoats' enemy, poor bastards!' said the Rose Inn's landlord, as he rolled down his new barrels of ale into the cellar for safe keeping. 'It's a waiting time for them either way, whether they swelter in the West Indies or freeze to death on the Waal!'

Not only were men freezing in the Low Countries as the flooded Waal became a sea of packed ice, but south-east England was having the coldest winter ever remembered there. The poor suffered terribly, and John, riding round Newington in a thick sheepskin jacket, knitted helmet and leather mittens, often dipped into his own pocket to help some poor soldier's widow or labourer's family buy coal or tallow for their candles.

As the old year ended and the bells rang out over the frozen countryside to herald 1795, it was the sheer necessities of life that many of the countryfolk were lacking.

Chapter 3

It was February before a thaw set in, and John was able to get over to Fordwich to see how his family were faring. He tried to take his usual cross-country route, but his horse slipped and slithered on the muddy tracks, the water in places reaching to her fetlocks. He decided to keep to the slower toll roads.

Upon reaching the Stour valley he was dismayed to find the former marshlands around Westbere completely under water, with only a hedge or a bare tree sticking up forlornly to break the surface. A squally south-easterly gale was blowing up, rippling the flood water into angry waves. The river was near danger level, and as John came up to the wooden bridge leading into Fordwich his horse twitched her ears apprehensively. She knew as well as he that warmth and a bag of oats were waiting on the other side of the bridge, where the lights of the George and Dragon were shining, but despite his coaxing she shied and refused to go any further.

The winter daylight was fading, and the noise of wind and rushing water combined to conceal the sound of running footsteps, so he only knew that someone was near when his horse's bridle was suddenly grabbed, and he saw a small, soaked figure standing beside him.

'Who are you? What the devil d'you think you're doing?' Instinctively he raised his whip and pulled his horse's head away from the grasping hands. In the half-light he could not see whether the hooded face gazing so beseechingly up at him belonged to a girl or a boy.

'Come quickly, sir, come quickly! 'Tis not safe for you to cross the bridge, it's on the point of breaking! Turn back, or you'll be swept away and your horse with you!'

There was no time to argue, or even to see who was warning him. He spurred his horse – she went willingly enough – and galloped back some hundred yards up the road on which he had just come. Turning in his saddle, he saw his rescuer scrambling after him. The hood had blown back, and as the fair hair tumbled loose he could see it was a girl, clutching something heavy in her arms. She was gasping for breath as she stumbled up, and leant against the steaming flank of his horse, staring backwards in horror.

Suddenly there was a great rending noise and the whole

15

bridge collapsed into the swollen river. John had, instinctively, flung himself off his horse and put his arm round the girl's shoulders, holding her close as they watched. There was a sound of rending timber and surging, sucking water; then the bridge was gone, its huge timber beams splitting into pieces that went tossing and crashing down-river. It all happened so quickly – one minute the bridge was there, the next it had disappeared – that John might have thought he had dreamed it but for the terrified girl in his arms and his horse whinnying in fear beside him.

'My God!' he breathed. 'My God! A minute later and I would have been on it!'

All at once he was conscious of two things: first, that the girl was sobbing against his jacket, and secondly that he had received a sharp kick in his stomach.

'What the hell – ?' He released her and backed away sharply, then laughed when he saw what she had in her arms. It was a new-born lamb, near-drowned and dripping, but with enough strength in its body to prove it had every intention of living.

'It's all right – look, you've saved it – and you saved me,' he said.

'But the ewe, she was swept away,' the girl said chokingly, 'and the magpie – the magpie that was on her back, she went too!'

'Magpie?' What on earth was the child talking about, and why was her face familiar to him? Those anguished blue eyes, dark now with tragedy, and the cheeks streaked with mud and tears. 'Why worry about a silly bird?'

She stopped crying and was looking up intently. Rooks and gulls were circling over the rushing river as if their lives, too, had been disrupted by the elements. Suddenly in a flash of black and white against the stormy sky there flew a magpie.

'Look, there you are!' He pointed, humouring her. 'See – and there's another!'

As the two birds flew away into the darkening clouds across the river a sudden change came over the girl. Fear slipped away and her whole body seemed to relax. She pulled her damp cloak lovingly round the still struggling lamb, whispered to it soothingly, then turned a radiant face to John.

'There's no more cause to fear, then, now we've seen the second magpie! My mother told me one magpie brings sorrow, but two bring happiness.'

Across the swiftly flowing water that divided them from the village John could make out people running up with lanterns, calling and shouting. They were waving their arms and pointing up-river towards Canterbury, indicating that he would have to go back to the city, to the next bridge.

As he turned to the girl again, he suddenly realized who she was. 'I'd forgotten that old Kentish saying, but I do remember who *you* are now! You're Bennett, aren't you?'

She nodded mutely, pushing back the damp golden hair under her hood once more, and he slapped his thigh, laughing. 'Well, by Heaven, that makes us even! I saved you from having your head cut off by my devil of a young brother, and now you've saved me from drowning!'

He whistled to his horse, who was nervously cropping some wet tufts of grass on the higher ground above them. 'Come on, then,' he said, grasping the bridle with one hand and holding out the other to help her up. 'It seems I'm fated always to give you rides home, my child. We'll have a long ride round tonight and I suppose if you hold me tight we'll have to take home that miserable-looking lamb as well!'

At midnight, sitting with his mother and sister in front of the fire at Fordwich Manor, and wearing Christopher's borrowed clothes, he asked them about Bennett. The hot mulled wine had induced a pleasant glow of well-being, and he began to wonder idly about the girl. It was so strange, the way she had appeared out of the dark, wet night to warn him of danger. Although she lived at Lewis's farm, she didn't look like one of their brood – or, for that matter, like any of the village children. Did they know where she had come from?

His mother, as always, had all the village facts at her fingertips. Bennett was an orphan, whom Farmer Lewis had taken in some years before to save her going on the parish. The poor child was always getting teased because her mother was the last wretched creature to be put on the ducking stool. People said she was a witch because she collected herbs and went about selling potions and cures, but Mrs Blaxland had always thought her harmless enough. They didn't make her wear the scold's bridle – so cruel, that iron mask and gag – but the ducking in the river as good as finished her even so, and she died a year later. The child was only four or five at the time – it all happened about ten years ago.

'Who was the father?' John interrupted.

'Probably a passing vagrant, nobody knows,' put in Bess. 'But she's quite intelligent. I've got my eye on her for my girls' classes later on. Did you know I'm starting them in the village, John?'

Her brother shook his head. How like their mother Bess was,

17

always looking for good causes! The thought reminded him suddenly of Harriott. Deliberately casual, he asked if she was landed on them for ever.

Mrs Blaxland bridled indignantly, and John winked at Bess. His mother's reactions were exactly as he had anticipated. He listened with the utmost solemnity as she extolled her young guest's virtues. She swept off to bed and John, alone with his sister, grinned affectionately at her departing back. 'I think mother would do anything for Lady Banks. She's never ceased to be impressed that her girlhood friend Dorothea should end up with such a famous husband – a baronet and President of the Royal Society into the bargain! I suppose she's right to keep in touch; they're a nice enough old couple.'

'Old?' Bess raised a questioning eyebrow. 'Sir Joseph can't be much more than fifty even now, and when you think of all he's done in his lifetime!'

'Bess, you sound like Gregory. He hung on Sir Joseph's every word last time he was here, telling us stories of his adventures in New Zealand and New South Wales, d'you remember?'

There was more than enough work to keep the men busy repairing the ravages of the flood and the bitter cold for all the year to come. It was a herculean task to get the land productive again, and John and his brothers worked hard, Gregory delighted to be doing a man's work when he returned home from school.

The constant drain of manpower to the militia made life increasingly difficult that cold spring and cool summer of 1795, and the war news continued bleak. Britain's allies were losing ground to the French on all sides. Spain, Holland and Prussia had given up the fight. Austria's position was precarious, and the French Army was casting hungry eyes on the riches of Italy. Far away in the West Indies British soldiers were dying in their thousands and, much nearer home, there were tragic losses amongst British convoys at sea.

John spent more of that year at Fordwich than at Newington. The family needed him after all the flood damage, he told himself by way of excuse. Christopher was not as experienced as he at making the most of what labour was obtainable. And he wanted to keep an eye on his younger brother: if Gregory was really keen to learn about cattle – and John saw that he worked well – he might take the boy over with him to Newington later to help with the stock down at Luddenham. Then, too, seeing him more often obviously gave pleasure to his mother and Bess. And he could also help them by entertaining Harriot – escorting her on the occasional drive to Canterbury, or just chatting to her

18

at odd moments – purely in an elder-brother capacity, of course.... She also served as a useful protection against his mother's infernal attempts to get him to mix with local society again.

'Save your matchmaking for the others, Mother,' he growled, coming in tired after a long day. 'I don't care whether the Cuffleys have a charming daughter or not, I'll not be here at dinner tomorrow to dance attendance on her.'

His mother smiled resignedly. 'Very well, dear, I'm sorry. It's just that I do so want to see you happy again.'

'Oh, for the Lord's sake, I am happy,' he retorted. 'Now leave me in peace, pray!'

But Harriot, one day after he had settled some trivial family disagreement, had complimented him on being *sympathique*.

'Sympathetic? How?'

'Well, I watch you trying to see that everyone in the household is content – your old grandmother, your aunt, your mother, your sister and brothers. I watch how you make peace with them all, and your labourers as well.' She looked out towards the river, once again flowing quietly between its banks at the bottom of the Manor garden. 'It is a pity there is not peace in the whole world also. There is so much trouble everywhere, even here in England.' She said 'trouble' with the slight French intonation that always fascinated him.

Earlier that day they had all been discussing the great mass meeting, calling for civil war, that had taken place the previous week in London, at Copenhagen Fields. Was it surprising there had been riots in some districts when there was not enough good flour for bread, and beef at the terrible price of sixpence halfpenny a pound? Hooligans had even hooted the poor King on his way to open Parliament, calling for 'Bread!' and 'Peace!' as if he could produce them on a platter. It was most disquieting.

He remembered that family discussion only too clearly the following summer when, back at Newington, he had a surprise visit from Sir Joseph Banks.

As the neat chaise and pair came up the drive he thought at first it was someone from Fordwich, until he noticed the unfamiliar livery of the coachman and the dark blue paintwork; then he saw the crest on the door, which betrayed the identity his distinguished caller.

'Why, Sir Joseph, this is indeed an honour,' he said, as the tall, well-proportioned figure of the baronet climbed stiffly out and grasped his hand in greeting.

'Not at all, my boy, not at all! It's good to see you. I have sent my wife on in the carriage to visit your lady mother at Fordwich where I shall join her, but first I wanted to have a talk with you. May we go inside?'

John led the older man in and sent servants hurrying for some refreshment, but Sir Joseph waved the food away and only accepted some wine. He had come for conversation, he said, not eating. John thought he had aged in the two years since he had last seen him, and under the brown wig the intelligent, shrewd face looked strained and tired.

'I know you'll be surprised that I call on you unannounced like this, John,' Sir Joseph began in friendly fashion, 'but I felt it my duty. I've known your family since before you were born and your father was one of my best friends, God rest his soul! I know your brother Christopher likes to think he's in charge at Fordwich, but you're the one that matters. You're the head of the family.' He winced as he shifted his weight in his chair. 'Damn this gout! It's time I left this lukewarm climate and went on another long sea voyage, if only it were possible!' He pulled his seat nearer. 'Now, my boy, what I've come to say to you is this: in certain circles you're regarded as a bit too radical – I could say unpatriotic – because you insist on staying on your land instead of rushing off to fight.' He put up a restraining hand as John began indignantly to protest; and went on to tell him in confidence that the Adjutant-General's office in London had started drawing up plans to defend the southern counties against invasion; that Pitt was planning to double the militia in the autumn; and that a new force of provisional cavalry might be formed. 'And that could mean your gamekeepers being drafted along with yet more of your best farmhands,' Sir Joseph warned.

'But I understood – the latest intelligence I had from London was that the Government was being prompted to put out feelers for peace?'

Sir Joseph gave a derogatory snort. 'Peace?' France's revolutionary government has made the country bankrupt! The Jacobins can't afford peace! That Corsican upstart, Bonaparte, who's spurring the French Army on in Italy, he knows how vital it is to achieve victory. But that's of less immediate import to us; what we've got to keep our eyes on are the ominous naval preparations going on at Brest....'

John listened with growing concern, and in silence. He respected the opinions of this man to whom experience and contact with famous men had given such breadth of vision.

'But you will not speak of this in such detail when you go to

20

Fordwich, Sir Joseph?' he said, after they had been talking together for over an hour. 'I would not wish my mother to be unduly alarmed.'

Banks stood up, his kind face solemn. 'No, my boy, of course not.' He limped slightly as he walked towards the door. 'Anyway, my wife went on independently because she had some sad news of her own to impart. One of the East Indiamen that docked at Tilbury last week had mail from India aboard, and we have learned that the father of Harriott de Marquet is dead.'

Chapter 4

After the baronet had gone John felt disturbed and restless, and could not settle down to anything. It was the war news, he told himself – nothing to do with hearing of the death of Harriott's father. Even so, he decided he would ride over next day to Fordwich. It was time, anyway, that he visited the family, he told himself – and if he could perhaps show his sympathy to the girl in some way...

'So Lady Banks and I have decided it would be best for her to stay on here for the present,' Mrs Blaxland was saying. 'Some instructions will probably come from her father's executors – she won't be penniless, of course, but now she's nearly eighteen, whether she can be made a ward or not we –'

'I'll go and see her,' John said briefly, and, still in his riding boots, strode through the house and out into the warm afternoon sunshine. It was a perfect summer day, with larks losing themselves in a cloudless sky and the river lazily lapping the bank at the bottom of the garden.

Harriott was sitting under the big walnut tree, the gently waving branches patterning her small, solitary figure with restless shadows. She was sewing some fine gauzy grey stuff that billowed round her, and her dark head with its frilled muslin cap was bent in deep concentration over her work. She did not hear John's approach over the soft grass until the clink of his spurs made her look up in surprise.

'Harriott,' he said uncertainly, 'Harriott – I'm so sorry....'

Her large eyes were sad as she asked, 'You came specially?' 'You are very kind – your whole family is very kind.'

John muttered something inaudible and lowered himself on to the lawn beside her.

She began plucking at her stitching with nervous fingers. 'Your sister Bess – she reminded me of this Indian muslin I had brought with me in my box – as it is a dark colour I intend to use it – it will be more fitting –' Her voice was un /en with suppressed tears.

Suddenly he felt angry and impatient, not with the girl herself but with everything that altered and ended with the finality of death.

'Oh, Harriott, do you really think your father would have wanted you to put on mourning clothes for him?' Seeing her

22

stricken face, he forced himself to speak more gently. 'Come down to the river with me. I believe there are kingcups – I'll get some for you.'

Reluctantly, she pushed aside her sewing and got up, refusing his outstretched hand. She was still wary of him, he could tell. She walked silently with him down to the path that ran along the bank and waited there while he climbed down to the water's edge to get her some of the yellow, glossy flowers. The leaves looked as if they were made of dark green wax.

She took the kingcups from him, her fingers barely touching his wet hand. 'You cannot understand what it is like,' she persisted, her expression almost stubborn. 'You have a family, but I – you see, there is nobody any more. From now on, I am quite alone.'

She stood very straight, her head tilted on one side and her face now looking slightly puzzled, as if, by concentrating, she could work out her life's pattern.

The sight of her standing there like that, so utterly desolate, did something to him. 'You silly little fool, of course I understand!' he almost shouted at her. 'Do you think you are the only one who has been left alone? Parents, children, wives, husbands: no matter whom you lose, you suffer. Don't think you have the prerogative of suffering!'

'What did you call me? I am not a silly little fool!' She rounded on him furiously and stood there like some trapped animal, her breasts heaving, staring at him with angry, passionate eyes. Her whole being seemed to have come alive. Then, as suddenly, she changed. She put up her hands to her face in an unconsciously childish gesture and burst into tears, backing away from him.

'Harriott, stop it, stand still!' He stepped forward and put both his strong hands on her slight heaving shoulders. He was half a head taller than she, and she had to tilt her head up to look at him.

'I'll say it again – you're a stupid fool! Don't you realize I know even better than you what it is to be lonely; and I know you have to fight it, show the world you don't care, learn to be independent! It's the devil of a task for a man and probably worse for a woman, but you can do it.' His voice was hard and harsh, but the touch of his big hands was surprisingly gentle. 'Harriott –' suddenly he spoke quite differently – 'Harriott, will you marry me?'

She gave a great choking gasp and pulled herself away from him, her face a mixture of bewilderment and tears. 'Marry you? But – you ask me from pity? You cannot ask from love?'

23

For a moment his face lost all expression. He might have been seeing her the first time: the dark hair falling loose under the cap, the red-rimmed eyes in the pale face, so lost and so appealing, made his heart give the sudden, half-remembered lurch he had thought he would never experience again. 'Love?' he repeated slowly after her – and just stopped himself from saying, 'But does that really matter?'

He did not see the shadowed withdrawal of her eyes as he made no answer to her question. Then, 'I think, between us, we can make a good life; and a good marriage,' he said quietly.

Only then did he think to kiss her.

John Blaxland and Harriott de Marquet were married in Canterbury in May of the following year. It was a quiet, brief ceremony with only a handful of close friends and family present. The times were out of tune for anything more elaborate, nor would it have been seemly. As a widower, John would not have had it otherwise.

At the wedding Harriott looked so youthful that for a moment he felt afraid. She wore a dress of cream Spitalfields silk over a quilted satin petticoat and a primrose-yellow silk bonnet. She made her promises gravely and clearly, but her nervous fingers gripped the beribboned stems of her small bouquet of primroses and lily-of-the-valley so tightly he thought she would snap the delicate stems.

Afterwards, when he teasingly said to her, 'Well, won't you look at your husband, Mrs Blaxland?' she gazed at him as if she could not believe it was true. It made him feel that the ten years separating them were those of a whole generation. Sarah had been eighteen, too, when they were wed but, however manly and handsome he might have looked in his cavalry officer's uniform, he was still really a boy only three years her senior.

To please the family, Harriott and John spent their wedding night at Fordwich. It was not a success. They were too conscious of knowing glances and coy whispers; and even when they were on their own at last, the rarely used guest-chamber at the Manor seemed unfamiliar and unwelcoming. The great four-poster bed with its ornate carvings too obviously symbolized all the past Blaxland births and deaths and marriages, and even the lovingly embroidered bed-hangings brought out from the chest in the attic hung stiff and self-conscious, as if they, too, were determined to emphasize the special occasion. The patchwork quilt made years before by John's grandmother was too warm and oppressive for the May night, and the scent from bowls of dried lavender and rose-petals on the bedside tables rose up overpoweringly.

When John snuffed the candles and climbed into the big feather bed beside Harriott, she lay there trembling, and as he kissed her he discovered that above the lace ruffles of her wedding nightgown her face was streaked with tears. Compassion overcame the desire that had begun to stir in him. 'Don't be frightened, Harriott.' He stroked her dark hair soothingly, as if comforting a frightened child. 'Everything comes with patience – even love between a man and wife.'

Next day was bright and sunny. They drove the long way out of the village, and as they saw the carriage pass by with its beribboned horses and cockaded coachman many cottagers ran out to wave and call out good wishes. At the ford by Lewis's, the farmer's family were gathered. John caught sight of Bennett among them. Her hands were shading her eyes from the bright sunshine so he could not see the expression on her face, but when one of the small children ran forward to toss Harriott a nosegay and they cried, 'Good luck, sir and ma'am!' Bennett was the only one who did not wave but stood silent, just watching, until they were gone.

Harriott began to relax once they were on their way, the telltale smudges under her eyes vanishing. In spite of the inevitable turnpike delays they made good progress. They stopped for an hour to change horses and have some refreshment at Faversham, but as they approached Sittingbourne, only four miles from Newington village, John saw the strained look come back to his young wife's face. She straightened herself against the velvet upholstery of the carriage cushions and he felt the grip of her hand tighten.

He put his arm round her shoulders and pulled her closer. 'Look,' he said, pointing out at the cobbled street down which they had just turned, 'my unobservant wife, this is *not* the road to Newington!' He laughed at her incredulous face. 'I have a surprise! We're not going home tonight – I'm taking you instead to Sheerness, on the Isle of Sheppey. There's an inn on the waterfront there where I've wanted to stay since I was a boy. The windows overlook the sea, we can watch the ships, and tomorrow we'll walk on the shingle beach in the sunshine! You'll like it, Harriott – it's a peaceful little seaside town where no curious eyes will watch us and we can be quiet together.'

Relief and a growing happiness shone in Harriott's eyes. 'Oh, John! You mean – at this place, there'll be no memories – ?'

' No, you silly goose, the only memories will be those that you

25

and I make together.' He put his hand under her chin and tilted her face towards him. 'A curse on this swaying carriage and your stupid bonnet, the cock-feathers tickle my nose and I can't kiss you!'

So it was that, on that May evening, just as the sun was sinking like a ball of fire into the marshes of the Medway, John Blaxland brought his bride to spend their honeymoon at the small Kentish seaport of Sheerness. To the east beyond the harbour lay the sea, and in the gathering darkness they could dimly make out the masts and sails of many tall ships riding at anchor. 'Some of Nelson's ships that defeated the Spaniards two months ago, no doubt,' John said confidently. 'Here at least we're safe enough from French invaders!'

Silently they gazed at the distant shipping, glad to stretch their cramped limbs and breathe the fresh salt air after being cooped up in the carriage. They heard a lot of noise and commotion farther along the seafront, but did not notice anything was amiss until the landlord of the inn came hurrying to fetch them in. He gave the coachman rapid orders about their carriage, hustled John and Harriott inside, then bolted and barred the door with a sigh of relief.

'You'll be the last of my visitors tonight, Mr Blaxland, sir,' he said agitatedly, 'and I'd have prevented you bringing your lady here could I have got a message to you in time.' His leathery face creased into worried frowns. 'Maybe you've not heard – the seamen have begun to rebel again, just like they did at Spithead. It started here on the *Sandwich*, Admiral Buckner's flagship, but now it's spreading throughout the fleet; only today Captain Bligh had to give up his command of the *Director*, one of the remaining two ships of the line. He'd been holding out against his men a week, but now he's come ashore. And the seamen are coming ashore, too, with their demands and petitions. There's danger abroad in the streets tonight for any honest citizen taking sides for or against them!'

From outside the hastily shuttered windows came sudden shouts and cries, and somewhere a drum was beating. He turned to Harriott and told her to go up to their rooms. 'We'll have food and drink sent up to us there, and I'll follow.'

When she had gone John turned back to the innkeeper. 'Speak freely now, my man,' he said tersely. 'Are you telling me that the seamen here have mutinied?'

The landlord nodded, picking up a cloth and miserably beginning to polish his tankards from habit rather than necessity. His eyes were concerned and unhappy. 'Oh, Mr Blaxland, sir, what's to become of our country? You're a gentleman, you

26

understand it all better than the likes of me – but where is the end of it all to be? Our allies gone – Spain, Holland, Italy. They do say Austria won't hold out much longer; and then there's all the unrest in Ireland as well. When will there be peace again? How can we fight the French with only Portugal on our side, and now our very navy in a state of mutiny?' He leant forward, thumping the table with his fist. 'There are four-and-twenty men-of-war lying off Sheerness, and the men have defied their officers and turned the forecastle guns on to the quarter-decks! The red flag's been hoisted and many of the ships have already been moved into the middle of the Thames to block the merchant shipping in and out of London. Some seaman named Joseph Parker's at the head of them – you'd think he was an admiral from the state he keeps! – and it's his delegates and committee-men that are making that row outside now, parading round the streets and singing. He sent a group of them to Admiral Buckner this afternoon with a list of grievances – Parker used to be a schoolmaster, so no doubt the words come easy – but for all their singing of "Rule, Britannia," when they come ashore, they look more like Frenchies than honest seamen, with their murderous cutlasses and pistols waving! I've heard tell that tomorrow two regiments of militia are to be sent for, and they may stop provisions to the Nore fleet.' He paused for breath, then shook his head. ''Tis no place to bring a bride, Mr Blaxland. In these troubled times Newington would be a safer place for your lady!'

When John finally escaped from the garrulous innkeeper and climbed the broad oak staircase to their bedchamber, he found Harriott waiting for him: she had changed out of her travelling clothes and put on a soft muslin wrap; and with her animated expression and hair hanging loose about her shoulders she looked like an expectant child newly arrived at a party.

'Oh, John, isn't it exciting? The maidservants have been telling me all about today's happenings as they helped me unpack, and about this Captain Bligh and the mutiny of the *Bounty*. He's acting as mediator between the rebels and the Board of Admiralty. And today one of the maids saw a poor officer from the *Clyde* cast ashore on the beach by two Irish seamen, and he was all tarred and feathered! There's a brass band playing along the street – can we open the shutters? I want to see –'

'Harriott, Harriott!' He grabbed hold of her hands and looked at her with a mixture of admiration and astonishment. 'And there I was downstairs, imagining you trembling with fear and furious with me that I had promised you a peaceful seaside visit!' He laughed, and led her away from the windows. 'No,

27

you can't look out, I'll not risk some drunken seaman saying he wants you! There'll be time enough tomorrow to see what's going on – that is, if you're not afraid?'

Supper was ready and the candles lit on a small table, but he disregarded it, pulling her instead across the room to the simple bed prepared for them.

'Last night, you know, you *were* afraid,' he whispered to her. 'Aren't you frightened any more, Mrs Blaxland, even though we are in the middle of a mutiny?'

Her confident smile and the invitation in her eyes were the only answer.

Chapter 5

In those first self-absorbed days of their married life, it was hard for John and Harriott to realize how breathlessly the whole nation was watching the small seaport of Sheerness. The newly arrived militia discouraged unnecessary road travel in and out of the town, so the newlyweds resigned themselves cheerfully to remaining at the inn until they could get back to Newington.

It was no great hardship. The kindly landlord made them comfortable, just as he did the officers of the militia, who arrived next day to be billeted on him. Later there was great excitement at the inn when three naval officers arrived after making a bold escape from the frigate *Clyde*, which lay outside the harbour. In the evenings, despite the ever present tension, there was almost an air of gaiety as all the guests sat round the flickering oil lamps in the landlord's parlour, animatedly discussing the rights and wrongs of the seamen's grievances.

Later still came other visitors, Admiralty delegates with cocked hats and grave faces, who had arrived from London for emergency meetings to discuss naval pay and conditions at the Dockyard Commissioner's House in Sheerness, but afterwards were glad to relax for a few hours' rest.

In the daytime, in the bright May sunshine with the seagulls swooping and crying, life seemed more normal; and the chanting sailors marching up and down the waterfront with linked arms looked little different from seamen on shore leave at any port. Only the ominous sight of their Jacobin-type headgear and their banners, and the tiny red flags still fluttering out to sea, gave any reminder of the mutiny. Harriott, shivering deliciously with John's protective arm around her, would have made light of it as some bearded salt blew her a kiss and leered at her knowingly, but John knew the events they were witnessing were no pantomime. However bad the war news, he had comforted himself up to the present, like all good men of Kent, that the sea would always be the barrier between his land and the French. Other countries might succumb, but not England, with her well-guarded Channel to protect her. But now, King George III's gallant navy was rebelling for the second time in a few months, and right here on his own Kentish doorstep. Could it open the way to invasion?

For a number of days it was a stalemate situation. Only

towards the end of the second week did the tension ease. The embargo on victuals to the rebel ships made itself felt. The seamen paraded with less enthusiasm. More officers escaped from the rebel ships and harangued the mutineers and, courageously, so did their colleagues who were still held captive on board. Finally the anxious watchers on shore saw a red flag come fluttering down from one of the mastheads, then another and another, and they heaved a great sigh of relief.

They'll be back to join Admiral Duncan with the North Sea fleet at the Texel any day now, you'll see!' said one of the militia officers jubilantly. John and he were on Sheerness beach looking through telescopes as the rebel ships weighed anchor and disappeared out to sea. 'It was stopping their victuals did it – no man could hold out for ever against that. But, for myself, I hope the seamen get something out of it – those poor devils have had worse conditions than the army, cooped up in their stinking ships; and it's as well the country hears of it and treats them better!'

Hundreds of the mutineers were arrested, and Sheerness jail was crowded with the ringleaders, many of whom were destined to hang. The rest would count themselves lucky to be sent to Newgate, or transported to New South Wales.

John and Harriott left the small white inn by the sea the next day, and returned to Newington. If those days at Sheerness had been a revelation to all Englishmen, they had also shown John a new side of his young wife. He had thought her timid; now he had found the proximity of danger brought out a new self-confidence and exhilaration that made her completely different. And, to his surprise, the old timidity never returned.

The servants had decorated the entrance of Newington Hall with branches of blossom to welcome them, and this delighted Harriott.

'You see,' John whispered, as together they smilingly acknowledged the bobbed heads, 'I was right about how everyone would receive you. Any girl who can face a mutiny as you did, can certainly face the prospect of being mistress of Newington!'

His encouragement was unnecessary. Harriott set about proving his words with a will, and astonished him by the able way in which she settled down to her new role of wife and housekeeper.

'Gregory wants to come for a long stay soon, I believe – but are you agreeable?' asked John one day shortly after their own arrival. 'He's a bit of a firebrand, as you know, and needs sitting on sometimes.'

'Of course he must come,' she replied warmly, adding with mock grandeur, 'but I can't promise to "sit on him", sir, for as you have reminded me often, I am a married lady now, not given to unseemly ways! Anyway, at least I can talk to him as an equal,' she continued airily, 'seeing we are not old like you, but near enough of an age together!'

John blessed his wife many times in the months that followed for her warmth and gaiety, and not least for the ready welcome she gave to her young brother-in-law. Having exuberantly kicked off the dust of Canterbury and his schooldays, Gregory flung himself into the freedom of life at Newington. He followed John everywhere, anxious to learn all he could about estate management, in readiness for the time when he would be considered responsible enough to take over the running of the family cattle farm at Luddenham. In the evenings at the Hall, he had Harriott rocking with laughter, her vaunted married dignity quite forgotten, as he regaled them both with tales of his school exploits.

'King's School must be a far more sober place since you've left,' commented John. 'You can scoff now, Gregory, but one day you may be grateful for the benefits of the classical education they—'

'Lord forbid!' Gregory interrupted unrepentantly. 'They never taught us the really useful things in life, like rounding up cattle; or how to tell the quality of one sheep's wool from another; or how to fight off a French invasion. By the way, John, did you know that Christopher has joined the Fordwich Volunteers? Last time I was home he was swaggering about like no end of a fellow in his new uniform—a blue jacket with scarlet facings. He looks fine as far down as the waist, but below that he's near bursting out of his white nankeen breeches! He even gets up at five in the morning to train: imagine it—old Christopher!'

'Not so much of the "old", sir!' John interposed. 'Remember he's a full year my *junior*.' He turned to Harriott. 'And there's no cause for you to laugh, ma'am, either. You may both pretend I'm in my dotage, but that's no cause for merriment.'

It was as well the three of them could have some lighthearted moments together, for the news from the outside world brought little to cheer them. The threat of invasion was growing. From Rye, from Dover, from Birchington, from Whitstable—each day came rumours of real or imaginary invasion craft on its way to England. John and Gregory spent several days down at Romney Marsh, arranging for their valuable herds of sheep to be moved farther inland, while Harriott, like other housewives, stocked up all the foodstuffs she could for the winter to come.

'We must fortify the menaced ports,' said Dundas, and the men of Kent rallied to his call. If Bonaparte was standing on the French cliffs of Cap Gris Nez and Cap Blanc Nez, looking towards England, the good citizens standing on the Dover cliffs looking towards France across that blue summer sea of 1797 would be ready for him. The Nore Mutiny, as everyone now called the seamen's rebellion at Sheerness, had in some strange way strengthened the purpose of the nation. Young men and old joined the Volunteer Corps in their thousands, proudly dressing up in an incredible variety of uniforms and rising at dawn each day to drill together.

Increasing numbers of John's labourers had their names posted up as volunteers on the church door in the village. He deplored the time they spent 'musket-rattling', but he admired their patriotism. But it was still not his personal way of expressing it. He stuck to his original principles: the plough and the pitchfork were equally worthy symbols of a British patriot as any sabre or musket.

At Romney Marsh he had listened grim faced when a smuggler told him that Napoleon was having gold medals struck with his garlanded head on one side and the words *'Frappé à Londres'* on the other. And the black devil of a Frenchman had given himself a new title, Citizen-General Bonaparte, Commander-in-Chief of the Army in England, the same man said.

There was one ray of hope in all the gloom. The news of a naval victory by the British over the Dutch at Camperdown brought a welcome respite – those men who a few months earlier had mutinied had now redeemed themselves tenfold, and made their country proud of them – but as winter approached, even the autumn gales blowing round the south-east coast could only partially lessen the continual fear of invasion.

The huge cost of the war and the national debt made Pitt demand ever higher sacrifices of his long-suffering countrymen. Everyone was talking about the latest taxes on wealth and property outlined in the budget, and when the Blaxlands met together at Fordwich that Christmas they were the principal topic.

The proposed window tax was Mrs Blaxland's chief concern. Her sons had told her that at least four windows would have to be bricked up at the Manor to avoid the increased tax, and she and her sister were having great difficulty in explaining the necessity to their old mother, who could not comprehend it.

'Christopher says we ought to get rid of one of the carriages as well,' she sighed to John and Harriott. 'This extra tax on our horses is monstrous – if we have to part with the two new bay geldings it will break my heart!'

Patiently John tried to convince his mother that the proposed tax increases were unavoidable if the country was to survive. He had seen for himself how much harder life was for the poor in their wretched town hovels than for those in the country. In rural districts each house or cottage might have to lose a few windows, but this was a small sacrifice compared with having insufficient bread. Mrs Blaxland remained unconvinced.

There was a general hammering and banging throughout the land in the first months of 1798 as the Blaxlands and house owners everywhere blocked up some of their windows, but there were far more serious things than that to worry about. The Channel fleet was lying off Brest, frigates and gunboats patrolled the Downs constantly, Kentish smugglers and fishermen enrolled themselves in the Sea Fencibles, and everywhere in the south-east plans were being drawn up for the erection of blockhouses and barricades in readiness for the hated French. Every day pamphlets were circulated with increasingly lurid pictures of what the invading craft would be like. John had to laugh at some of the illustrations his gullible farm workers brought him. 'Why,' he said, 'that wouldn't even float!'

But invasion fears, alarming though they were, could be shared by everyone; John had something far more personal to worry about. Harriott was with child. She had kept it from him until it became obvious, sensing his reactions, and even in the final months was continually telling him not to be anxious about her. But as the weeks went by and he watched her figure growing heavier and more ungainly as she moved about Newington there were moments when he felt a panic greater than any fear of French invasion. Sarah had laughed and chided him, too, and said all would be well, but she had been wrong. He had married Harriott for companionship, sympathy, affection. In the ten months since she had given him all these and much more – a love that he had accepted too casually. A cold dread suddenly gripped him that this pale, grave-eyed girl might suffer as Sarah had.

But when the blackthorn was bursting into flower in the Kentish hedgerows and the sheep were complacently suckling their lambs beneath the cherry-trees, Harriott Blaxland was safely delivered of a healthy daughter, who was given her mother's name. And a week later came the surprising news that Bonaparte had temporarily taken his eyes off England, and instead was sailing to seek glory in Egypt, with Admiral Nelson in hot pursuit.

Chapter 6

It was New Year's Day, 1800. Outside it was very cold, but in the dining room of Fordwich Manor it was bright and warm. The women had all been busy since early morning preparing for a family gathering in the evening. Now that all three sons were married or betrothed more places were needed at table, and Bess, with Harriott to help her, was hovering round like some flapping bird. The wide sleeves of her best gown dipped like wings as she happily swooped to straighten a knife here, a crystal tumbler there, until she was satisfied with every detail.

With a little sigh of relief, and looking very tired, Harriott subsided into a chair. Bess glanced at her anxiously. 'That's right, my dear, you rest awhile. Another baby on the way so soon is really too much for you – but there, 'tis the Lord's doing, and I know how much John wants a big family, so no doubt he's delighted.' Having allocated responsibility where it properly lay, she turned round to busy herself at the table once more, stopping only with an exclamation of pleasure as John came in, carrying his baby daughter on his shoulders.

At sight of her mother young Harriott clamoured to be put down and was immediately gathered up in a lovingly maternal cuddle. Her father was spoiling her, Harriott crooned over the little dark head: this was a special grown-up party, and she would have to be a good girl and understand and let her nurse look after her....

'Come, let me have her and take her back to the nursery.' Bess held out her arms invitingly to the child and Harriott thankfully handed her daughter over. 'I really think you ought to get another nurse, Harriott, when the new baby arrives; this one you've got wastes far too much time mooning about her soldier husband in Ireland instead of looking after your child.' She paused, rocking her niece to and fro over her shoulder, then turned to John. 'Now *I* know who might be a help to Harriott! D'you remember that girl Bennett who used to be at Lewis's farm? When she came to my classes here at the Manor I got to know her quite well. An intelligent child. She never learned to read or write, but she worked well as a nursemaid in Canterbury when she left here. Now the family are no longer needing her and Mrs Lewis asked me if I could help find another situation for her. If you like, I'll interview her when she comes back to Fordwich and see if she might be a possibility for you.'

Harriott smiled ruefully after the pair of them as Bess bore off the child. 'What a pity it is that Bess cannot find a husband, John! She's so admirably suited to be a wife and mother.' She paused, then went on tentatively, 'I had hoped, when so many of Lord Abercromby's men were stationed round here in August that Christopher ...'

'Christopher?' John laughed shortly. 'He'd be too puffed up with his own importance in the local militia to go matchmaking for Bess, my dear! And too occupied with his own courting – with Sarah Cuffley near swooning with admiration at all his scarlet and gold braid every time he rode over to Canterbury. In any case, the officers he met had more important things to think on than wife-seeking.'

He frowned unconsciously, his mind travelling back to those vivid autumn days when the countryside had suddenly sprung alive with gaily uniformed troops. The huge invasion force gathered at Barham Down, near Canterbury, was itching to get back to the Continent again after four long years' marching and drilling in England. Too long had they been on the defensive, waiting for the French to invade. But the French had not come; now at last the British army was offered a chance to fight back.

Eagerness and enthusiasm were everywhere as the people of Kent had watched the final preparations for a victory that seemed almost assured. Even the Prime Minister had made a special journey from London to his home at Walmer Castle to wish the Duke of York and his troops godspeed as they confidently set sail for the Dutch coast, well primed with liquor to help them on their way.

But where had it got them, after all? They and their Russian allies had fought bravely enough as the golden days of autumn gave way to the mud and slush of the Low Countries in winter, but courage was not enough to counteract mistakes in timing and strategy. The Dutch were not as welcoming as their exiled Prince had anticipated; military muddles prevented the hoped-for capture of Amsterdam, and appalling weather conditions had finally driven the invaders back to England. By November those troops that had survived the disastrous campaign were home again, leaving the Dutch still under French control, and – crowning disillusionment – Bonaparte was back from Egypt, appearing triumphantly in Paris once more.

'John, don't look so despondent!' Gently Harriott summoned her husband's thoughts back to the present. 'Isn't that a carriage outside? Gregory must have arrived from Luddenham.' She pulled aside one of the long curtains and waved, smiling. 'Yes, it's Gregory. At least you ought to be pleased your youngest brother is safely off your hands and into the arms of his Eliza. And I gather the determined Miss Cuffley has finally conquered Christopher, despite his protestations that he would remain a bachelor.'

A few seconds later Gregory bounded into the room. He slapped John exuberantly on the back and greeted Harriott affectionately. The last three years had changed him; the over-grown schoolboy who had stayed with them at Newington had developed into a strong, broad-shouldered young man, exuding health and confidence. Though a inch or so shorter than John, he was more powerfully built. He was clean-shaven, but the thick brown hair that curled down either side of his rather full cheeks made him look older than his twenty-one years.

'It's good to see you both – how are you? John, when are you going to ride over to Luddenham to see my new cattle? Magnificent beasts, though whether I can keep them in fodder this damnable winter, or must salt them down for beef, there's no telling. Harriott, you're looking peaky. My brother driving you too hard, eh? He needs me to show him how to care for a wife!' Grinning, he looked over his shoulder. 'Eliza, Eliza, where are you? Stop gossiping to Bess and come and show yourself – John and Harriott are here.'

Mrs Gregory Blaxland tripped gaily into the room. She was a small vivacious blonde with a retroussé nose and a wide-eyed, innocent gaze for every man she met. Gregory had married her after a whirlwind three-month courtship that had surprised them all. Eliza now rushed at John and Harriott with effusive greetings, then gazed adoringly at her husband.

'Did you tell them how abominably we were delayed in Ford-wich at the new tollbridge, my love?' Her voice was quick and light with the suspicion of a lisp that John suspected was more fashionable than genuine. 'Do tell me, John, is it really true, that Christopher is formally betrothed to Miss Cuffley?' She clasped both hands together ecstatically. 'Oh, I think it's too, too delightful, don't you, Harriott? 'Tis a pity she's so old – twenty-eight is far too late to get married – but, as Gregory says, perhaps she has money, for had she had good looks she would assuredly have married long before. But then you know how wicked my Gregory is, don't you?' She ended in a gurgle of laughter.

Over her head John's eyes met Harriott's in mutual amusement. Thank the Lord his own wife was quiet and tactful, he thought.

Mrs Mary Blaxland picked up the silver nutcrackers in veined hands that shook slightly. She chose two cobnuts from the dish in front of her, then passed them to one of her sons to crack for her. Strange, she reflected, such a short number of years since she had to do everything for them, and now, children no longer, they were doing the same tasks for her. The formalities of the meal over, she sat back and quietly surveyed the family seated at table about her. At sixty-two it was time to take stock, and to wonder. What better occasion than this New Year's Day, the first of a new century.

She was lucky, she knew, that so many of her family were with her. Only her husband and her son Samuel, who died as a schoolboy, were missing, and time had softened these griefs. There where absent places in many homes this day, and widows who mourned not only husbands but children. Yet she still felt afraid. What would the coming century mean for them? Of recent years life had been moving too fast for her. Events made her feel confused and bewildered – the revolution in France, a near-revolution at home, wars and divisions everywhere. How different from the settled days of her youth when her sailor father had captained his ship in safety on the high seas, and her young husband had carried her triumphantly home to Fordwich, hoping that life would not be 'too dull for her in the garden of England'.

She sighed nostalgically. Yet, despite everything, there were still these bright, familiar faces around her. What would their future be? Suddenly she saw them all as the spokes of a wheel, radiating outwards, herself at the hub. Where would they go, and how many years could she count on having them?

'Mother, you shivered suddenly – are you all right?'

Bess was looking at her anxiously, but Mrs Blaxland shrugged off the shawl her daughter pulled up round her shoulders and told her to stop fussing. She wanted to hear what Christopher was saying: some story from a brother officer in the militia that the King had received a personal letter from Bonaparte on Christmas Day, suggesting there should be an end to the eight-year hostilities; and that George III had promptly rejected it.

'And quite right, too,' concluded Christopher, stoutly. 'Who does he think he is, dictating to our Sovereign? Upstart little Corsican! First Consul he calls himself now – it will be Emperor next, I'll be bound! There's no stopping the scoundrel!' He glared round the table for approbation.

It was not forthcoming from her other two sons, Mrs Blax-

37

land noted silently. Their faces showed that they saw the situation differently. Continuing the war wouldn't help the farmers, John was insisting. Scarcity of grain might put higher prices in their pockets, but what use was that when the cost of maintaining the land rose equally?

'Even so shrewd a man as Sir Joseph Banks is against prolonging the war,' he went on. 'He has the King's ear, though he wisely takes no part in politics; and from the farming point of view they both know we cannot hope to improve the strains of our cattle and sheep unless we import from abroad. It must be ten years already since we first imported those merino sheep from Bilbao.' He smiled, remembering. Those sheep had caused quite a sensation. They travelled by road, wintered in Portugal, then came right across Spain and France, doing some twelve miles a day. They had survived the journey all the way to Calais and on the packet boat to Dover, whence they eventually reached Romney Marsh. But, because of the threat of invasion they had had to move inland a few years later.

'"Fresh fields and pastures new",' murmured Gregory suddenly. 'That's what *we* need, John, to make our mark as farmers. If we can't find them here I say we should contemplate seeking them elsewhere, what say you?' He raised his glass: 'I give you a toast – to the nineteenth century, and to the success of the Blaxlands, in pastures old – or new!'

The others lifted their glasses and joined in the general laughter. But his mother only pulled up the shawl she had earlier scorned, and, though her children did not notice it, she was trembling.

Chapter 7

It was one thing to welcome in the new century with optimistic toasts and village bonfires; quite another to accept the fact that a change in date was no magic password to peace and prosperity.

Almost two years had gone by since a laurel-decked mail coach from Dover had raced through Newington with post-horns blowing on its way to London to announce preliminary peace negotiations with France – at last. But hopes of an eventual end to the war did nothing to improve the economic state of a country burdened with high taxes, everlasting price increases and petty restrictions.

There was a new Prime Minister, Addington, but nobody had much faith in him. Billy Pitt might well have demanded greater sacrifices and produced the biggest budgets in the country's history, but everyone was familiar with him, and understood why he was asking it of them. But now, after sixteen years of leadership, he had retired to Kent to lead the quiet life of a country gentleman at Walmer Castle, and a new flag was fluttering uncertainly over Westminster, to signify the Act of Union with Ireland that had caused his downfall. The same Irish troubles had not only divided the nation but had driven the kindly old King to his first bout of insanity; and now he lay seriously ill at Kew.

In Kent, the Blaxlands had their own problems. Christopher was less affected than his brothers by external pressures, because he had brought his docile bride to the family home at Fordwich and life continued in much the same pattern as before; but for John and Gregory, struggling to maintain large estates at Newington and Luddenham, it was a different story.

Gregory rampaged impatiently round his pastures, cursing the restrictions that continually hampered him whenever he wanted to introduce any new methods of farming cattle or sheep, and even his gay Eliza was hard put to distract him from black periods of depression at the frequent frustrations. Instead of settling him, the son she gave him within a year of marriage made him more restless than ever.

John was concerned to see his brother so despondent, but couldn't say much to cheer him. He felt a greater concern than

Gregory's about the future and what heritage they would have
to offer their children, but was less inclined to talk about it.
For his volatile younger brother an extrovert temperament was
a safety valve. But John, with both feet on the ground and
greater experience behind him, suffered a steadier, less variable
disillusionment. He knew they were both doing their best to
help the country by keeping their prices as low as possible; but
in some parts people were near starvation and farmers were
being forced to reduce the price of grain after the sixth bad
harvest in succession.

Had Harriott not become so rapidly immersed in bearing
his children and running their large home, John might have
had more opportunity to discuss the troubles with her, and find
in her some measure of sympathy and understanding. But in
those difficult early years of their marriage, partly because she
was so young, domestic affairs preoccupied her. They both had
their own problems, and neither realized they were drifting to
a dangerous state of apathy in their personal relationship. Even
the initial fears for his second wife in childbed had now lessened
for John; the nursery of small Blaxlands certainly made him
a proud father, but the children by their very existence also
made him less aware of Harriott as a wife, rather than a mother.
He was not to know that often when she knelt meekly beside
him in the Squire's pew at Newington church she was
desperately promising to fulfil whatever role her husband
demanded of her, if only he would give her the idealistic love
she heard he had given to Sarah – that unknown first wife who
lay buried under the chancel steps only a few yards away.

Surprisingly, the danger to their marriage that Harriott had
unconsciously feared came from quite a different quarter, and
it was Bess who unwittingly sent it to them. It was in the autumn
of 1801 that a message arrived from Fordwich that the girl Bennett, about whom Bess had spoken the previous winter, was now
free to come and help with the children, if Harriott still wanted
her. Ever glad of reliable nursemaids now that they had two
young children and another on the way, John told Bess to send
her to his wife.

The day Bennett was due to arrive Harriott, feeling unwell,
was resting, so it was John who went over to Sittingbourne one
golden October afternoon to meet the new nursemaid. His
thoughts were on the disappointing harvest prospects – if only
all the days of autumn had been as perfect as this! – and when
the stage coach arrived from Canterbury he was unprepared
for the sudden, surprising sight of Bennett. The child he
remembered had grown into a beautiful young woman, so start-

ling in her unaffected grace that he caught his breath. Standing there in the late sunshine, regarding him uncertainly from deep blue eyes as the coachman lifted down her boxes, she looked like the personification of all that had ever been conjured up by the phrase 'fair maid of Kent'.

They spoke little on the short journey along the country lanes to Newington. He drove the small open chaise himself – on small trips he often preferred to do this rather than have the company of a talkative coachman – and for once was glad he had something to do rather than make conversation. She asked some commonplace questions about the children, and when the new baby was due, to which he replied briefly. Her voice was quick and low, with less of the Kentish country accent than formerly – that would be the result of Bess's elocution lessons, he thought with amusement. He kept his eyes on the road ahead, his strong hands gripping the reins firmly – no need to remind his neatly dressed passenger of those earlier rides when, ragged and barefoot, she had sat on his horse behind him. and yet . . . 'You still like brown mares, sir?' she suddenly stated rather than asked; and though, when he glanced at her, she was gazing straight ahead at his horses' twitching ears, he knew she had not forgotten. Suddenly, he was more aware of her proximity, with the space of their seats separating them, than he had been when her child's arms had encircled him so tightly all those years ago.

'Yes,' he replied, whipping up his horses, 'and you, do you still collect flowers and rescue half-drowned sheep?'

'Of course, sir,' she replied solemnly, as if it was an unnecessary question. 'One should love all things of nature, as I will teach your children.'

In the days and weeks that followed he saw her only briefly, occasionally running into her by chance on the staircase, or when Harriott told her to bring the children to him. The nurseries were in a separate wing of the house and Bennett's quarters were there, too. Harriott did not say much about her, but he could see for himself how excellent she was with the children, keeping them happy and amused in the dark winter months, where past nurses had failed. When their second son, George, was born on a bleak November day, it was Bennett who calmly helped with the delivery, replacing the assistant midwife who could not get there because of the icy roads. It was she who took the squealing baby in her arms and placed him with infinite tenderness in the crib beside his mother. But when John later praised her in front of Harriott for her help, he did not notice that from the bed his wife's dark eyes were gazing apprehensively at him from an exhausted face.

41

George's arrival was jokingly described as a good omen, and a turning point in the affairs of the nation. Within a few months of his conception in the spring of 1801 came news of a great naval victory for Britain at the Battle of Copenhagen, with the surrender of Cairo by French troops soon afterwards. King George III's recovery and renewed talk of peace proposals cheered everyone at the end of the year. In March 1802 the Treaty of Amiens was signed, and the embattled nation emerged as if from an endless tunnel into the light of day.

Although many regarded the peace with scepticism, to a man of Gregory's temperament the news was electrifying. He galloped over to Newington, expressed astonishment at finding his brother calmly seated at his desk as if the day was nothing out of the ordinary, and immediately burst out with a whole list of plans. At the first opportunity he would take Eliza over to Paris – tourists would certainly be scrambling over themselves to get passages on the Dover packets. He wanted to see if the First Consul was really the monster everyone had said. He planned to visit Frascati's and the Tivoli, and to try to get an introduction for Eliza to the salon of Madame Récamier. Afterwards, perhaps, he might travel on to Spain to see if there was a chance of buying any of their Merino rams cheaply for stock. Now how about John coming with them, and Harriott, too, if she were well enough?

John's reaction was to hoot with laughter, put both hands on his excited brother's shoulders and push him firmly down on to a chair. 'Calm down, hothead! The ink's barely dry on the Treaty and you talk as if peace were settled for ever. Mark my words, this is a truce not a real peace. The French won't consider themselves victorious until they have conquered England, and we won't feel we've won until all the subjugated nations are free.'

He sat down again at his desk, picked up a letter and pushed it across to Gregory. It was an invitation from Sir Joseph Banks to visit him in London next month for a dinner at the Royal Society. Sir Joseph was expecting several interesting guests newly returned from overseas, and had also some new theories on the improvement of wool he wanted to discuss with the brothers. 'Well, how about it, Gregory?' said John. 'Don't you agree that a trip to France can wait?'

As he had expected, Gregory jumped at the suggestion. Both brothers knew that an invitation to Sir Joseph's house in Soho Square was not one to be lightly ignored, for where else could you meet and exchange ideas with such a variety of eminent men from all walks of life? Explorers, botanists, naturalists and inventors were all made welcome at the home of the kindly, bluff baronet who was a close friend of the King, and was recognized as the leading international authority on the natural sciences of his day.

At the age of twenty-five Banks and his Swedish friend, the eminent naturalist, Dr Solander, had sailed with Cook in the *Endeavour*. The notes and drawings they brought back had formed the beginnings of Banks's famous library at Soho Square. At Kew, George III had made him Royal Adviser-General of the Botanic Gardens, where he had been so successful in establishing exotic plants from distant lands that the gardens were achieving a world-wide reputation amongst botanists.

Now approaching sixty and frequently crippled with gout, a lesser man might well have thought it time to retire from public life to his country estate in Lincolnshire, but Sir Joseph's quick brain was as alert as ever; and although he had many interests, his overriding passion still remained the distant land he had first visited with Cook and Solander – New South Wales.

The name 'Botany Bay' was associated with the most glorious period of Banks's life as a young man, and he could never forget it. As far back as 1779 he had pushed for its settlement and recommended to the House of Commons Committee on Transportation of Felons that the eastern coast of New Holland, which Cook had named New South Wales, was very suitable, with fertile soil and a moderate climate. The first settlers had arrived in 1788, at Botany Bay. Finding this unsuitable, they discovered, a few miles to the north, a harbour equal to any in the world: Port Jackson. There they settled around Sydney Cove. In the following ten years Botany Bay became more notorious as a convict settlement than a future colony, but Sir Joseph never lost faith in its potentialities. In 1797 he had written out to Governor Hunter, 'I see the future prospect of empires and dominions that cannot be disappointed. Who knows but that England may revive in New South Wales when it has sunk in Europe?'

He was interested in a young naval lieutenant, Matthew Flinders, who, after sailing his small sloop *Norfolk* around Van Diemen's Land in 1798–9, had returned to England with so much valuable information that Sir Joseph had personally sponsored the fitting-out by the East India Company of a new ship, the *Investigator*, in which Flinders had left Spithead in the summer of 1801, on a voyage of scientific exploration up New Holland's coasts.

It was clearly the subject uppermost in Sir Joseph's mind when John and Gregory arrived at Soho Square to see him. After a few words with Lady Banks, who inquired affectionately after Harriott, they were shown into the large library where her husband usually received his visitors. Servants had pushed his wheelchair into the recess by one of the tall windows, and he was seated in front of a large globe with a group of young men gathered round him.

'Given favourable winds, Flinders's ship should now be about here and approaching the Great Reef,' he was saying. 'See, just off that coastline. This piece of coral mounted in the head of my cane came from there, by the way, and I'm only hoping the botanist and gardener he has on board can bring me home fresh specimens.' He paused. 'If only by some miracle of science I could see where his ship is now, and what they are all doing, instead of having to wait the best part of a year for news of them!'

Suddenly he caught sight of the two brothers standing deferentially in the doorway, and at once struggled to manoeuvre his wheelchair towards them. He held out both his hands in welcome. 'How are you, my boys, how are you? Good of you to come. Gentlemen, may I present to you two farmer-landowners, John and Gregory Blaxland from Kent.'

The brothers found themselves quickly drawn into the animated group round Sir Joseph. Later Lady Banks and his sister came in to dispense tea, and before retiring showed them the beautifully illustrated catalogue of botanical specimens they kept in order for him. Afterwards, the gentlemen adjourned for the Royal Society Dinner, which was to be followed by a meeting at the Club.

The banquet itself was a friendly, informal occasion, the food and drink as stimulating as the conversation. Just before they sat down Sir Joseph called John over to present him to someone whom he called 'a great and esteemed friend of mine who was elected as a Fellow here last year for his distinguished services both to navigation and to botany – Captain William Bligh'.

They shook hands, and John found himself looking into the rugged face of a naval officer of about forty-eight years. They exchanged a few polite words – Captain Bligh mentioned that the Admiralty was sending him down to Kent shortly to examine and survey the harbour of Dungeness with the Dover revenue cutter *Swallow* – and as they chatted John was trying to think where they could have met before.

Not until later, when a fellow-guest enlightened him by saying, 'Surely you know who that is – old "Breadfruit Bligh" of the *Bounty* mutiny,' did he remember. Of course – Sheerness at the time of the naval mutiny, when he and Harriott had frequently seen Bligh come ashore. Since then the captain had received great honour for the brave part he had played in the Battle of Camperdown with Lord Nelson, and several times during the course of the evening John found himself glancing across at the famous sailor with interest.

At the dinner John found himself placed next to a young landowner who shared his, and their host's, interest in sheep-breeding. He began to speak with enthusiasm about some samples of Merino wool recently sent to the Colonial Office by a certain Captain John Macarthur, who had been establishing flocks of these sheep in the distant Colony of New South Wales.

'The fleeces were excellent, far better than anything I have seen here, but I understand the gentleman in question, Captain Macarthur, an army officer, is not in high favour and is returning to England under some sort of cloud.'

An hour later, still mystified by his new acquaintance's remarks, John settled himself down next to Gregory at the Club with keen anticipation. Royal Society Meetings were always well attended, but tonight the Club was packed to capacity. The guest of honour was an old friend of Sir Joseph's – John Hunter, a naval officer and former Governor of New South Wales.

During his five years' tenure of office Hunter had had a running battle with the officers of the New South Wales Corps – those 'soldiers from the Savoy', as he disparagingly called them – who since their formation in 1789 as a garrison and police corps had grown too rich and powerful. In the former Governor's view they had come to have too great a control over law courts, public stores and convict labour for the Colony's good.

Many of the officers had used free convict labour to grow grain on their grants of land, but instead of grinding it into flour for the use of the settlement the more unscrupulous ones, under such men as Captain Macarthur, had converted it into spirits, which, with rum imported from Bengal, they had since used increasingly for purposes of barter. That was why they had achieved the doubtful distinction of being called the Rum Corps.

'Had a body of Marines been permitted to embark for the Colony to replace the Corps, as Sir Joseph knows I wanted, this situation might not have arisen, but as you are all aware' – Hunter shrugged his shoulders and raised his hands

45

expressively – 'here at home such men were needed, since we were at war. However, it was not my object tonight to come and tell you of the difficulties, but rather of the wonders and attraction of life in this young Colony of ours.'

Interested though he was, John found the warm room was making him sleepy. He closed his eyes, and from then on only the occasional phrase such as 'wonderful climate', 'fertile, well-irrigated land', 'great potentialities once the present teething troubles are over' and 'fine pastures for cattle and sheep' percolated through to him.

He did not notice that beside him Gregory was gripping both arms of his chair in determined concentration, as he drank in every word, with parted lips and shining eyes.

Chapter 8

John had been right to distrust the peace treaty with France. A little over a year later, in May 1803, Britain declared war on her old enemy. With a sigh of resignation, not unmixed with pride that there was still enough solid determination left in their countrymen to push for real victory, everyone settled down to the familiar pattern of war.

Again there was talk of Napoleon's assembling his forces for an attack on England – French soldiers were beginning to gather at Boulogne, people said – and Billy Pitt was happily reorganizing the local militia at Walmer once more. Before long it was hard to remember there had ever been anything called 'peace'. But for Gregory, not actively engaged in fighting the enemy, the prospect of returning to the endless difficulties of life at home was one to fill him with impotent rage.

'What future is there here for us and our children, everlastingly cooped up in this corner of Kent?' he exploded one day, as he and John walked through the cherry orchards of Newington. 'I know all our land has been in the family for generations, but how can we ever develop it and expand as we would like, with these damnable wars sapping the country's prosperity? Who knows, even these acres may be grabbed from us one day if the French are victorious and then where shall we be, all the Blaxlands? I won't have my family growing up any Frenchman's vassals; I want them to grow up in a land that is free. Perhaps we'd better consider going elsewhere.'

John stared at Gregory as if he had taken leave of his senses. 'Go elsewhere – what sort of damfool notion is that?'

'No damfool notion, common sense! Just think, if we were to sell Newington and Luddenham now, we could get high prices for our land and set up in another part of the world – New Holland, for instance – and ...'

John wondered if it was the conversation at Sir Joseph Bank's house and John Hunter's talk at the Club later that had unsettled Gregory. They walked on a few minutes in silence, and over the trees ahead of them the square flint tower of Newington church came into view. For seven hundred years it had stood solidly there, resisting change, watching generations of the same families come and go. . . .

'Why have you not spoken of this before?' John asked quietly.

'You're really interested? You really want to know?' Gregory spoke eagerly as they both began to stride on again. 'Well, last week I had a visitor at Luddenham. It was the Captain John Macarthur from New South Wales we heard talked about in London. He's travelling round the country visiting farmers to compare different methods of sheep-breeding.' As John looked astonished Gregory continued hurriedly, 'I only received intelligence the previous day of his visit, otherwise I'd have asked you to come over to meet him. There wasn't enough time, he had to travel on later to Tonbridge.'

'Well?' John's voice was curt. He remembered Hunter's views on the gentleman in question, and felt far from pleased that his brother had given him such an apparently ready welcome.

'For the Lord's sake don't scowl like that, John! I can tell you, he's an incredible man.' Gregory's face glowed with admiration. 'I've rarely met anyone with such energy and enthusiasm – and keen as a razor. He's thirty-six, he told me, and obviously in his prime – a powerful-looking man with a swarthy face and a determined jaw. His one desire is to get back to New South Wales. He says there's a fortune to be made out there in sheep and cattle by men prepared to work. His army friends –'

'I understood his army career was now somewhat in jeopardy,' John interrupted dryly. 'I'm told there's a case coming up against him in connection with a duel; also for trying to discredit the civil administration in New South Wales. Isn't there to be a court martial?'

Gregory dismissed such a trifling matter with a wave of his hand; then went on enthusiastically, 'John, he really convinced me that no other part of the world holds such prospects for farmers with capital and ambition. He said that manufacturers all over England are becoming interested in his wool, now that the war is making supplies from Spain so uncertain again, and soon he's to submit evidence about it before a committee of the Privy Council. *Now* can you see what I'm getting at?'

John was disturbed: he had met his younger brother's enthusiasms so many times before – the whole family joked about them – but he had never known him speak with such serious conviction. Gregory was nearly twenty-five now, no longer a schoolboy but a man to whom marriage, fatherhood and the responsibility of a large estate had given maturity. It was not easy to brush aside such strongly expressed views.

John would have liked to discuss the matter with Harriott, but an affectionate intimacy had sprung up between her and her sister-in-law, and he didn't want to burden her with a confidence she might find embarrassing. She was spending a lot of time now at Luddenham, where Eliza was expecting her third child and welcomed Harriott's company. Though they were of very different dispositions, marriage into the same family and the similar situations in which they found themselves as mistresses of large country houses had drawn them together. The arrival of their children brought them still closer – young Harriott, Johnnie and George at Newington now had two small cousins, also John and George, at Luddenham, so the young mothers had much in common and often made the half-hour drive to visit each other.

One wet afternoon when Harriott was spending the day with Eliza, John wandered into the nursery. The problem of Gregory was still occupying him and he felt restless and alone. One of the labourers had given him a stray ginger kitten that he thought might amuse the children. But when he got to the nursery he was scarcely noticed: George was asleep, in the care of an under-nursemaid in another room, and Johnnie and his sister were sitting at a table with Bennett, so engrossed in an album of pressed flowers she was helping them to make that she had to prompt them to look up and greet him. But when he released the kitten they wriggled down from their chairs willingly enough, and promptly scampered off after the small creature.

John stood there awkwardly for a moment, feeling lost without the kitten clawing him and half wishing he had not come. The children were all right. They had been perfectly happy. Nobody had any need of him.

And then – 'You are troubled, sir?' Bennett said.

He started. She was standing by the table holding the album of flowers, quietly looking at him. He was used to her presence in the house now; when the children were there, or Harriott, it had always been easy to nod or smile, and think of the passing remark. But to be suddenly quite alone with her like this, seeing her standing there in her neat grey dress, noticing the way the small blonde tendrils of her hair escaped from under the white frilled cap, and the question in her blue eyes – suddenly something stopped inside him.

Involuntarily he took a step towards her. 'You are very – perceptive, Bennett,' he said.

It was a remark that to any of his own kind would have emerged as a joke, left on the air as an unfinished exchange of words between them. But to this girl, he knew it was not

49

enough. She was still looking at him, gazing up into his face as if she would find the answer written there.

'I have known you most of my life, sir,' she said simply, 'and something is wrong. I can sense it. It is something I have inherited from my mother, to be able to understand such things.'

She looked away from him towards the window, where the rain was making rivulets down the glass and distorting the branches of the trees outside into grotesque, fanciful shapes. 'They persecuted her because she had the gift of prophecy,' she went on softly, 'but she passed it on to me, and it is a wonderful gift, but sad – because it tells me I shall lose for a time all I hold dear – you, your children – and there is nothing I can do to prevent it.' Her beautifully proportioned face was hauntingly sad.

'Bennett, you little fool, you don't know what you are saying!' He spoke roughly, purposely misunderstanding. 'Surely you must realise you are of great service to us here – to my wife, to the children – why, I could see only this afternoon how fond they are of you! My wife tells me Johnnie already knows the name of many birds, and that you are teaching young Harriott to ride side-saddle, and how well she manages. . . . There is no question of your leaving us, we all need you.'

'And you, sir?'

'I? Dear Lord Almighty, silly wench – have I not said so? What more must I do to convince you?'

In answer she moved close to him, put her hands up to his face, and pressed her body invitingly against his. With an expression of yearning wonder in her eyes she touched his lips lightly with her fingers, then put both hands behind his head to pull his face down to hers. She kissed him fully on the mouth, then with a half sob, broke from him and ran out of the room, calling to the children.

Some time later a servant arrived from Fordwich with a letter from Bess, asking John to come over and see her. 'It is a matter of some urgency,' she wrote, 'but come alone if you can – I prefer to discuss what I have to say privately.'

He rode over at the first opportunity, thinking possibly to find his mother or aunt ill, but after their first greeting Bess set his mind at rest on that. As he would presently see for himself they were well and in good spirits, her mother delighted at the news that soon Christopher, like his brothers, was to become a father.

'I am so pleased for her,' she went on with a certain wistfulness, 'because it seems probable in the future she will not have the chance of seeing some of her other grandchildren.'

'What do you mean?' John asked, but even as he said it he realized the question was unnecessary. His sister's strained, concerned face told him. Frowning, he took hold of her hand and pressed it – an unusual gesture. 'Let's go into the garden, shall we? We can talk alone there, and I'll see Mother later.'

Together they walked down the flagged path to the circular white seat under the walnut tree and sat down side by side, as they had done when they wanted to exchange confidences as children, long ago.

Bess spoke first. 'It's about Gregory,' she said, and then hesitated, looking at the river rippling peacefully between its banks at the bottom of the garden. 'He's quite serious, you know. He spoke to me of his intentions several months ago, before he even told Eliza.' There was an unconscious hint of pride in her voice, which for all her good nature she could not quite banish, as if it proved an unmarried sister still had some value. 'He said he thought I might understand, better than the others, and he asked me to pave the way gently with Mother and Aunt and Christopher. He never mentioned you, but I take it you knew already?'

Bess in a roundabout fashion was referring to Gregory's plan to sell up his possessions in England and take his wife and children to New South Wales to start a new life there. John admitted that Gregory had, indeed 'discussed it endlessly' with him.

'Christopher has some idea already of Gregory's plans,' Bess continued, 'and of course thinks the whole idea utterly preposterous. At least nothing will ever uproot that dear stolid brother of ours from Fordwich and his property here and at Westbere! Mother knows nothing yet: bless her heart, she thinks that, come peace or war, come trouble or prosperity, our family life will go gliding along the same course, as unchangingly as the river Stour at the bottom of the garden!' She stood up, shook out the folds of her gown, and then, as if she must be active about something, walked down to the path by the river and stared down into the green water.

John followed her, and stood for a moment beside her without speaking. Then he put his arm around her shoulders and squeezed his sister affectionately. 'Dear Bess, where would we all be without you? You're the salt of the earth and not nearly enough appreciated.' Her plain, kindly face flushed with pleasure at the rare compliment.

'Whether Mother should be told yet I don't know,' he went on, 'but the last thing I heard from Gregory was that he was

51

going to London this week to have another talk with Sir Joseph. Then, if everything is favourable, he intends to apply for a financial grant from Lord Castlereagh to sail out to New South Wales as a free settler, taking Eliza and the children.' He paused, then added with feeling, 'God grant his decision is the right one!'

Chapter 9

It was in the late spring of 1804 that Gregory finally rode over to Fordwich to break the news to his mother that he had applied to go out with Eliza and his children as a free settler to New South Wales.

What went on in the hour they were closeted together the rest of the family never knew, except that Bess – who had been tiptoeing about the house rather as if a death was being announced – afterwards told John that their mother had seemed quite calm afterwards, almost as if she had already guessed! Perhaps she drew strength from childhood memories when her own mother had had to part with her father for long periods when he was at sea. Or perhaps the sight of Gregory's eager face as he spread maps and plans in front of her stirred enough of the dormant adventurer's spirit in her to make her understand the gamble he was prepared to take; and secretly to admire him for it, however much personal anguish the parting with him would mean.

She had barely registered the news before she had another visitor; Lady Banks arrived at Fordwich, sent by the thoughtful baronet to ease her old friend's mind as far as possible over Gregory's decision. Nothing had pleased her husband more than to hear he had really made up his mind to go out to New South Wales, she said. Sir Joseph had come hurrying back from a meeting of his newly formed Horticulture Society to tell her, he was so very delighted. 'The young Blaxlands are just the type of men the Colony is needing – honest, upright, resourceful and experienced farmers, good family men. . . .'

A sudden thought struck Mrs Blaxland, and she frowned. Surely dear Dorothea had made a mistake in referring to the Blaxlands in the plural.

'Sir Joseph is not anticipating John would go out with his brother as well?' she asked anxiously.

It was Lady Banks's turn to look embarrassed. 'Oh, you know Sir Joseph!' But Mrs Blaxland's eyes were fixed on her face, and she knew she must say something. She smiled brightly and leant forward, confidentially. 'My husband is always such an idealist as far as New South Wales is concerned, you know that! Now, my dear, don't you worry about Gregory! If you will keep it to yourself, I can tell you that by the time he and his family are established there, things should be vastly improved.'

Governor King was being recalled from the Colony: no doubt he himself would be thankful – he had had such a worrying time with problems between the army, convicts and farmers; and, like dear Sir Joseph, he suffered so badly from gout. His successor had yet to be publicly named, but Lady Banks felt sure she could tell Mrs Blaxland in confidence that her husband's choice had fallen at once on Captain William Bligh.

Mrs Blaxland looked up with interest. Of course the name was familiar to her, as it was to most of her countrymen. Her sons had often spoken of the famous Captain who had been master on the *Resolution* under Cook before his name was on everybody's lips because of the shocking affair of the *Bounty*. John had seen him at Sheerness, she remembered, at the time of the seamen's mutiny; and she had heard he had won much distinction since then for his gallant conduct in various naval battles.

Lady Banks's flow of information was unceasing. 'Dear Betsy Bligh, his wife – such a sweet woman, most intelligent, but unfortunately not blessed with a strong constitution, and it is unlikely she will be able to accompany her husband on the long journey out to New South Wales if he does accept the post of Governor.' She stopped, hoping she had said enough to divert her friend from her gaffe about the Blaxland sons.

Mrs Blaxland remained silent, and Lady Banks continued more gently, 'It will be hard for Betsy Bligh, too, Mary, when she has to part with her husband again perhaps for several years, whereas you – you still have other sons.'

'Sons?' Mrs Blaxland murmured, almost to herself. 'Christopher – yes.' She smiled faintly. 'He thinks his younger brother has taken leave of his senses, but then he himself never wants to go anywhere, nor does his young wife. But John ... John?'

They were busy getting the harvest in when the news came from London. Gregory had been waiting in Luddenham in a fever of impatience, alternately driving Eliza mad by his restlessness or else dashing over to Newington to spend hours discussing the future with John.

He read eagerly the official confirmation that his application to the Colonial Office had been granted. In his usual fashion he wanted to do everything at once – put the house and estate up for sale at Luddenham, catch the next stage to London to go to the East India Company to make inquiries about the voyage and possible dates of departure. His thoughts went racing ahead of his words and poor Eliza was in a frenzy. It was John who took control of the situation.

'Leave everything to me,' he said firmly. 'Gregory, you go off to London and start making arrangements for the journey – but remember, every East Indiaman's voyage is dependent on the convoys, and the whereabouts of the French Grand Fleet, so you must be prepared to wait. I reckon it may be nine months or more before they can promise you a passage. Meanwhile I'll begin things this end. There'll be a lot of negotiating to do if we're to get the best prices, and we may find it's better to wait until the spring before we put Luddenham on the market.'

'And Newington as well, John!' pressed Gregory. 'With the joint capital from the two estates, you've already said ...' But John refused to be drawn. Harriott was expecting another child in December and, as he told Gregory, he didn't think this was the moment to talk to her about emigration.

'But it would be the very best time to do so! Does this not offer your children the chance of a brighter future than anything one can see ahead in England? Good God, John, surely you are as sick as I of the same wearisome pattern of the news!' He pulled a face. 'French assault troops assembling at Boulogne, the hourly watch all along the Kent coast for their coming, the new fortifications being built – what are they called? Martello towers. War, war, war! That's all one ever hears about, and no end in sight! Even with Billy Pitt back in London as Prime Minister nothing changes for the better. No wonder the poor old King keeps losing his sanity!'

'That may be, but these are hazards we all share.' John spoke quietly. 'The hazards you are choosing – the prospect of a long and uncertain sea voyage in wartime, then starting a new life in an unknown colony the other side of the world – these will be yours alone.'

'I'm no fool, John. D'you think I've not weighed all this up before deciding? But look at Macarthur – I know Sir Joseph doesn't hold much brief for him, but there's a man who's seen both worlds, he knows where the opportunity lies, and can't wait to get back! I hear now I'll be too late to meet him in London, he sailed on the *Argo* last week. He got the additional grants of land he asked for: five thousand acres in the most coveted district of New South Wales. And he's taken with him eight Spanish rams he purchased at twenty-nine pounds a head at a sale of the King's flocks at Kew last month, lucky devil!'

'So I heard from Sir Joseph,' John replied laconically. 'And

55

I also heard something of far greater import. News has just reached London that poor Matthew Flinders was detained by the French at Ile de France a year ago, when he was on his way home with all his precious charts and journals for which all London was waiting. He's been cooped up there ever since – damnably frustrating for a man of his type.'

But Gregory was undaunted. Whistling cheerfully, he set off exuberantly for London, leaving his brother to set things in motion for the sale of his estate.

John had always been a shrewd businessman and enjoyed a transaction he could get his teeth into, but he never before had to arrange anything on such a scale as this. Christopher had no wish to take on Luddenham as well as his own property; he lived comfortably enough on the proceeds of the family land round Fordwich and Westbere and, when asked, replied irritably that 'if Gregory was fool enough to think he'd buy his estate in north-east Kent from him, he must think again'. So that disposed of Christopher, and casting sentiment aside John set his agents the less embarrassing task of seeking buyers outside the family. He spent long hours at Maidstone with estate valuers and bailiffs, working out the potential value of, first, the land itself; then the Hall and the farms with their barns and outhouses and stables, the carts, ploughs and those tools Gregory would not need to take with him, and finally all the livestock. The more he went into the financial side of it the more aware he became of what Gregory had said all along: if they sold their two adjoining estates together, the proceeds would be much more. Prospective landowners who were prepared to pay out the sort of money he and Gregory wanted were no fools, especially in wartime; they knew that land must supply a diversity of needs, and they had to be convinced they were investing wisely and well.

'Damn them, they're all trying to force the issue on me!' John muttered to himself, and galloped home, angry with everyone. He went to seek out Harriott, only to find her resting. The strain of her fourth pregnancy was beginning to tell, and under the thin coverlet her body was full and ungainly; even in sleep she was tossing restlessly, as if already wishing to be freed of the burden of the child she carried. Her face was turned from him and her dark hair spread over the pillow. He knew he had only to go to her and lightly stroke her face for her to wake up at once, smiling and reaching out her arms; but it would be her eyes and not her lips that would ask the questions. Damn a woman's eyes, he suddenly thought irritably: for the past weeks

56

whenever he was at home he had been conscious of Harriott's questioning look following him everywhere, constantly appealing. At twenty-six her eyes were as darkly beautiful now as they had been when he first met her – more beautiful, perhaps, for now there was greater wisdom in them. The rest of her pale face was of no consequence compared with those lovely eyes.

He looked out at the autumn afternoon, hearing the distant screech of a pheasant and noticing the way the trees were already beginning to lose their leaves. The hazy shafts of sunlight slanting down through the branches were already turning the neatly swept leaves along the drive into mounds of gold. From here, whichever way he looked, it all belonged to him. The orchards stetching away to the left, as far as you could see; the barns on the right, now filled with all the summer's hay; the thatched cottages where the name of every tenant's child was known to him; the hopfields beyond, where the oast-house vents pieced the blue September sky. His, all his, and always had been. Now, at thirty-five, could he give them up for ever?

Three riders were coming up the drive, the sound of their horses' hooves muffled by the fallen leaves. He saw it was Bennett with his two eldest children whom she had taken out for a promised afternoon ride. He smiled at the sight of them. How beautifully she sits her mount, he thought and what a picture she makes in her blue riding coat (one that Harriott, so often pregnant, could no longer wear), with her bright blonde hair and sun-flushed cheeks. She may not be capable of teaching the children what Harriott calls 'the finer accomplishments', but by her very way of existence she is teaching them much more – the love of flowers and animals and all wild things, and the beauty of the countryside we live in.

They were riding now just below the window where he was standing, and Bennett must have sensed he was watching because she suddenly looked up and saw him, the colour of her face deepening. She lifted young Harriott and Johnnie down and they scampered off, but she still stood there, staring at him with her strange, half-inviting, half-wistful smile. A light breeze played in her fair hair, lifting it in a golden cloud about her shoulders. It suddenly seemed to John she symbolized all that his world stood for; was an indivisible part of the beauty of the whole familiar scene in front of him. Could he really choose to reject all this – this beauty that was his for the taking?

A movement behind made him swing round quickly. Harriott was awake and sitting on the side of the bed pulling on her wrapper, looking at him.

'I thought you were never going to stop staring out of the window!' She felt for her slippers, put them on, then patted the bed beside her. 'Come and kiss me and tell me how it went at Maidstone.'

He crossed over to her and did as he was bid, glad, as he buried his face in the dark hair falling loose round her shoulders, that she could not look too closely into his eyes.

When she was dressed they went downstairs together, talking, and were met by young Harriott, who ran towards her mother with a happy smile. 'Mama, Mama! We found so many interesting things – conkers, and hips and haws, and even Old Man's Beard! Bennett says if we had looked longer we would have found more flowers and berries, almost as many as in spring. Bennett says that here in Kent is the best place in the world to live, because nowhere else are there so many beautiful things. Bennett says the blackberries here are the biggest...'

'Yes, my child, but Bennett doesn't know everything.' Harriott's voice sounded brittle, lacking its usual patience. 'When I was a little girl I lived in a country called India, and there my nurse, too, would show me flowers and plants that she said had no equal anywhere in the world, they were so beautiful!' She broke off, shrugging her shoulders and spreading out her hands in one of her typically French little gestures, and turned helplessly to John. 'But she can't understand what I'm talking about, poor scrap, how could she? She'll never see them here; there's not enough sunshine.' Suddenly she turned away, her voice choking her, and to her little daughter's surprise burst into tears.

'Run along to the nursery, little one,' said John quickly. 'Mama is tired – Mama has a headache.' He put his arm round his wife's shoulders and led her gently back upstairs.

'I'm not tired, John,' between sobs she struggled to speak evenly. 'It's not that, nor the baby. It's just, oh, another winter; and the war; and Gregory and Eliza going, and – and – sometimes I long so much for us to get away and start a fresh life. Away from everything and everyone here – and to feel again some really hot sunshine!'

They talked late into that night together. When they finally put out the lamp and snuffed the bedside candles Harriott fell quickly into a deep sleep, her face against her husband's shoulder, relaxed and at peace. But John lay awake listening to the owls in the beech trees outside until it was almost sunrise. When he shut his eyes at last there was no more questioning. His mind was made up. And because the weeks of agonizing decision were now behind him, he too slept.

PART II

... That upon the faith of an agreement with the Secretary of State, your Memorialist quitted a very good situation in Kent, and ... that the Governor, in violation of the faith of His Majesty's Government, and in contempt of the orders from the Secretary of State, did refuse to carry the agreements into effect....

–(JOHN BLAXLAND, Memorial to the
Colonial Office, October 1809)

... Damn your laws of England! Don't talk to me of your laws of England! I will make the laws of this Colony, and every wretch of you, son of a bitch, shall be governed by them!

–(GOVERNOR BLIGH, to his Chief
Commissary Clerk, December 1807)

Chapter 10

John's prophecy of a nine-month wait for Gregory proved to be over-optimistic. In fact it was exactly a year before the two brothers travelled down to Deptford together for a first sight of Gregory's ship.

She was the East Indiaman *William Pitt*, of eight hundred tons, newly returned from the Bengal run, and now preparing for her first voyage to New South Wales, busily loading up stores and provisions. As John and Gregory arrived at the wharf some sixty water-butts were being hoisted aboard, and the ship's guns were being filled and holed – a lengthy business but a very vital one, as John pointed out, with rumours growing ever more conflicting each day as to the whereabouts of the French Grand Fleet.

As soon as he heard the Blaxlands had come aboard, the ship's captain, Captain Boyce, invited them to his cabin, and at once sent his servant off for glasses and wine. The long wait was being damnably tedious – he had written the same words, 'At Deptford', in his log daily for most of April and May now – and it was a relief to be able to meet the first of the passengers

59

who would later be joining the ship. Most of them were due to come aboard at Gravesend. This was as well, for the carpenter was still hurriedly building the passenger's cabins, although the convicts' quarters had been ready for some time.

The master looked up with interest as the two well-dressed men entered. 'Gentlemen? I understood only one Mr Blaxland was travelling?'

Quickly John explained that he had only accompanied his brother to Deptford to have a look at the ship and to help him check the loading of his stores before his family came aboard. 'I myself will be travelling out to New South Wales with my wife and children by another ship, later.'

'A family exodus, then?' The master's curiosity was increased. He had expected to carry convicts, he had taken that for granted, and he knew there would be a handful of ordinary passengers travelling as well. When he had seen the words 'Free Settlers' on the list against the names of Gregory Blaxland and his family, he had assumed they would be like those he had met previously – people of not much substance, or low-grade government officials. But these self-assured young men before him were of a different type: these must be the new 'gentlemen settlers' he had heard the Government was trying to encourage to go out to New South Wales. Well, good luck to them, he thought – they'll probably find it tougher than they think! 'Why aren't you travelling together?' he asked.

'Because my brother decided after I did,' said Gregory. 'In any case there are still many family matters to attend to here in England. Winding up the sale of our property here, and all that: we intend to make the Colony our permanent home.' He dismissed further questions with a wave of his hand, and asked one of his own. 'How many passengers are you expecting to have aboard, and how many convicts?'

'Twenty-two passengers including yourself and your family, Mr Blaxland, but thirteen of those are children.' The master's not very happy expression inferred that he hoped the little devils would behave themselves. 'Then there'll be about a hundred convicts waiting for us when we get to Spithead and Falmouth – we'll be taking their provisions on board at the same time as we load your livestock and goods at Gravesend.'

'Has your first officer shown you my brother's bill of lading, sir?' John refused Captain Boyce's offer to refill his glass. If the master was going to turn this into a drinking session, however well-meaningly, they would never get all the business sorted out that afternoon, and now he had seen the ship for himself he was anxious to get back to Kent.

As Captain Boyce began to rummage amongst the papers under the log book on his table, John signalled to Gregory to produce his own copy out of his pocket, and handed it to him. 'This will save time, sir. Here it is. We would like your approval.'

'Thank you.' Quickly the master ran his eye down the carefully noted items:

12 Trunks for cloth and haberdashery
10 Iron Vats for tallow
 4 Tons of iron hoops and rods
 1 Plough
 1 Tent
 1 Case of nails
 2 Cases of field and garden seed
 1 Case of groceries
 1 Case of shoes, soles, shoemaker's and saddler's tools
 2 Sets each of carpenter's, blacksmith's, cooper's and wheelwright's tools
 5 Cwt. compressed hay for cattle fodder.

Captain Boyce looked up. 'Is that all?'

'The cases of books and pens are to go in our cabins,' Gregory answered, 'and the medicine. As for the livestock' – he smiled apologetically – 'I understand my four bulls will be stowed in pens on the maindeck just for'ard of the poop, with the two sheepdogs chained in their kennels alongside. I hope they will not disturb you?'

'Many years at sea have accustomed me to a variety of travelling companions, Mr Blaxland, and I've had stranger ones than that. There's but one request I would make you, however' – the master's voice was gruff but his eyes had a twinkle in them – 'pray keep control of your swarm of bees! I'd rather meet the entire French fleet than have *them* loose all over my ship!'

Gregory looked at John, who was smiling, and bowed solemnly. 'Sir – I will take special note of that!'

They went on to discuss the prospects of the voyage ahead. Gregory was fetching Eliza and the children to join the ship at Gravesend, but John was hoping to travel down to Portsmouth after that to see them all off finally when the *William Pitt* left Spithead. 'Have you any idea when this is likely to be, sir?' he asked. 'Is there a definite sailing date?'

Considering all things, it was not the most tactful question. Captain Boyce produced a good nautical expletive before replying that their sailing date would depend on wind and weather; on the French; and on how soon the convoy would muster.

*   *   *

The visit to Deptford, seeing for himself all the various preparations for the *William Pitt*'s departure, infected John with some of his brother's unbounded enthusiasm and made him eager to put his own resolution into effect. After a couple of days at home in Kent he travelled back to London again, to visit various ships' brokers, compare their prices, inspect some of the different vessels they had on offer, and begin negotiations.

By the end of the week John had decided to become part-owner with Hullett Brothers of London of a ship he had not seen. She was still on her way back from China, but due to dock at Tilbury early the following year, 1807.

It was a big decision, for it meant that he was tying up a considerable part of his capital in her, but he trusted the brokers' drawings and descriptions and he was sure she was worth it. Hurrying back to Newington to be in time to see Gregory and his family before they left for Gravesend to embark, he spoke about his ship enthusiastically.

'She was built in London ten years ago and is similar in design to the *William Pitt* – roughly the same tonnage and a length of about a hundred and fifty feet. Appropriately enough she's called *The Brothers*! What do you think of that? The great thing about her is that with my half-share of the vessel go the sealing rights! That means that Hulletts will man the vessel and provide the master, I'll have management and direction of the ship until she reaches Port Jackson, and then she'll go on to carry on seal-fishing in New Zealand waters and I'll get half-profits. It promises very well – sealskins are fetching high prices now in England – so you'll agree I've not made a bad bargain?'

Gregory looked respectfully at his brother and let out a low whistle of admiration. He turned to Harriott, who, with Eliza, had been listening intently. 'Lord, Harriott, I always did say John had all the brains of the family! By chartering the ship you'll be able to bring out extra provisions and all else we need, won't you – a manager, a carpenter, a skilled farmer, not to mention the extra furniture, and servants –'

Harriott spoke for the first time. 'Oh, I don't know that we'll trouble to bring many servants,' she said lightly, 'at least, not domestic ones. I certainly don't think we'll need Bennett, for instance – it'll be far better for the children to start afresh with someone new.'

For a moment John looked across at his wife in angry surprise. 'Well, I think that's downright stupid, Harriott. While the children are still so young, surely it's better to take a girl they're used to rather than –'

'No, John.' Avoiding his eyes, she turned to Eliza and smiled sweetly. 'I think you're so sensible, Eliza, saying you'll train convict girls to help when you get there. That's what I'll do, too. As for the voyage out, if we take the farm bailiff I'm sure his wife and daughters will help me with the children then, don't you think? Yes, my mind is quite made up. I know Christopher and Sarah will be glad if we leave Bennett behind to help them!'

Gregory with unusual tact decided it wiser to change the subject. He asked John if he had had any news as to when the future Governor of New South Wales was likely to be leaving England. Bligh was due to set sail early in the new year with his eldest daughter, who was to act as Governor's Lady in place of her ailing mother, John told him. 'So it looks as though he'll probably arrive at Port Jackson about half a year after you – and Harriott and I, God willing, another half year after that.'

The next day passed all too quickly; then Gregory and his family were gone, and Luddenham without its squire was quiet and empty. John had so many business affairs in connection with the property to clear up after they had left that he almost regretted his promise to go down to Portsmouth the following week for a final leavetaking when the *William Pitt* arrived at Spithead, and he regretted it even more when he had been lodging at a Portsmouth inn for a further week without sight of her.

Impatiently he whiled away the time reading the various broadsheets that were circulating. Each day they were sent out on the ship's chandler's boats to the many vessels lying at anchor in the Solent. They were full of rumours and counter-rumours – 'Napoleon arrives at Boulogne to see his invasion barges leave', 'the French Emperor promises the destruction of England', 'After fourteen thousand miles Lord Nelson still sees no sign of Admiral Villeneuve's two-decker battleships', 'the sugar fleet in danger on its way home from the West Indies' and 'the outgoing East India Fleet still waits at Plymouth'. Everyone, all the time, speculated as to the whereabouts of the French Combined Fleet.

'Blast the French Navy!' thought John. At this rate, he despaired Gregory – let alone himself – would ever leave England. But at last the sails of the *William Pitt* came into view, and she dropped her anchor. John was ferried out by watermen ahead of the convicts, and found Gregory eagerly looking out for him.

'Damnably slow progress so far!' he greeted John. 'Even Eliza has had time to get her sea legs by now, and we've only

63

come a small way along the south coast.' His face brightened. 'But I hear a cutter is arriving later today to convoy us to Falmouth, where we join the India Fleet. But tell me, John, what news? It's so good to see you again this last time!'

High above them some of the seamen, agile as monkeys, were employed about the rigging. Others were assisting with the many convicts who were being brought aboard. Earlier, John had seen them sobbing on the quayside as they bade farewell to friends and relatives before being pushed into the small boats taking them out to the *William Pitt*, and farther along the deck-rail he could see Eliza compassionately watching them.

The brothers talked together for about an hour before they saw the pilot boat approaching and knew that soon John would have to go back ashore. Suddenly the moment of parting seemed very near.

'There's a rumour going round in Portsmouth that Lord Nelson's somewhere in the Channel and on his way to join the *Victory*,' John said. 'You can see her lying over there.' He pointed, then gripped Gregory's hand with unusual emotion. 'God grant the name may be a good omen – for us all.'

The next day, 17 July, John prepared to return alone to Kent. He waited to watch His Majesty's cutter *Chance* come astern of the *William Pitt* before she weighed anchor and then, with the other vessels which had been waiting, set out towards the open sea. It was a perfect English summer day, with a light breeze and high fluffy clouds scudding across the sky, and the white sails against the soft green hills of the Isle of Wight made a sight he would never forget. As he shaded his eyes to catch a last glimpse of his brother's ship he saw, in the far distance, the whole of the India Fleet sailing majestically out of St Helen's Roads.

Gregory and his family had left.

Chapter 11

The following January, John received a message from Hulletts in London that *The Brothers* had arrived safely back in England after her voyage to China, and was ready for his inspection.

He had been waiting impatiently for the news, but now he hesitated: Harriott was nearing the end of her fifth pregnancy, and however anxious he was to inspect the ship, he didn't like to leave until she was safely delivered of the child.

Harriott scoffed at his concern, and insisted he go immediately to Tilbury. 'You can do nothing for me by staying here,' she said. 'The best news you can bring me back is that you like what you see and that you've been able to fix our departure date.'

He went with some reluctance; and when he hurried back a week later to Newington – eager to tell her that, with a few minor reservations, the ship was everything he had hoped for – she was lying against the pillow of their great bed, cradling their third daughter in her arms.

It was freezing outside, the February sky lowering over the stark, bare trees. But the servants had lit a log fire in Harriott's bedroom and it was casting a cheerful glow over the intimate scene – his wife smiling at him in welcome, fourteen-month-old Anna was crawling at the end of the bed, peeping at the baby, and young Harriott, with elder-sister authority importantly restraining her.

Coming so suddenly upon the happy domestic picture of his wife and little daughters, John felt a rush of doubt and misgiving. What was he doing – asking a woman to uproot herself and travel with five young children to the other side of the world? Gregory had done it, certainly, but Lord knows how he and his family were now faring, or whether they had even reached their destination – the five months since they'd left seemed an eternity. But when John put his thoughts into words, Harriott swept them aside indignantly.

'Of course we are going, John!' Her dark eyes were alarmed and angry. 'How can you say such a thing? A new baby makes no difference. I thought we might call her Jane – Jane Elizabeth, after your aunt – would that please you?' She pulled him down beside her. 'Now, tell me about *The Brothers*. When will she be ready for us to leave?'

65

Her enthusiasm was infectious. John stopped frowning and smiled. 'At the latest, next September.'

It was almost a year to the day after the *William Pitt*'s departure that *The Brothers* sailed from England. There had been so much to do in preparation the previous six months that the leave taking was upon John and his family almost before they realized it. Harriott's unquestioning confidence in the rightness of their decision was some comfort, but the parting from everyone in Kent was hard, and John was glad when it was behind them.

There was one reassurance he had been able to leave with his anxious mother. The French Navy should not be such a menace to British shipping as it had been on Gregory's outward journey. The previous October, Lord Nelson had caught up with the French Combined Fleet at last off the southern tip of Spain and, as he himself lay dying, had achieved England's greatest victory. Now the convoys leaving British ports this autumn of 1806 still kept a wary lookout for the enemy, but sailed less apprehensively.

Captain Russell was the master of *The Brothers*. John did not greatly like the man; he was a surly fellow, clearly resenting the fact that the part-owner of the vessel was on board as his passenger; but he seemed competent, and Hulletts had faith in him as a master. Apart from the Blaxlands and the bailiff's family and servants, John had agreed they should take on a few other passengers: a Mr Bates and his wife on their way to Hobart Town, Derwent, where he was to take up the post of Deputy Judge-Advocate; a Mrs Reynolds travelling with her four children to join her husband; a Mrs Harris and child, servants to the Bateses; and Mr and Mrs Thompson with five little Thompsons, travelling out as settlers. At the last moment before they left Falmouth a neatly dressed woman came running along the quayside, sobbing and holding out a bag of money, imploring them to take her on board. She wanted to go as a free settler, she cried, and could pay her way. Captain Russell was all for ignoring her, but John, curious at her desperate insistence, sent a servant to find out more about her. He returned to say she was the wife of the only male convict on board – he had been taken on an hour earlier, and was now down below in company with the ninety women convicts who had been brought aboard at Gravesend from Newgate and Maidstone jails.

When Harriott heard the story, she pleaded with John on the woman's behalf, so he sent word to the master to take her. 'The lady won't have much cause to be grateful to you, sir,' was Captain Russell's terse comment. 'When she finds out how

many women convicts we're carrying she'll wish she was travelling on the orlop deck as well!'

Once they had left the shelter of the south and seen England disappear into the autumn mists behind them, a favourable northerly breeze sprang up, which brought them within sight of the Irish coast after three days. They picked up a pilot, then dropped anchor at Cork on the fourth day. John felt more cheerful as he stood on deck with young Harriott and Johnnie, watching the now familiar routine of loading stores, which included water in barrels, fresh bread in baskets and the convicts supply of beef.

'Look, Papa,' said Johnnie. 'They're bringing the convicts up on deck again, just like they did before! What are they carrying?'

'They're bringing their bedding up so that their berths can be fumigated,' John patiently explained.

'What's "fumigated"? And what's that funny smell?'

'They're cleaning the convicts' quarters. That's what makes the smell.'

'But why – ?'

His sister came to the rescue. 'Oh, Johnnie, stop asking Papa so many questions. Let's go and see how the dogs are today.'

The Brothers left Cork a week later, together with five ships of the line, ten East Indiamen and a fleet of transports. As they sailed out into the open Atlantic, leaving war-torn Europe behind them, there was a visible easing of tension. There still might be French ships about, but the sun was growing warmer each day, the sea more blue, and the constant sight of their escort ships brought peace of mind.

The days at sea began to develop a familiar pattern: the crew working up junk and employed about the sails and rigging, the carpenter busy caulking the decks, and the women convicts brought up twice a day for exercise. Harriott walked the decks in the sunshine talking to Mrs Reynolds. Mrs Bates had given birth to a healthy daughter in the middle of a gale off Cork. 'The pitchin' and tossin' made the birth quicker, that's for sure!' said Mrs Reynolds knowledgeably. All the children were enjoying the weekly practice of running out the guns for which their mothers were thankful, as at other times they were becoming increasingly mischievous. Harriott thought it might be a good idea if the mothers took turns in giving the older children lessons.

As for the men, they read and talked and discussed and debated their way through the long, sunny days. Time hung

less heavily for John than for Mr Thompson and Mr Bates because he had his animals to look after as well as his family, and he also spent a certain amount of time each day with Captain Russell. To the delight of the male convict's wife, John arranged for her husband to be allowed up from the convict quarters each day to feed and water the bulls for him – 'although why it takes that man and his wife an hour to feed compressed hay to my animals when I can feed them in ten minutes, the Lord only knows!' he grumbled. Harriott only smiled.

They had been at sea for three weeks when the cry of 'Land on the larboard bow!' brought everyone to the ship's rails. On the right the island of Porto Sancto rose mistily beautiful out of the blue sea. Beyond was the loftier outline of Madeira. As they approached the port of Funchal they saw in the distance the homeward-bound fleet returning from the West Indies.

They lay at anchor off Madeira for three days, taking on fresh fruit and vegetables and wine, as well as beef and water, then stood six miles off from the island, waiting for a signal from the Commodore of the convoy. When it came, it requested that all the masters should wait upon the Commodore. The passengers of *The Brothers* watched with interest as their longboat was lowered and eight sturdy seamen rowed Captain Russell across the mile of clear blue water to the Commodore's ship to receive his sailing orders.

The convoy left the following day, but by noon the West India Fleet parted company from them. As the sails dipped over the horizon one by one and disappeared into the sunset, *The Brothers* turned south-west with the rest of the convoy and, with the prevailing winds behind her, began the long voyage to South America.

The weather was becoming hotter all the time. There was a burning, timeless quality about those late-autumn days in the South Atlantic that was like nothing they had known before. The sky overhead was a fiery arc of blue, under which lay the immeasurable expanse of the sea. Some days, with a good north-easterly behind them, they covered as much as a hundred and fifty miles or more in close convoy. On others, as they approached the doldrums, the wind would disappear, the ships drift far apart with sails hanging limp. Then for everyone on board it was as if they were suspended in a motionless, unalterable vacuum of sky and glassy sea, their world reduced to the size of their own small ship. With no other sail in sight there was no past, no future – only the burning present of themselves, their ship and the endless, indescribable blue that surrounded them.

68

The pale-faced women convicts stumbled when they were brought up from the half-light below for exercise; the vivid glare dazzled them, and they shielded their eyes. But the passengers' children, long acclimatized, ran barefoot and free across the warm decks, their skin salt and their sunburnt faces glowing almost as brown as those of the smiling Portuguese children who had helped stow their fresh water-butts on board at Funchal – was it ten, twenty, thirty days ago?

One day a convict died in childbirth in the suffocating stench of the hold below, and they stared in silence as the waves parted briefly to receive her body as it slipped thankfully into the cool peace of the deep. But at other times there were better things to watch. The way the canvas above them suddenly filled with life-giving air when a breeze came, and cut into the purple-blue of the high noon sky; the antics of a school of porpoises playing round the bow of the ship in the sunshine; and at night, when inky blackness had replaced the vivid blue, the silver streak of flying fish that jumped towards the lantern hung over the rail amidships and then lay thrashing and gasping their last on swabbed decks – a free meal for next day.

The convoy reached the coast of Brazil late in November. After passing the sobering sight of two newly wrecked British transports on the dangerous sandbanks of the Roccas islands, they anchored six leagues off the port of San Salvador. They waited there for a fortnight doing the necessary repairs, caulking the ships' sides and sending their longboats ashore for water and supplies; then set sail again, bound for the Cape.

The weather grew cooler the farther south they went, which was a relief, but as they neared the African continent their progress was delayed by thunderstorms and squalls. The slow progress was frustrating, and tempers on board grew short. Intimacy had not improved John's liking for Captain Russell, and although he had complete confidence in him as master, he thought the man rather too fond of drink.

'Oh, John, do stop pacing up and down the cabin! It's bad enough with everything else on the move in this dreadful storm! Stop worrying about what will happen after our arrival – for myself, I'll only be too thankful if we reach Sydney at all!' Harriott's usual calmness had deserted her and she sounded worn out and exasperated. With the constant pitching and tossing of the ship, the children whining because they had to be confined to their cabin, and the baby cutting a tooth and whimpering in her crib, she had as much as she could stand without an ill-tempered husband as well.

69

She had tried to be loving and cheerful, heaven knows, but this long voyage to the Cape was getting on top of them all. The convict girl John had got to help her with the children was little use – she was seasick most of the way – and Harriott missed Bennett's quick instinctive help more than she would admit. But however busy she might be without Bennett, she didn't care. She had had her way – Bennett had been left behind in England! It was a gamble, she knew, and even in these long weeks at sea, when she had John to herself more than ever before in the eight years of their marriage, she was not sure she had won. For the most part, except when his annoyance with the master reflected on everyone, he treated her with kindness and consideration. But when his face was turned away or she caught him in an unguarded moment, where were his thoughts, she wondered? One day, when he was extra silent, she challenged him straight out; never so much as mentioning Bennett, only asking him if he were homesick for England. But all he had done was to laugh defensively, avoiding a direct answer. He said no man could be homesick when he was between two homes, as it were, at sea; and with that she had to be content.

After a week of storms the weather quietened, and it was a calm and sunny day when *The Brothers* sailed slowly into Table Bay. Harriott's spirits lifted at the sight of land once more and she gazed eagerly at Table Mountain with its low bank of white cloud. Ahead of them lay their longest sea journey of all. There would be no turning back after leaving the Cape – when they next saw land they would have almost reached their destination.

John and several of the men went ashore at Cape Town. It was a welcome break, made even more welcome by the sight of the parcel of mail he found waiting for him. When he was rowed back in the jolly-boat to *The Brothers*, where Harriott had preferred to remain resting, she was astonished at the change in him. He was lively and cheerful, exhilarated beyond measure to have some lines from Gregory at last – the first news he had had of his brother since they had said good-bye at Spithead that September sixteen months ago.

'– and there's a letter for you, too, Harriott. From Eliza. From the thickness of it she must have sent you all the gossip of New South Wales!'

Harriott opened the letter and read:

Sydney, September 1806

DEAREST HARRIOTT,

A vessel is leaving Port Jackson in a few days for the Cape, so I write these lines hoping they will reach you there. We could not write ourselves from Cape Town or go ashore because as we arrived (January 4th) a war was going on between British and Dutch, and all we could do was anchor in the Bay and watch, which – for Gregory – was most frustrating! The constant firing of cannon and musketry quite terrified me, but when we saw the British flag hoisted over Cape Town Castle and knew the Dutch had surrendered we were very proud, and the *William Pitt* joined with all the men-of-war and transports in firing a salute. The children were delighted when the gunfire echoed all round Table Bay!

But enough of that. Our journey was safely accomplished, and now there is so much to tell you, where shall I begin? First let me say Gregory and I pray you are safely on your way at last – surely even your cautious John cannot regret the decision to leave, now that poor Pitt is dead as well as Nelson! Poor England! What leaders now are left to fight the French?

We are all well, but find the heat here very enervating. The next few months – summer here – they tell us may be worse, and already flies and mosquitoes bedevil us.

Since our arrival we have rented a temporary house. By English standards it is very primitive – single storey, made of wooden slabs, with verandahs all round. A rough track leads to it from the road and we are surrounded by the bush, where the constant laughing of the kookaburras disturbs my rest. But it is better and more accessible than the homes of many of the poorer settlers and ex-convicts, who have only bark or daub-and-wattle huts to live in.

Gregory has purchased a herd of eighty cattle for £2000, but I can tell you privately he is very disappointed in our poor grant of land. It has certainly not come up to expectations, nor has the number of convicts granted to us. However, he refuses to be downhearted, and keeps reminding me of Captain John Macarthur, who they say arrived in New South Wales twenty years ago in debt and is now worth £20,000! Gregory has had several conversations with Mr Macarthur (as he is now called, and who returned to the Colony a short while before our arrival) and is most impressed by him. He is hand-in-glove with all his former associates of the New South Wales Corps, who in practice run the Colony, and he remains their virtual leader. These men have the best land, the best cattle and have a complete monopoly, engaging in the most varied enterprises – they are sheep-breeders, farmers, merchants, shipbuilders – even publicans, with rum the main currency! The officers buy all the spirits and goods that arrive in port and prohibit any but themselves to purchase the cargo; thus some three-quarters of the whole quantity of spirits imported fall into their hands; and they also own and operate numberless private stills.

Captain Bligh, the new Governor, arrived with his daughter Mrs

71

Putland and took up residence at Government House here last month on the 14th. It was quite an occasion – parades, military bands, and an address of welcome presented to him on behalf of the military, civil and free inhabitants here. Gregory has waited upon him, and Mrs Putland – who says she once met you at Tunbridge Wells with her mother and sisters, when they were staying in Kent – invited me and a number of other ladies to tea at Government House.

I think the poor Governor has arrived at a difficult time, as assuredly did we! In March, a month before we reached Port Jackson, there were disastrous floods here. Water flowed down from the Blue Mountains (which form the barrier of New South Wales) and the Hawkesbury River overflowed its banks. The water level rose forty feet and submerged all the fertile areas where the settlers had good land – livestock drowned, all wheat lost. Rationing and even famine in some areas have been the result. Imagine it, the coarsest flour soon sold for as much as 2s. 6d. a pound, and up to last month I had to pay 5s. for a two-pound loaf!

Governor Bligh left for a tour of the devastated areas as soon as he took office and he is receiving thanks from all the poor settlers for the way he is trying to help them: instigating clearance operations and seeing they get cheap provisions. But there are others, Gregory says, who are less happy with our new Governor: they dislike him because a naval officer has been chosen yet again for this position instead of an army officer – which I think, considering his gallant reputation at Camperdown, is most unfair! Also, only last week, he promulgated a General Order prohibiting the exchange of spirits or other liquors as payment for grain, animal food, labour, clothing or anything else. This will surely set the cat among the pigeons of the merchants and traders of the New South Wales Corps!

At present the grumbles are only under the surface, and outwardly all seems well; and I hope things will be happier by the time you and John arrive. The differences I speak of are perhaps mere gossip of which I should not have written. Suffice it to say the Governor is trying harder than his predecessor to get on well with everyone: Mr Macarthur dines from time to time at Government House, and Major Johnston (Macarthur's great friend and Commanding Officer of the Corps) also waits upon the Governor frequently.

Dear Harriott – there are many things here for which I should prepare you, but I cannot list them all. Soon – and how I look forward to the day! – I pray God you will be safely here and then you can judge for yourself. You will find many everyday necessities lacking that we took for granted in England; it will take time for you to grow accustomed to the sight of the gangs of convicts, many of them chained, working about the place; and the rough language and behaviour, the frequent drunkenness, and the many prostitutes. I was told that at a recent count the total number of married

women in the Colony was just under 400, while concubines numbered 1.035. So there is much competition!!

I can write no more, for Gregory is waiting for my letter. I send my affectionate greetings to John and all your sweet children, and to you, my love – until we meet here together.

Ever your devoted sister-in-law,
Eliza Blaxland

Chapter 12

The Brothers finally sailed from South Africa on 9 February. The stop at Cape Town and the letter received improved the health and spirits of all. Harriott kept Eliza's letter stuffed in the pocket of her muslin gown, to pull out and re-read whenever she had an opportunity. Now, remembering Eliza's every detail, she could always have something to talk about with John – something to make him think of all that lay ahead.

He seemed more relaxed, less inclined to talk about England and the family 'at home', now that he knew for certain that Gregory was established in New South Wales and waiting for him. He laughed more readily, and played with the children. It helped Harriott very much. She had not told John, but she was almost sure she was pregnant again, and was thankful that the enervating heat of the South Atlantic was behind them. Now the weather was growing cooler as they sailed into the path of the Roaring Forties, and although her childhood in India had made her accustomed to oppressive heat, she was glad in her present state that here it was less so.

Knowing they were on the last long stretch of their journey the passengers were less lethargic, and even when the master's entry in the log read 'Confused sea', they were no longer troubled. Their ship was home, every pitch and toss and groan of her; they knew the creak of every timber, the rub of rope straining against the masts, the music of every wind-filled sail. They trusted her as implicitly as they trusted the Good Lord to bring them safely across the vast expanse of ocean, even when the time came for them and the rest of the East India Fleet to part company. Captain Russell was rowed across to the Commodore's ship for a final rendezvous when they were four weeks out of Cape Town; when he returned to his ship he brought with him final messages and dispatches from the Commodore for the Governor at Port Jackson, and official permission for *The Brothers* to part company from the Fleet next day. Forty-eight hours later he wrote in his log, 'March 9th. Saw the Fleet hull down astern.' When the sun rose next morning there was not an accompanying ship in sight. *The Brothers* sailed on alone. . . .

One early April evening John and Harriott were in their cabin carefully measuring out the children's ration of drinking water when a shout from the deck made them hurry outside. It was five o'clock, and the late sunlight on the water was dazzling. They could see nothing unusual, but high on the masthead above them the lookout was pointing and laughing. 'Land ahoy, land ahoy!' he cried, and like an echo his call was taken up the entire length of the ship. Everyone began to laugh and exclaim and point excitedly. From below decks the news was received with a strange sound, half-cry, half-moan. It rose to a crescendo until John told the master to give orders for the convicts to be brought on deck. Throughout the voyage he had insisted that Captain Russell should show more humanity and consideration than most masters of convict ships, and he would not go back on his humanity now.

The hatches were opened and the women came shuffling up; they were thin and pale and their clothing was in rags, but as they pushed and shoved their way on to the main deck they had the same eager, half-disbelieving look in their eyes as the poop-deck passengers, the cook who ran out of the galley wiping his hands, and even the cabin boy who, against all orders, was jumping up on the taffrail and beginning to cheer.

On the horizon, still almost ten leagues away, was a faint, thin line that looked at first like a wisp of cloud but now, unmistakably, was land, journey's end.

Harriott, clinging to John and the children, stared as intently as everyone else, but felt suddenly afraid. This ship had become home. She understood life here and had grown accustomed to the pattern of the days. For the past eight weeks time had gone on stretching ahead as endlessly as the sea. Journey's end was something invisible, an intangible future that they talked about most of the time, but nobody could really comprehend. But now, minute by minute, that distant streak of land was getting nearer, and soon it would be the future no more. What would it be like when it was the present, and the present was life in New South Wales?

John's arm tightened around her waist. His strong, suntanned face was shining with excitement, his eyes as eager as his children's beside him. But Harriott, overcome with emotion, buried her face in his shoulder and burst into tears.

Now the last days, the last hours, of the voyage seemed to telescope. The children who had played and fought together through all the long weeks abandoned their games and stood with John and the other men, chattering excitedly as they pointed out the different features of the coastline. At first the land had been high and hilly; now it was low, with long, white sandy beaches on which the rollers were endlessly breaking. The colours were so intense they almost hurt: the huge arc of burning blue that was the sky, and the deeper cobalt of the sea below. The only break in all the blue was that made by the distant shore, where the surf-raked silver beaches were crowned by scrub that stretched back into the horizon and infinity. It was not like any English coastal vegetation. No fresh green here of chalky down or clifftop wood, but a drab, exhausted olive, as if the primary colours had been sapped by the sun's burning heat. The illusion was made stronger by thin skeins of smoke drifting up from Aborigines' fires here and there into the still, blue sky.

Harriott came out on deck and joined John and the children. 'Oh, John, I feel like a sleek cat in this wonderful sunshine! I'm almost sorry that when we arrive and I walk the streets of Sydney I shall be expected to act the English lady again and unearth my parasol! Look at those cliffs.' She pointed into the distance.

'Yes, they're the sandstone cliffs that form the entrance to Port Jackson. It won't be long now, Harriott, it won't be long!'

Harriott leant against him, breathing quickly, her lips parted. Tomorrow, tomorrow – Sydney at last, and Gregory and Eliza waiting. A fresh start, a new beginning; a challenge, but she was ready for it!

The following day, at midday, they docked at Sydney. It was 3 April 1807; only one week short of a year since Gregory and Eliza had arrived here. The arrival of any ship was an event, particularly one out from England, and at first it seemed as if all the population of Sydney had come down to the quayside to greet them. There was the naval officer, stiff and erect, waiting to be first aboard to examine the ship's papers and cargo. There were farmers, settlers poor and prosperous, with their wives; storemen who had raced each other down from the Commissary to be first to get news of the cargo; soldiers in uniform well to the fore, assertive and self-confident; three drunken men in rags, taking it in turns to play a trumpet; gaping women in torn dresses pushed imperiously aside by casually curious army officers on horseback, and children – tow-headed children everywhere. They were entangling themselves in the quayside ropes and sitting astride the hot stone bollards, waving, whistling and shouting, as prolific and cheeky as Cockney sparrows in the streets of London. There was a gang of shaven-headed convicts with picks and shovels and emaciated faces; they fur-

tively stretched their aching backs and stood erect in their chains, chancing a lashing in the hope their bullying overseer might find the newly arrived ship a better distraction. Everywhere on the rough stone quayside of Sydney people pushed and shoved and barged into each other in their eagerness to look as *The Brothers* was made fast amidst shouts and whistles and cheers.

'Look! Look! There they are at last, I can see them!'

'There's Gregory, there's Eliza!'

Voices grew inarticulate, words were lost in other words, cries were muffled in kisses and hugs, hands were pumped up and down as if they could never have enough of the wonder of renewed feeling and touching.

'How elegant your dress is, Harriott! Is that a new material?'

'Your plumpness becomes you, Eliza, it does really!'

'Harriott, you'll never guess – Governor Bligh is planning to give a special dinner in your honour next week at Government House – imagine that! – so that you can meet all the ladies of the Colony!'

On, on the voices went, rising and falling, as if there would never be an end to all the joyous commenting and asking and exclaiming. The sweat ran unnoticed down their faces and their overheated bodies as the hot New South Wales sun beat down upon them all. The sails of *The Brothers* hung limp and forlorn against the blistered masts. On the Sydney quayside, the two Blaxland brothers and their families were together again.

Chapter 13

It had been arranged that for the first few weeks John and his family should stay with Gregory and Eliza at their farm on the north side of the Parramatta River – 'to get their land legs', Gregory said, a mental and physical necessity after seven months at sea.

They were glad it was the beginning of autumn, with weather no warmer than a pleasant English summer. They talked and exclaimed and asked each other constant questions, in their initial eagerness hardly waiting for the answers. But it was not easy for Eliza, in the final month of her pregnancy, to have so many in her house for long. The two families had a total of eight small children between them, and with the eldest only ten these lost no time in forming passionate cousinly loves or hates for each other. Eliza's convicts soon made life disagreeable for the Blaxland servants who had travelled out on *The Brothers*, so before long there was not much peace for anybody.

John was anxious to get everyone established as soon as he could. His concern was not only for his own family but also for all the workpeople he had brought with him. He was impatient to inspect the land he had been thinking about for so long, to see what houses and huts there already were and what should be built, and he could not understand his brother's reluctance to take him to see it.

Gregory caught hold of his brother's bridle. 'Listen, John – before we go – it *is* fertile soil along much of the south side of the Parramatta, right enough – but not the land you've been granted. I wasn't going to spoil your first days here by telling you in detail, but now you'd better have it straight. It's nothing like the promised eight thousand acres: nearer thirteen hundred. It may look fine enough on the plans, with Duck Creek on the north-west and the Parramatta road to the south, but it's very different when you actually see it. It's damn poor swampy land with nothing fertile about it!'

A muscle in John's face twitched. 'Let's see it, anyway.'

After the convicts had ferried them the sixty yards across the river, they remounted and made their way along a muddy track along the south bank until they reached John's land. The whole area had been roughly pegged out by stakes cut from the surrounding bush. The beginnings of a boundary had been marked

78

between the stakes by rough stones, on the warm surface of which an occasional sleepy lizard basked motionless in the sunshine. The sky above was large and overpowering.

The little party of men reined in their glistening horses and surveyed the marshy brown acres in front of them. A magpie flew overhead in a commotion of black-and-white wings, then settled in the branches of a dusty gum tree some distance off and stared at them. Apart from the river, the only sound that broke the vast silence was the everlasting buzzing of the flies and the gentle swishing of the horses' tails.

'I'm sorry, John.' Gregory's eyes were on his brother's face as if desperately trying to read his thoughts. Little trickles of sweat ran along the creases of his forehead. 'To travel thirteen thousand miles and then be confronted by – this!' He spat contemptuously on the ground, and the globule of spit landed on an anthill where it lay like a gleaming eye, looking reproachfully back at him. 'This is not what I hoped to show you!'

Surprisingly, John's only answer was to laugh. It was a big, rolling laugh, a laugh with no pretence, coming from deep inside him, shaking his whole body until the buckles on his horse's harness jangled. If there was a touch of grimness, too, Gregory didn't notice: all he knew was that John remained undaunted. All through the years of his own childhood his elder brother had been behind him, encouraging him, restraining him, picking up the pieces when he was in any scrape or trouble. If John could laugh now, confronted by his unpromising land stretching into the shimmering distance, well, by God, there was hope yet!

'It reminds me of some of the land along the Thames,' he was saying. 'This river is tidal, isn't it? And subject to flooding? Well, we often tackled similar problems at home at Westbere when the Stour flooded, so this shouldn't be too difficult.' His eyes narrowed. 'Let's see now, if we could make an embankment and enclose about a thousand acres and get some salt-pans going and build a boiling-house, then we could make good salt for meat preserving here. And once the cattle are established we'll get a dairy going and build a slaughter-house. Now, where are we going to live?'

He turned to gaze speculatively at the few run-down buildings dotted about the area, and the larger, crude-looking house set farther back from the river. 'That's our place, is it, Gregory? No palace – but given time doubtless we can build on to it and Harriott will be able to make something of it.' He put up his hand to shade his eyes from the merciless glare of the sun and looked farther on to where the river bank sloped up to higher hills. 'Who lives in that homestead over there, Gregory – some two miles away?'

'Oh, that's Elizabeth Farm, a well-established place, where John Macarthur and his family live.' Gregory began to grin. 'See, I told you the Parramatta area was where all the best people live!'

'Well, this will be all right in time.' John paused as an idea struck him. 'We might even call it Newington!' He laughed. 'Now, where do I apply for my cattle, and those eighty convicts I've been promised?'

There were fewer cattle allowed to him than expected, and there were not eighty convicts. That was the worst blow of all. In spite of all the official documents from England, and the pledges signed by Lord Castlereagh, only twenty-three men were offered to John when he got back to Sydney.

'. . . And two of them are in their dotage, one coughs continually, another has only one arm, and the third is a gibbering idiot! What price all the indulgences of a grateful Colonial Office in England if that's how we're treated when we get there – poor land, inadequate labour and precious little else!' John flung down some building plans his overseer had given him, and glared in disgust at Gregory and Eliza and Harriott.

They had never seem him so angry, and with reason. The thought that in all good faith he had turned down the offer of a free passage out for his family and servants and all his farming equipment and stores rankled most of all. Because he had been obliging enough to charter his own ship, their voyage had cost the Government nothing. Certainly he had promised to invest six thousand pounds in the Colony, but the way things looked he would have to invest a damn' sight more. At the very least he had expected to be able to count on the Colonial Office's promise of eight thousand acres. As to the firm guarantee of eighteen months' free supply of food and clothing for his eighty non-existent convicts, when he thought of the twenty-three wretched downtrodden creatures allocated to him, that was the most damnably funny statement of them all! He wished he had both Sir Joseph and Lord Castlereagh in front of him now, he would have a few home truths to tell them – they with their assurances that 'settlers of responsibility and capital' were needed, stressing his 'property and education', and saying that he and Gregory would 'set useful examples of industry and cultivation, and be fit persons under whose authority the convicts may be safely placed'!

Eliza, sitting in a basket chair and fanning herself, was regarding him with cool amusement. At the time of her marriage John had held no particular brief for his sister-in-law. Privately he had thought her pretty but ineffectual, with few original opinions of her own and too many affectations. But now she was changed. The blonde curls that had been so elaborately dressed were pulled back into a knot on top of her head; and the face thus exposed had developed a greater understanding. In the short time since their arrival several of her remarks had shown she had become a far more practical woman. Harriott was certainly right: Eliza was proving herself a better wife for young Gregory than he had prophesied.

'Don't you see,' she was saying, folding away her fan, 'there's a perfectly ordinary explanation? I've been trying to tell Gregory, but he won't listen! The very reason you haven't been given all that was promised you in England is that everyone here is suspicious of you. Nobody like you and Gregory has ever come to the Colony before, so nobody knows what to make of you. You're an entirely new breed – gentlemen farmers with money – and so far they haven't got a category to put you in! The army, too, will be suspicious of you – your capital will make them fear you'll steal a march on them if you have too much land; the poor settlers won't be able to compete with you; the ex-convicts who have already acquired land and positions here by unorthodox means will dislike you. You're not even honest-to-goodness convicts to be bullied and lashed and told what to do!' She put up a protesting hand to stop their laughter. 'No, wait, I'm not being stupid! You must face it – to everyone here you're intruders come into this tight little Colony with its neatly organized corruptions and vices, and they'll all be watching you out of the corners of their eyes to see which group you'll settle for.'

Gregory looked at his wife with proud affection. 'She's right, you know, John – she's summed it all up admirably. The question is, whom do we join?'

There was soon to be an opportunity for John and Harriott to size up all the leading members of the Colony. Eliza pointed to a card with a heavily embossed crest, lying on a side-table near them. It was the Governor's invitation, delivered that morning by special messenger, for a dinner to be given in the newcomers' honour the following Saturday at Government House.

Harriott chose her gown with infinite care. Not the yellow, that was too simple, nor the blue, which was too elaborate, and rather too close-fitting, since she was pregnant again. She would

81

be quizzed from every angle, Eliza said. The 'ladies of the Colony' were very jealous of their privileges, and any newcomer who showed signs of trying to be too *haut ton* would be regarded with much cattiness and jealousy.

'Save the blue till next year,' advised the practical Eliza. 'That fashion may have reached here by then and you'll be able to produce it in triumph – that is, of course, if you're not pregnant yet again.' She heaved a small self-pitying sigh; she was likely to be preoccupied with other things when her sister-in-law was introduced into New South Wales society.

They settled finally on the rose silk, as being not too dressy. Eliza giggled, 'You've no idea, Harriott, the ridiculous rivalry there is here among the women. "Ladies of the Colony", indeed – some of them are more like fishwives. When a trading ship comes into Sydney Cove they'll even steal their husbands' rum to barter for a length of Indian muslin or Chinese silk!'

When the evening came Harriott was grateful for Eliza's warnings and advice. With her hand on her husband's arm, excitement lending a most becoming colour to her face, she walked up the verandah steps of the simple white building that was Sydney's Government House. In the drawing room Governor Bligh and his daughter were waiting to receive them. The Governor was in full naval uniform, his campaign medals gleaming on his chest. A thickset man of average height, with dark hair greying over the temples, he looked strong and well preserved for his fifty-two years. He had a prominent nose, firm mouth, and eyes of a very noticeable blue. His daughter's eyes were the same colour, Harriott noted; she liked the look of Mary Putland, a young woman in her early twenties, who came forward at once to greet her.

'Mrs Blaxland – welcome! My father and I have been eagerly awaiting your coming. You had a good voyage? I must thank you and Mr Blaxland most sincerely for so kindly bringing out the letters and parcels on *The Brothers* from my mother. When you have been here a little longer you will know what joy such links with home are. Have you met my husband yet? Mr Putland, my love, come over here and meet Mrs Blaxland before the other guests monopolize her.'

Lieutenant Putland, a young naval officer who had come out to New South Wales on his father-in-law's staff, came forward to be presented. He did not look very strong, and coughed a great deal, which caused his wife to watch him anxiously. He spoke pleasantly, and asked Harriott if she was getting acclimatized.

'Yes, but my children are still distinctly puzzled at not seeing the sun in its accustomed place in the sky at midday.' She laughed. 'When we drive out into the country we are continually losing our sense of direction!'

Guests began to pour into the room, and the next half-hour was so filled with introductions and presentations that Harriott, standing at John's elbow, grew quite bewildered. Uniforms predominated amongst the men. She thought the women a mixed collection, and decided Mrs Putland was the most agreeable.

Not until they were seated at dinner, and she found herself in the place of honour next to the Governor, did Harriott have an opportunity to study the guests. At first impression it was hard to remember that she was not at a large dinner party at any county home in England. His Excellency was clearly determined to bring some style to colonial living – the Waterford glass chandeliers, the Doulton dinner service, the silver candelabra, the English crystal, even the tablecloths of Nottingham lace – all these could have been found in any well-appointed house in England. But here the illusion ended. The guests were far more varied, as proclaimed by their voices as well as their conversation. There were accents from Scotland, Ireland and the West Country, as well as from southern England. When the Governor turned aside from her for a few minutes to engage his daughter and John in conversation, Harriott tried to memorize the names.

Mr Palmer, the Commissary of the Colony; Surgeon John Harris, who also acted as the Governor's naval officer and checked exports and imports; Mr Gore, the recently appointed Provost-Marshal who had come out with Governor Bligh; the Reverend Henry Fulton, who had replaced the Reverend Samuel Marsden the previous year; Mr Divine, the Superintendent of Works – she had already seen him several times riding about on a white charger – and near him Mr Oakes, who they told her was the Chief Constable of Parramatta.

'Who is the gentleman seated near Mr Gore?' she whispered to the obliging Lieutenant Putland, who sat on the other side of her.

'That's Mr Atkins – Richard Atkins, the Judge-Advocate,' he whispered back. 'A gentleman rather too fond of the bottle, as you may observe.' He frowned. 'John Macarthur's a fool to see that his glass is refilled so often!'

She looked, and noticed the way the Judge-Advocate's hand clutched his glass. His face was dissipated, and his red eyes puffy. So that dark, curly-haired man opposite him was the well-known John Macarthur! She might have guessed, from what John and Gregory had told her. Obviously a positive, dominant personality – anyone could see that, even from a distance – and she could easily imagine the attraction such a man would have for her brother-in-law. As she watched, a shout of laughter rose from the group seated round Macarthur; it was easy to guess from the hurried glances and the hands covering mouths that it was probably some bawdy joke about the Governor.

Harriott glanced at Captain Bligh, and saw his eyebrows drawn together in a quick frown, his mouth hard and the blue eyes narrow. She remembered some gossip Eliza had been telling her of a story that had been going round Sydney a few months before they arrived. It was said that Macarthur and the Governor had a violent altercation about the former's grant of land and large flocks of sheep, during which the Governor was supposed to have said, 'What have I to do with your sheep, sir? What have I to do with your cattle? Are you to have such flocks of sheep and herds of cattle as no man ever had before? No, sir!' And then gossip had it that he added furiously, 'Damn the Privy Council, and damn the Secretary of State, too; he commands at home, I command here!' Whether true or not, it was clear just from looking at them, Harriott decided, there was little love lost between the two men.

'And the officer who is in command of the 102nd Regiment – the New South Wales Corps – he has been here with the army a long time, under previous Governors?'

'Major Johnston? Yes, indeed, he was aide-de-camp here under Governor Hunter. He's not a bad fellow, but he has a very mixed collection of men under him, many of them no better than common criminals – but you must remember the Corps was not enlisted as a fighting unit, only for garrison or police service. All the best men stayed in England. These rum-drinking soldiers wouldn't put up much of a fight against Napoleon! Major Johnston's great friend and confidant, Mr Macarthur –

'Mrs Blaxland, will you not try some of this pineapple?' the firm voice of Governor Bligh deliberately interrupted his son-in-law. He was bending towards her and holding out a basket of fruit. He glanced across her at Lieutenant Putland, who had flushed with embarrassment, and was beginning to cough again.

'My son-in-law is quite right,' the Governor went on calmly. Although he was looking at her again Harriott had the impression his words were for everyone. 'I was just telling your husband there's far too great a dependence on liquor here in the Colony, and I am determined to suppress the rum monopoly, whatever the cost. There's no popularity to be gained by it, but then life has already taught me that if one does one's duty one is rarely liked for the execution of it.' He gave a short laugh. 'Most of the Army here, and others besides' – his eyes strayed briefly to the Judge-Advocate – 'have all tried to convince me and my predecessors that drunkenness is the permitted vice of a gentleman. I happen to think otherwise, and so does the British Government. My aim is to see honest law and a stable currency, and I want to help the oppressed poor settlers like those on the Hawkesbury who have no hope here without proper support. With the backing of the Government at home and the support of men like your husband and his brother, I intend to see justice done, whether some like it or not!'

Chapter 14

They could put up a roughly carved wooden sign with the name 'Newington', and they could plant an avenue of young English trees leading up to the house, but to think of it as home was something that took much longer. John installed Harriott and the children in the low-built, slab-like edifice at the beginning of the winter. She was as glad as he to have somewhere of their own at last; Eliza was busy with her new baby and they had all been at close quarters for long enough.

Nothing was finished when they moved in, and she had to put up with much sawing and hammering the first weeks as Gregory's workers as well as their own built new timber-framed rooms on to the existing house to fit their needs. But the work took longer than they had thought; the carpenter and his men fresh from England were not used to working with hardwood and it took them time to adapt their tools. There were delays until a couple of craftsmen experienced in working with the local wood could be fetched over from Parramatta to instruct them.

Harriott had other difficulties, too. With fewer convicts than he had calculated for, John needed all available workers on the land, so she was left with the two servants she had brought out from England to help with the house and children, and a couple of convict girls from Sydney to do the laundry and the dairy. John promised her more help later, but for a start these had to do.

It took all her time in the beginning deciding how best to organize her days. The solitude of country life held no fears for her; in many ways she was glad to escape the social distractions that had inevitably been part of their life in England. But there were so many adjustments to make that sometimes she wondered if she would ever get used to them all. People had complained of the shortages in Kent caused by the war, but how many things that were taken for granted there were unobtainable in this new land!

'Never mind, it will make the children more self-reliant,' said John optimistically. He had just restored an uneasy peace between his son and daughter at the end of a childish squabble. 'Young Harriott only threw the slate at George because he was trying to melt the wax face of her favourite doll – now they know they'll get neither new dolls nor new slates here as easily as in England, perhaps they'll learn their lesson.'

86

They were sitting in the big living room having their evening meal. Young Harriott had been sent to bed with the younger ones as a punishment, but Johnie was allowed to sit up with them, and was determined to take full advantage of it.

'Father, can I come with you when you go over to see Uncle Gregory at Brush Farm tomorrow?'

'And miss your lessons?' John asked. The bailiff's wife, who was established in a house half a mile away from them, had just begun classes for the settlers' children in the area with a widowed friend, Mrs Flower, who was a governess. Johnnie and Harriott and George went to her for a few hours' simple instruction each morning. 'What does your mother say?'

'It's quite rough going,' she said anxiously. 'Will it be safe, and won't he delay you?'

Johnnie hotly denied the suggestion, and begged so hard that his father gave in.

'How long will you be away, John? Will you stay overnight?' She had heard stories of blacks coming in from the bush at night to spear the settlers' cattle, and she was apprehensive.

'Yes, probably, but if you lock up properly and keep the dogs in the house with you, you'll be all right. The overseer down at the convict hut is a reliable fellow – no trouble there – and anyway Mr Hopper will be bringing his gang over early tomorrow to start building the new cow-bails. I'll certainly be glad when they are ready, then we can really get the dairy working and sell the produce.'

'We'll grow grain, won't we, Father?' Johnnie asked.

'Some, of course – enough to feed the animals – but I think it's best we do as Uncle Gregory suggests and invest in sheep and cattle rather than grain. The people here need good red meat in their bellies, and at a price they can pay – and if we can give them enough of it, then we'll get rich.'

'That's what Mr Macarthur says too, isn't it?' Johnnie looked thoughtful for a moment, then began to grin. 'I know a song about him and Major Johnston – shall I sing it?' Without waiting for invitation he began to pipe, '... That turnip-head fool, Jack Bodice's tool ...' "Jack Bodice" is what they call Mr Macarthur, Mother, because he was once apprenticed to a staymaker in England, and Tom told me that he saw Major Johnston last month when he was riding with some of his officers, and it *is* true, his head *is* shaped like a turnip –'

'My God, who taught you that scurrilous ditty?' thundered John. 'And who's Tom, in Heaven's name? You haven't been playing with that convict's bastard again, have you? If so –'

'John, John!' remonstrated Harriott. 'Johnnie didn't realize

87

the implications. . . .' She turned to her son who was cowering in his seat, looking frightened. 'Where did you hear that, anyway?'

'It was – I read it – they were using old newspapers – the *Sydney Gazette* and pages of old journals from England, and – and leaflets, and any paper there was, and they were pasting them over the walls of the room over the barn, and I was helping. I – I just read it. . . . Tom didn't tell me, he can't read, and when I'm with him we always play with the animals instead.'

His father looked less angry. 'All right, then,' he said, regretting the fear he had seen in his son's eyes. 'Go to bed, then, and we'll start early tomorrow. But mind you don't let me catch you quoting lines like that again, and when you want playmates don't go seeking out the convicts' children; they're not for you.'

'But, Father, Tom's not a convict's bastard! His father's got a free pardon, he told me so, and the woman who lives with them, she's nice, too, she keeps a grog-shop in the Rocks district, Tom told me. His mother doesn't like her, but he does, and she's got a lovely new baby . . .'

'Johnnie, go to bed!'

Not daring to catch her husband's eye, Harriott bundled their informative eldest son out of the room. But on her return she was relieved to find John roaring with laughter.

'Out of the mouths of babes and sucklings, indeed!' he said to her, slapping his knee. 'He'll do all right, that boy. He's got the situation here in a nutshell, and he's got the wit and intelligence to deal with it.'

John was away very often those early months, but Harriott soon grew used to his frequent absences. She kept the two guard dogs, Keeper and Watcher, always in the house at nights, and in the daytime, though she missed John, she was inwardly content. Here in this new land she knew her husband was doing what he wanted, without constantly being hampered by the restrictions of war-torn England. There, frustration had made him seek other – and far more worrying – distractions.

Looking back, afterwards, she remembered those first weeks of winter as the happiest times, in spite of all the early difficulties. John would come in, muddy from a three-day visit to Cockle Bay at Sydney where his new dairy and slaughter-house were being built, and would tell her all about it between hungry mouthfuls of the meal she had got ready for him. With baby Jane bouncing up and down on her knee, she would sit and watch him, his eyes full of enthusiasm as he described to her

88

fresh plans for extending farm buildings or diverting the course of some stream for better irrigation. She would try to look intelligent, but privately she would be thinking, 'How like he is to Johnnie and George when he has that eager expression!' or 'Would he be angry if I told him how distinguished those first threads of grey in his thick brown hair make him?' Then she would look at the dirty old broad-brimmed hat he had tossed down on the seat beside him; she loved to see it there, that hat, because it typified everything that was new and different in their lives. In Kent she would long ago have made him throw it out, muddy and sweat-stained as it was, but here, on the long days when he rode out with his bailiff and graziers, the hat was part of him. He was working harder than he had ever worked before, but he was strong and healthy and he revelled in it.

Her own days were never long enough. The birth of the new baby, Louisa Australia, made only a brief interruption; Harriott was soon up and about again, busier than ever. Caring for the children, planning the meals, experimenting with the making of pumpkin preserve or quince jelly; seeing that the girls scalded the milk pans properly and put enough salt in the butter, making up the yards of curtain material she had brought from England – the jobs were endless, this first winter. Sometimes she went down to Sydney with John on the packet-boat, and occasionally to visit Eliza at Brush Farm, but for the most part she was fully occupied learning about this new world they'd come to.

In Kent, she had been far less aware of farm life: the formal gardens and cherry orchards had provided a barrier. But here, where nothing was established unless by nature, she was conscious of the animal life about them. Sheep were everywhere. It was the crutching season, and the hot, musky smell of their bodies rose up in the air from their thick fleeces. Cattle, too – fine herds, which John said held great promise for the future. By June he had collected his share of government stock and got his drovers to bring them up to Newington, after which it was a full-time job to see none of them strayed or were stolen before the fences were up.

Sometimes Harriott would take the children to watch the cows being driven into their bails for milking. The older ones would try to help; the younger ones would stare, solemn and round-eyed, as the cow-hands pulled the stiff teats and the milk foamed into the pails; and then they would all compete with each other for the first taste of the warm, frothing liquid.

'You need stronger stuff than that to make a man of you!' whispered one of the men to Johnnie and his young brother one day, after their mother had gone back to the house. 'You come round to the back of the barn there after milkin' time!'

Johnnie and George looked excited and smiled at each other. Young Harriott overheard, and being the eldest thought it her duty to tell her mother. Harriott, preoccupied, forgot all about it, but when the two boys had not returned some half-hour later she remembered and felt anxious.

'Where did you say they were going?' she asked.

'Behind the barn,' said her daughter importantly. 'The man said it was stronger than milk, what he'd give them!'

John was away somewhere, there was no use waiting for him. And it had begun to rain – heavy, slashing, soaking rain, quite different from the gentle rain she'd known in England. The gum trees to the side of the house looked black against the sullen evening sky. She tied a shawl anyhow over her head and shoulders, looped up her skirt, and ran the couple of hundred yards across the rough, stony ground to the newly erected barn. There was nobody in sight and the door was shut, but, hearing noises inside, she pushed her way in.

As her eyes got used to the half-light she stood transfixed, the rain dripping off the fringe of her shawl and her sodden skirts in little pools amongst the fowl-droppings. There indeed were her sons, rolling helplessly about on the straw bales at the far end, squeeling with laughter. Beside them were five men she recognized as John's farm labourers. They were all squatting round an unmistakable bucket of rum. The smell of it rose in the stuffy air, mixed with that of cattle manure, damp straw and sacking, and wet human clothing. The men all had pint-pots in their hands and were using them to ladle out the liquid, slopping it round in drunken abandon. Even as she watched, one of the men – she recognized him as the one-armed convict John had originally complained about – was holding out his pot unsteadily to George and saying, 'C'mon, boy, drink it! This is whatcher need t'make a man o'yer – yer'd better get ter like it while yer young! This country wants no milksops – it wants real men!'

'... It was awful, Eliza, horrible! One of the men fell over insensible soon after that, and I had to drag the children away. All George would do was laugh and sing, and Johnnie was promptly sick on the doorstep as I tried to hurry him in out of the terrible rain. Oh, you can't imagine with what relief I saw John come in! The overseer had the ringleader of the men thrashed that night — a good thing, too – but I'll never forget the sight of my children being forced to join in that drunken orgy!'

90

'Well, at least they didn't have any women with them. That *would* have completed the boys' education,' commented Eliza philosophically. 'Take comfort, Harriott. Children's memories are short and at least now they – and you – know a little more of the country you've come to live in. Rum is what half the Colony lives for, and they'll get it by hook or by crook no matter where they are. Anyway, after that experience I guess the boys slept so well that next day they'd forgotten all about it.'

Eliza leaned forward, looking serious. 'Has John told you about Gregory's idea that they should start a distillery together, along with all their other interests? Gregory's very keen – he says everyone else in the Colony manufactures the stuff, so why shouldn't they – but what do you think about it?'

It was the end of July, and John had brought Harriott over to Brush Farm on a visit. She had not seen Eliza for six weeks, and they were sitting together on the verandah in the bright sunshine, sheltered from the cool westerly wind that was blowing down from the distant Blue Mountains.

Harriott looked concerned at her sister-in-law's question. 'I really don't know what to think,' she replied slowly. 'I had heard something of it, but hoped they wouldn't pursue it. From what the Governor said that night at the dinner, he is entirely against such private speculation, particularly in the manufacture of spirits –'

'Oh, Harriott, don't be so stuffy! Gregory says that *everybody* does it!' Eliza's light laugh floated up unconcernedly into the branches of the wattle tree, where the first yellow flowers were showing.

Harriott said nothing. She knew perfectly well that almost all the army officers had their private stills, it was the only way to make money. But defiance of the law could cause trouble if found out. Only a month before they arrived in the Colony, Macarthur had been involved in just such an affair. There had been a great fuss over a ship called the *Dart*, jointly owned by Macarthur and Hullets of London, when she arrived in Sydney. The ship's manifest had revealed that there were two stills on board on arrival, and the larger of the two – a sixty-gallon one – was destined for Macarthur. When it was found out, only the coppers were allowed to be delivered to his personal store; the heads and worms of both stills were confiscated and put into King's Stores, to be returned to London. As a result of it all Macarthur was furious, and now everyone was saying in Sydney that he had ceased to visit Government House.

Eliza must have read her sister-in-law's thoughts.

'If you're thinking about Mr Macarthur, Harriott, he

91

protests his innocence over the accusation made against him, and insists he never ordered those stills to be sent out from England in the first place! *And* he's taking every opportunity now to point out the arrogance of the Governor; how high-handed he is, and how tyrannical. Gregory says the fact that Mr Macarthur was only granted five thousand acres on the Nepean River instead of the promised ten thousand is at the bottom of it all. But I can't see, myself, he's any cause to grumble: after all, what with Elizabeth Farm and his land at Camden he's got far better land than Gregory or John were given. We can all raise a grudge against old Breadfruit Bligh if we look for one!'

'That may be,' replied Harriott, frowning a little. She was remembering the kindly manner in which Captain Bligh had gone out of his way to entertain her at Government House, and his daughter's friendly smile. 'But it seems to me,' she added, 'nobody in the Colony is helping to make the life of the Governor very easy. . . .'

Chapter 15

Their first winter in New South Wales was ending: life was again stirring in the dormant earth. Those plants and seeds that had somehow survived the journey from England were beginning to push their way up through the sandy, stony soil, and the grass was growing again. In the winter months John had got his convicts to fence off an area by the house for Harriott's garden, so now she would spend satisfying hours planning how to lay it out, knowing that cattle could no longer roam everywhere.

But it was hard to convince herself that September was springtime; it lacked the miraculous awakening of an English spring. Here there was none of the vivid fresh green that at home predominated: instead there was a perpetual parched, coppery-olive look about the tufted grass and the eucalypt trees that changed scarcely at all, even after the winter's torrential rains. The wind and the strong sun dried up everything too quickly – or was it the magnetic pull of the sky's astounding blue? That she loved and revelled in, the vastness of the huge blue sky above them as the sun grew warmer each day. She was sorry when the wattles stopped flowering; the clusters of fragrant, fluffy, yellow flowers were something she never ceased to marvel at, and she took a sensuous delight in the perfume on the air about her as soon as she stepped outside.

In that first year, the altered timings and seasons were a constant confusion and novelty. The children, quicker to become acclimatized, noticed the differences less. A lamb was welcome whether born in February or August, and it did not seem strange to them that it was September when the swollen cows were dropping their first damp calves. For John Blaxland, the increases in his sheep and cattle meant extra vigilance. At such a time there was greater danger of would-be marauders, black or white. He sent his men out in pairs on patrol by day and night; armed with stout sticks, they constantly rode round the perimeter of his land to keep off intruders. Night attacks by the Aborigines were what they feared most, for spears could find their mark in men as well as cattle, and could be deadly. Gangs of marauding ex-convicts were another danger. Many of them lived wild in the bush, or roamed through the valleys stealing what livestock they could, and good luck to those who were quick enough to drive off a couple of milk-cows or a few stupid sheep and get them safely to another farmer's territory before they were caught. There was usually a good pot of liquor waiting as payment.

From the blue springtime sky there were other hazards. Crows swooping purposefully down with angry, cruel beaks to peck out the new lambs' eyes, leaving them to stagger off bleating and mutilated to die a slow death at their helpless mothers' sides. At other times they landed almost unnoticed on sheeps' backs, there working their systematic way through the thick fleeces to catch and eat the ticks. But not all birds brought torment. The happy chattering of magpies floated down from the gum trees and sometimes there were the bright green and red-and-yellow flashes of parakeets' wings. As the birds settled among the dull leaves, long tails twitching, the children would call to each other to come and see; but dispersed by their eager shouts, the birds would fly up in a swiftly vanishing cloud of colour.

With the late spring and early summer days visitors arrived. Merchants John had got to know in Sydney came in their boats, traders rode out from Parramatta, and New South Wales Corps officers from their lands farther afield on the Nepean and Hawkesbury. The smaller settlers with their mules and bullock carts dropped by also, curious to see this newcomer who, people said, had brought out more capital to the Colony than any earlier settler from England. Under their broad-brimmed hats they sized him up with sturdy independence, chewing slowly on a reed or cud of old tobacco as their horses' reins lay slack in their calloused hands.

With undiscriminating friendliness John invited them to ride round with him to see his new shearing-sheds, his barns and his cattle. They restricted themselves by tacit consent to farming talk – safe subjects of crops, and flocks, and weather – but all the while their narrowed eyes watched him shrewdly from leathery, sun-lined faces. They assessed him not as an equal might have done in Kent, by the stable he kept or the cut of his hunting jacket or how familiar he was with the nearest titled landowner, but by what sort of man he was himself – his seat in the saddle, the strength of his muscles, and how well he held his liquor when they shared round the rum.

While the men sized up this John Blaxland who had chosen of his own volition to come and live amongst them, their sturdy, sunburnt progeny were satisfying an equal curiosity in their own way about the Blaxland children. They lured them down to the muddy river bank and tested them by catching snakes

94

and lizards and water-rats to set loose among them, squatting back on bare heels to watch with brightly hopeful eyes for any sign of cowardice in their reactions. But, surprisingly, these paler, more cosseted English children disappointed them. They gave their colonial-born inquisitors no cause to snigger, for they exhibited a toughness and resilience all their own. So that once the introductory tribal rites of children were dispensed with, they quickly accepted each other for what they were, and became friends.

John Macarthur rode over sometimes in semi-regal progress, impressively jingling on his fine sleek horse, with a retinue of army friends. As one of the largest landowners in the Colony he could afford friendship, and was quick to realize the advantage of claiming it. He had already won over the younger Blaxland by the sheer force of his personality, but his shrewd brain told him it was not wise to delay in also making overtures to the older brother. He had heard that John Blaxland might be a tougher nut to crack – less easily swayed, and slower in forming his opinions. So he went out of his way to exert his not inconsiderable charm when he visited Newington. He praised John's cattle, praised the homestead, praised his children – and would have praised Harriott, too, had she not studiously avoided him.

In the wake of the male inhabitants of the Colony, the ladies began to find their way to Newington. Harriott was secretly amused by the incongruous formality of their visits compared with those of the men. They would come up the river on the Sydney ferry, or ride out on the rough track from Parramatta in their gigs, wearing their best dresses and hats, with parasols at the ready. They settled themselves sedately in the basket chairs and made polite conversation and drank tea with carefully crooked little fingers, for all the world as if they were paying a formal visit in an English country house. But over their teacup rims their eyes would dart about curiously, quick to note the various pieces of furniture, the draperies, and the mantelpiece that it was said Mrs Blaxland had brought out all the way from England. And while they were talking, she knew, they were struggling to memorize every detail of her house to take back and report to friends in Parramatta, or Camden, or Sydney.

'And are you now receiving news from your family in England?' inquired one such visitor, a Corps lieutenant's wife.

'Oh, yes, indeed, we had letters and parcels with the last transport arriving at Port Jackson. It is so good to get news from home!'

It was the expected reply, Harriott knew, but did she really

95

mean it? Their life in England was past, finished, and no amount of correspondence could resurrect it for her. In her heart she was glad to push it behind her. They wrote letters home in turn, she and John and Gregory and Eliza, but of them all she was the one who took longest about it. Of what interest to the family in Fordwich was news that would be six or seven months out of date before reaching them? The children's minor illnesses, the new cattle John and Gregory had just bought from Government stock – all was stale news by the time it got to Kent, so what was the purpose of writing it? Another baby might be on the way, or the cows might be dead, by next March or April. . . .

Dutifully Harriott wrote, and made the older children pen laborious messages to their grandmother, but privately felt she was writing to people who had been frozen into immobility. When she thought of them, she could only imagine them in the situation in which she had left them, grouped as if for a family portrait – John's mother and aunt, Bess, Christopher with his meek wife and baby – all of them looking at her with unseeing eyes from their Kentish background of oast-houses and cherry orchards and muted, set way of living. But usually it was Bennett's face that came, uninvited, most vividly to mind – the over-abundant gold of her hair, the way the girl's blue eyes followed John around like a wretched dog – but she no longer feared the memory; instead she almost cherished it, resurrecting it triumphantly as something that had once tormented her but now, thank God, no longer threatened her happiness.

Even the war news from Europe was too far removed to have meaning. In the two years since they had sailed away from England the general picture was much the same. Only the personalities changed: not Pitt and Nelson, but Castlereagh and Sir John Moore were the names they read most frequently now when the out-of-date papers arrived in Port Jackson from England. There had been no invasion. The theatre of war was shifting to Spain. British soldiers were still dying in their thousands, Napoleon still straddled Europe like a stocky giant, the war still continued. . . . But the war, just like their immediate family, ceased to be uppermost in their thoughts any more.

'But you will send your sons home to be educated?' the lieutenant's wife was persistent in her questions. 'Mr D'Arcy Wentworth's boy William was sent home for schooling, you know.' She coughed discreetly into her handkerchief before going on in lower tones, 'It was dreadful, the humiliation to which Governor Bligh subjected his father last month, wasn't it?'

Harriott was immediately on her guard. Her visitor had the reputation of being one of Sydney's worst gossips.

'I heard something about it,' she replied casually, 'but really took little notice.'

Surely Mrs Blaxland must have heard how the Governor had taken the unprecedented step of suspending D'Arcy Wentworth, the surgeon in charge of Parramatta hospital, a most respected doctor and a man of wealth and influence in the Colony? Not only was he court-martialled – some ridiculous charge of misappropriating convict labour: he was said to be employing convicts for private labour after receiving them into hospital as sick men – but was sentenced to be publicly reprimanded on the Garrison Parade.

'My dear husband says he thinks the Governor is really trying to set himself up as a dictator, like Bonaparte! Do you know what he replied when the Judge-Advocate remonstrated with him? It's so shocking I hardly like to repeat it!' Although they were alone, she put her hand up to her mouth and dropped her voice to a whisper. 'He said, "Damn the law; my will is the law, and woe unto the man that dares to disobey it!"' She sat back and stared at Harriott dramatically, rearranging her skirts and giving the folds angry little shakes as if thereby she could remove all perfidious rulers and their autocratic ways.

'Indeed?' was Harriott's non-committal reply. 'But, of course, it's so difficult to judge without hearing both sides of the story, isn't it? And we're such newcomers here that even after five months I would not presume to express an opinion.' She smiled disarmingly. Nothing would make her admit that John had told her all about the colourful Mr D'Arcy Wentworth. She knew that he had come out to Botany Bay as a surgeon on the notorious convict ship *Neptune* in 1790, only narrowly escaping coming as a convict himself because of his highwayman activities earlier. What neither she nor her visitor knew was that the son referred to earlier was the result of a liaison formed with a young girl transported on the same ship; she had lived with him as his mistress until she died.

Later, when her visitor had departed and John had returned home, she turned to him in exasperation. 'What is the matter with them all, John, these army wives? They seem to spend their days doing all they can to spread malicious gossip about the Governor! I'm sure he *is* autocratic – but how could any sailor who has led the life he has behave differently? They criticize him because he talks as if he was still on the quarterdeck, and his language is blasphemous, and they say he is against all the Corps' trading activities here, but what *do* they want?

97

He may be stern, but at least he's temperate in his drinking – not like that awful old Judge-Advocate! Sir Joseph Banks had the highest regard for his capabilities –'

'Banks?' John said the word with such derision that his wife looked at him amazed. 'That man has no idea what the Colony is like. I can see myself how wrong he was in many instances. His New South Wales is the vision he had as a young man with Captain Cook all those years ago – a land of Aborigines and fertile valleys and exotic botanical specimens with which he can everlastingly stock Kew Gardens!' He turned aside and spat, as if to relieve his feelings. 'I tell you he's old, out of date! His views on what's needed here and how the Colony should be run are as antiquated and obstructive as – as those bloody Blue Mountains over there that hem us in!'

'Oh, John!' Harriott's distress was clear. 'Before we came out here you admired him so, you thought him so wonderful! After all, it was he who backed us –'

'Yes – and he sponsored His Excellency, too, and the more weeks go by and the more I travel about this Colony the more I realize your Captain Bligh's no help to us.' He spoke bitterly. 'Oh, Harriott, can't you see? On all sides he's making himself increasingly unpopular. He interfered with the New South Wales Corps so much that Major Johnston told me privately the other day he's thinking of writing a complaint to the Duke of York. He gives orders in direct contradiction to Major Johnston and other Corps officers, and often abuses the soldiers for utterly trivial complaints. He doesn't carry out promises of land grants on the ridiculous excuse that he has received no official instruction to do so. He is jealous of any man of consequence. He's been upsetting everyone in Sydney that has leases of land in the Domain. Did you know he issued a General Order in July saying that all leaseholders who had built houses there must quit them by the first of November? He says that the land is a Crown reserve, and although Governor King granted the leases, they are worthless now.'

Harriott made no reply. What had happened to all their high hopes if John could speak so bitterly now? Lately she had noticed how cynical he was becoming; there was an impatience, a greater ruthlessness in his attitude, that was new and alien. Now that he was having to spend more time in Sydney, where their new stockyards were being built, she saw less of him. When he was at home he was still loving and considerate to her and the children, but the other changes in him were beginning to worry her. She did not share the unspoken fear of so many other wives of the Colony: she was fairly certain that the easily obtainable convict mistresses and lights o' love in the Sydney grog shops were not for him. Her fears were of something less tangible and more insidious – the slow corruption of the standards and values that were the very thing they had been sent out to represent. It was so easy for a man to get caught up in the web of unscrupuulous self-seeking which enmeshed the Colony. She did not often come into contact with John's new associates in Sydney, but there was one particularly, an emancipationist named Simeon Lord, whose growing friendship with her husband concerned her. He had been transported to Botany Bay in 1790 for stealing cloth, but was now a prosperous merchant, trading in coal, sealskins and whale-oil, and was a ship-owner as well. That he belonged to the anti-Bligh, pro-Macarthur faction she felt certain....

'John,' she began tentatively, 'this Mr Lord that you and Gregory see so often, is he the one who is turning you against the Governor, he and Mr Macarthur and others like him? And this distillery you and Gregory are setting up –'

'Good God, woman! For heaven's sake leave me to do what I think is right and stop interfering! We came out here to farm and raise cattle and help this Colony get on its feet, so that we can make it a fine land and a worth-while country for our children and our children's children. We both agree on that?'

She nodded mutely, her eyes wide and troubled.

'Well, then, let me judge the best way to go about it!'

Chapter 16

Of all the women she had met since arriving in the Colony, Harriott felt most closely drawn to the Governor's daughter. After their meeting at the dinner at Government House just after their arrival there were not many opportunities for contact; Harriott was busy settling in at Newington, and Mary Putland had to divide her time between Sydney and her country home on South Creek. Official duties as hostess for her father often kept her at Government House, but when she could she was glad to escape to her home near the small township of St Mary's, where she and her husband had the six hundred acres given to Mary as a parting gift by her father's predecessor, Governor King.

It was from there that, one day in October, she wrote to Newington – to ask if Harriott felt her help was reliable enough for her to leave her large family and pay her a short visit.

'Oh, John, I would so like to go! May I accept? Mrs Hopper will keep an eye on the servants and the children, I know, and if I am away not more than two nights ... She suggests the middle of this month, before the weather gets too hot.' She scanned the letter again quickly. 'She had heard that you and Gregory might be going over in the direction of St Mary's to look at some land you were interested in, and thought I might come with you. She says she hasn't invited Eliza as well because she knows she's occupied with the baby.'

'Eliza would probably have more sense than to want to go anyway,' he growled, 'or she would listen more willingly to Gregory.'

She flinched momentarily at his tone of voice, then drew herself up with chin in the air, dark eyes determined. 'Why shouldn't I go?' she demanded coolly. 'Perhaps you sometimes forget I'm making my life in the Colony as well as you, so why should I not choose my friends also?'

John put down the hunk of bread he was chewing and gazed at his wife in astonishment. What had given his meek Harriott, with the grave pale face and quiet manner, this sudden urge for independence? After ten years of marriage and six successful childbearings, what was causing her to show the self-will he had always thought of as a masculine Blaxland prerogative? This was a new Harriott!

100

But not lastingly so. Within a minute she had changed her tune. With feminine astuteness she was full of self-reproach and affection again. Of course she would not think of going if John did not want her to, the last thing she would like would be to upset him! It was only that she felt so sorry for poor Mary Putland, knowing how increasingly troubled she was over her husband's ill-health, and with few friends outside government circles she could turn to.

'. . . And there's not a great difference in our ages, John – she's only twenty-four, and I'm sure she sadly misses her mother and all her sisters. It must be so sad with no children and an ailing husband, and her only other relation here her father. . . .'

She knew she had achieved what she wanted before the grin began to appear on John's face. It was the familiar amused grin that made him look as young as Gregory, crinkling the skin round his grey eyes into a hundred suntanned lines of laughter.

'And a bloody difficult father into the bargain, poor girl! Yes, I can see your point. With such a parent Mrs Putland needs the fullest commiseration and sympathy – and how right she is to turn to you, my love, rather than most of the empty-headed females in this Colony!' He looked at her, suddenly serious. 'But don't get too involved with them, Harriott. Remember, Governors and their families come and go, but this country is now our home.'

He was right, she knew, and she appreciated what he was trying to say to her. But he need not have worried on that score; already the fascination of life in New South Wales was daily exerting an ever stronger pull on her. Other wives might be homesick, but she was different. From the moment she had arrived she had instictively known that this was where she wanted to put down her roots. Here there was a newness, a feeling of fresh beginning, that she found constantly exhilarating. Perhaps the fact that she was an orphan with no personal ties outside the Colony had something to do with it, making her the more determined to create a new life here for herself and her family the way she wanted it.

She could not grapple physical obstacles with her bare hands the way the men did, pushing through the scrub or hacking down the bush to make tracks, or moving rocky boulders from the sandy soil to make pastures fit for grazing. But she could achieve her own small triumphs of creation. Each time they could have fresh vegetables on the table grown from her garden, or goat cheese produced from their herd in the paddock, she felt a triumph all her own – just as she did in a much stronger way when she looked at her healthy, laughing children.

Yet this awareness of her own powers of creation in the nature of things also brought its own independence. Just as John was changing, so was she, she knew. She was dependent as ever on his love, but less on his judgment. Marriage in a country like this demanded less subservience. It was more of a partnership in which she must learn to think increasingly for herself, and form her own opinions. And, sometimes, make unpopular decisions.

Ten days later she arrived at the Putlands' home on South Creek. Mary welcomed her with friendliness, but Harriott was concerned to see that there were shadows round her eyes, and in the bright sunshine her face looked strained and anxious. She told Harriott that her husband was confined to bed again with a fever, and the worrying cough he could not get rid of.

Looking back afterwards on her visit, Harriott decided it was the mountains that left the most lasting impressions on her. It was their ever-present nearness that captured her imagination. Beyond the Nepean valley they were like a solid wall, an impenetrable barrier only a few miles to the west, completely hemming in the small Colony. At Newington she had been less conscious of this natural boundary; the rise and fall of tides and the river flowing seaward made her more aware of the easterly limit, where the ocean incessantly pounded the sandy beaches with long white rollers. From there the mountains to the west were no more than a distant range of hazy blue which blended as the clouds did into the deeper blueness of the sky above.

Riding out that bright October day with Mary Putland, she saw for the first time the sheer impenetrability of the Blue Mountains. They were not high – no more than four thousand feet at most – nor did they have any dramatic peaks such as she had always imagined when people had talked to her of mountain ranges in Europe. No Matterhorn nor Mont Blanc here, but instead a long, seemingly endless flat-topped line of great cliffs with gullies cut deep into their perpendicular walls. The very sight of them made her draw her breath. No wonder all attempts to scale this vast barrier had failed: how could any man ever hope to find a way over such a rugged wall?

'You are like everybody who sees the mountains closely for the first time,' Mary Putland said quietly. 'I know exactly what you are wondering – what happens over the other side?'

The servants who had come with them had laid out a picnic for the two young women beside a shallow watercourse that ran between boulders and trees. It was a pleasant spot, shaded from the direct heat of the sun, with a couple of bullocks standing ankle-deep in the water and staring at them expressionlessly, tails gently swishing. The sun shining above the perpendicular face of the mountains made the gullies appear even more black and impenetrable.

'But men have tried to find a way through, haven't they?' Harriott persisted. 'John told me. It was about eighteen years ago that Lieutenant Dawes made the first attempt, wasn't it?'

'Yes, then Captain Paterson, and Hacking and Bass after him. Barallier penetrated much farther through the valleys than the others in 1802, but he still came up against the same obstacles – valleys of rock and impossible precipices.'

'My brother-in-law thinks Mr Caley's idea of following the ridges north of the Grose River was the best plan yet – better than always trying through the valleys,' Harriott commented idly. The warm day and the excellent cold meats and wines were making her feel sleepy. She turned to her companion, relaxed and smiling. 'Gregory is always full of enthusiasms, you know – he loves impossible challenges. He has only to be told that something cannot be done to want to do it at once! John is very different. He can be equally determined, but in a different way. Once he gets an idea in his head nothing will stop him; but Gregory goes at things like a rampaging bull – and when he can he drags John after him.'

'Yes, so my father complains,' said Mary Putland. For a moment her discerning blue eyes met Harriott's brown ones in a long level gaze.

For an instant neither woman spoke. Then, simultaneously, they began to laugh – relieved, infectious laughter. There was understanding as well, born of the age-old knowledge of women's greater wisdom and the need, therefore, to be patient with masculine foibles.

It was as well they could laugh together. However relaxed and easy they might feel that peaceful, sunny day, idly discussing the different attitudes of people in the Colony, it was as if they both sensed it might be a long time before they would find another opportunity to talk so freely.

As soon as she got home to Newington, Harriott knew from John's face that something was wrong. He kissed her briefly, reassured her about the children, but made only the most perfunctory inquiries about her visit. When she started to tell him he barely listened to her replies, except to ask scathingly, 'And did she also take you to her father's farm?'

She looked at him, puzzled. 'What do you mean?'

'Only that John Macarthur was telling me that for all his pious moralizing His Excellency is as unscrupulous as any when

103

it comes to taking grants of land and stocking his farm.' His voice grew increasingly angry as he went on to retell Macarthur's story of the 'fine old fiddle' Bligh and Governor King had engineered when Bligh arrived in the Colony, confirming unauthorized grants of land for each other. 'Not only your friend Mrs Putland but also Mrs King benefited – did you know those eight hundred acres in Evan, named "Thanks" were given to her? And King in return quite illegally gave Bligh the land where he's built "Camperdown", not to mention the thousand acres near Rouse Hill and other grants besides!'

He had learnt a lot more from Macarthur, but Harriott was looking so impatient that she would probably say it was all an exaggeration and not believe him. Her friendship with Mary Putland would like as not make her biassed.

He, personally, had no reason to doubt Macarthur's words; he was sure the man knew what he was talking about. Macarthur had told him for a fact that the Governor had been increasing his own herds by taking government-owned cows in calf into his own paddocks, then sending back the dams without their calves! And yet the unscrupulous fellow had only allowed him, John, sixty cows and said that all the female calves for the next four generations must be returned to the government herds! These herds totalled some three and a half thousand already, but he and Gregory – experienced graziers – were refused any more, even for good payment. Did the Governor himself pay anything into the public stores for the value of the stock issued to him, he wondered? He very much doubted it.

His wife looked at him in exasperation. 'John, what *is* the matter?'

'Matter? The matter is that the more co-operative we try to be with the Governor, the more arbitrary he becomes!' He went on to tell her about the 'most uncivil' letter Gregory had just received from the Governor, flatly turning down the brothers' offer of a partnership in their distillery.

Really, men are illogical, thought Harriott. Knowing the Governor's frequently expressed views on the manufacture of spirits, what else could they expect? She could see no reason for John to be so indignant.

'Anyway, that's over and done with,' he was saying impatiently. 'I'm going down to Sydney tomorrow to attend the legal action John Macarthur's bringing over the stills affair. At least he'll know from my presence in court that he has my support – as he will have that of most of Sydney. It's time the Governor sees he cannot ride roughshod over everybody!'

* * *

The legal proceedings which took place that October in Sydney attracted most of the leading members of the Colony. Because of the Governor's order forbidding their import, parts of John Macarthur's stills had been lying in the King's Stores all through the winter. When the *Duke of Portland* was due to sail to England in October, Governor Bligh gave orders that the complete stills should be put on board and shipped home. As Macarthur personally held certain parts of them in his own store, these had to be collected from him, and this unfortunately was done without written authority. It was the chance Macarthur had been looking for to stir up trouble against the Governor. He brought a case against the poor young man who had innocently taken the boilers from him without permission and instituted proceedings against him in Sydney before the Bench of Magistrates. This consisted of Macarthur's friend, Major Johnston, commanding the New South Wales Corps while Colonel Paterson was in Van Diemen's Land, and Mr Palmer, Commissary of the Colony; the chairman was Richard Atkins, the Judge-Advocate.

The court was packed with a tense and interested audience. Not only the Blaxland brothers but everyone in the Colony knew what was the real issue. It was not an argument about some insignificant boilers, but a test of strength between two powerful men, one the Governor of the Colony, the other the richest and most influential man in it.

The courtroom gave Macarthur exactly the stage he was looking for. In an impassioned speech he appealed for his rights as a British subject, living in a British settlement, with British laws established by Royal Patent, who had 'had his property wrested from him by a non-accredited individual', without any authority being produced other that it was 'the Governor's order'. Then, with eyes flashing and tossing back his dark hair, he demanded of the entire assembly 'to determine whether this be the tenure on which Englishmen hold their property in New South Wales.'

The tense silence that greeted him as he stepped down was as good as applause. Gregory and John, sitting at the back of the courtroom amongst the spectators, looked at each other significantly. If John Macarthur thought this, was it not time they all took stock to see if they were losing their civil liberties? By the time Atkins gave the deciding vote in Macarthur's favour – a foregone conclusion, anyway – everyone was so swayed by Macarthur's rhetoric that nobody paused to question whether there had possibly been a miscarriage of justice, least of all his friends and admirers.

105

'This means a fight to the finish, John!' whispered Gregory triumphantly. 'The Colony's not big enough for them both!'

In Government House, a short distance away, Captain William Bligh sat at his desk in the window overlooking Sydney Harbour and eased his feelings by writing in a dispatch to England that he was disgusted with his Judge-Advocate. Then he penned his signature with a flourish. For a moment he was swept with a sense of isolation. It would be seven long months before anyone in the Colonial Office in London would read his complaints, and as long again before a reply came back to him – but then he squared his broad shoulders and smiled to himself, reconciled again. The *Bounty* Mutiny, the Nore Mutiny, Camperdown – had he not always been at his best when he had to fight for the right against heavy odds?

Chapter 17

Daily the summer grew hotter, and so did men's tempers. In those last months of 1807 it was obvious to everyone that the Governor and John Macarthur were now in open conflict.

On all official occasions Governor Bligh rode in state 'like a great planet', with coach and four, six or eight light-horsemen with a sergeant, and two or three outriders and footmen. But when he drove out informally, in a small sulky with canvas awning, the more observant noticed that there were always pistols and a blunderbuss, within easy reach, beside him.

In arrogant contrast, John Macarthur rode his horse through the Sydney streets laughing and unarmed, with a group of friends usually pressing close around him. He could afford to be contemptuous for his own safety – how could it be endangered now that he knew he had not only the army, but most of the merchant traders of the capital and all those wealthy settlers, behind him? In Sydney itself lived three thousand people – that was getting on for half the population of the Colony – and of these three thousand, five-sixths were of convict origin. John Macarthur with his dashing air was a man after their own heart, cocking a snook at authority for any chance of gain – and, sometimes, it was said, just for the daredevil fun of it.

Throughout the Colony, opinions about the two men were sharply divided. The poorer Hawkesbury settlers, remembering how Bligh had gone out of his way to help them after the disastrous floods, were still in favour of the Governor. Even in Sydney, where the complaints and mutterings were growing, few would deny that he was doing his best to improve the look of the place. Some of the shabby public buildings were being restored and put in order; St Phillip's church, derelict before his arrival, was being rebuilt and several of the streets were already looking tidier. The town had grown over the years round Sydney Cove. Now it was about a mile long, with the Tank Stream running through the middle of it and the slopes on either side housing the officials, the army and the convicts. Government House stood on the west slope of the eastern hill, with other officials' homes near by.

In common with several of the other wealthier merchants and settlers, John Macarthur had a small house in Sydney as well as his home near Parramatta. This was in the centre of the town, in the High Street, the long road that ran parallel with the Tank Stream from behind the dockyards, past the Market Place, then south in a straight line through the town to become the only track leading inland to the country and Parramatta.

Along this road one day Gregory came riding into town, and was flattered to be hailed by John Macarthur and invited to come into his house for a glass of grog: a surprising honour since he knew that Macarthur himself did not drink.

'Your brother is not with you? A pity, I had news of a sale which I thought might have interested him.'

Gregory was all ears. 'He is down at the wharf with Mr Lord. Is there some message I can give him?'

John Macarthur shrugged, elaborately casual. 'Possibly it would be of no appeal, but I heard today of some property – two houses either side of the High Street, farther up – coming on the market shortly. The owner is a former sergeant-major of the Corps – he came out to the Colony as a convict some sixteen years ago, but has since done very nicely for himself, partly thanks to some little speculation I was able to put him in the way of – and now he wants to sell up and return to England. It occurred to me it might be doing a good turn to you and your brother if I told you about the property. I remember hearing John once say he would be glad of a base in Sydney to trade from, as well as your homes in the country.'

'How much is he asking?'

'Nine hundred pounds – with eleven years of the lease to run.'

Gregory pulled a face. 'The price is high for that, sir.'

'Admittedly. But I think your brother has a sufficiently good business head to realize that there would be – advantages.'

When Gregory finally ran John to earth an hour later, he was standing talking with his merchant friend, Simeon Lord, on the quayside with a crowd of other men, watching crates of tea being unloaded from a ship just arrived from India. He greeted Gregory cheerfully.

'With luck *The Brothers* should be on her way back to Sydney soon with a good cargo of sealskins, then you and I can be like some of these other plutocrats.' He thumped Simeon Lord laughingly on the back.

Lord laughed cynically, 'You'll certainly need the luck, my friend, the way things are going! Old Bounty Bligh with his straitlaced views and his damn' rules and regulations against barter is making every trader's life hell.' He turned to Gregory, winking broadly. 'Have you heard the latest pipe about him, young Blaxland? It's damned appropriate – "*O tempora, o mores!* Is there no CHRISTIAN in New South Wales to put a stop to the tyranny of the Governor?" Good, eh?'

He went off into a roar of laughter in which everyone round about joined, but Gregory scarcely listened, and was busy trying to get the attention of his brother.

'John,' he demanded urgently, 'forget the future for a moment. Have we nine hundred spare here and now? Listen . . .'

John was more than interested in Macarthur's suggestion. Increasingly he had been thinking it uneconomic to have all their capital tied up in farming. If he and Gregory could have somewhere of their own in Sydney they could enlarge their milk-house sheds and sell much-needed milk to the poorer inhabitants; they could open a butcher's shop; they could bring fresh vegetables in from Newington and Brush Farm and sell them to the townsfolk; they could extend their trading interests, being nearer the harbour, the focal point of everything. . . . All the other successful men in the Colony realized the advantages of not having all their eggs in one basket, so why not the Blaxlands, too? If Bligh still made no attempt to ratify their further land grants, well, they could show him that wealthy settlers had other uses for their money than being made mere stock-breeders for the Colony.

He began to smile broadly. 'Yes, Gregory, I can see many advantages, as John Macarthur has pointed out. We'll take on the lease between us. Two houses near together in the High Street – what could be better? And how pleased Harriott and Eliza should be at the prospect!'

But there John Blaxland was mistaken. Increasingly these days he found he was misjudging his wife's reactions. Harriott was not only against the idea of coming to live in Sydney, at first she absolutely refused to do so. She liked life in the country, she told John. She was not lonely. Of course it would be nice to be so close to Eliza, but they could all meet fairly often as it was. She had no wish to uproot herself and the children and be packed into a small house in Sydney just when she had got the farmhouse at Newington exactly as she wanted it. Besides – she produced her trump card – she had not thought to tell John before, but she was practically certain she was pregnant again, so before long she would not be able to take part in any social life in the town, and would therefore much prefer to stay quietly where she was.

Fate – and Eliza – made her change her mind. First, a miscarriage was threatened, which not only alarmed John dreadfully, but made Harriott realize that for the next few months she would be wiser to live in town within closer reach of midwife or doctor. Then Eliza, possibly prompted by Gregory, came over to enthuse over the prospect of having second homes in Sydney.

'We've both got good governesses and nursemaids now and can leave the children on the farms, which will be much healthier for them, so why shouldn't you and I have a few weeks together every now and then in Sydney? After all, my dear, you may feel your John is safe enough, but however much Gregory may profess his love to my face I wouldn't count on his not falling for a bit of fun in town with some of the convict trollops if he thought I was safely out of the way at Brush Farm with the children.' She tossed her fair head, giggling, then pronounced solemnly, 'After all, a wife has a duty to her husband as well as to herself and the children, Harriott; and better safe than sorry!'

Harriott could not explain to Eliza that her own fears were different. It sounded complacent to say that she was sure her only real female rival had been left behind in England. Temptation now for her husband lay in quite a different direction – in wealth, power, self-aggrandizement, ambition. His new associates in the Colony were all luring him to join with them, and it was their influence that she feared far more than any passing feminine distractions.

She felt this influence increasingly after John had taken her to stay in Sydney. Not only the heat but the whole humid atmosphere of the place oppressed her: rumours and counter-rumours rose up and drifted around as insidiously as the stench and mosquitoes from the sluggish, dirty Tank Stream that ran at the end of their garden. Certainly, as Eliza had predicted, they saw more 'society'. But she cared little for these hard-headed, hard-drinking merchants and traders and army officers; their laughter was too loud and their language as coarse as that of the Governor whom they constantly criticized.

Harriott saw Bligh from time to time riding by in his carriage with Mary Putland, pale and drawn, beside him. She longed to let Mary know she was in Sydney, but dared not risk John's wrath. She had been distressed to hear that Mary had been so upset by the way some rough soldiers of the New South Wales Corps had ridiculed her and her father during the service at church one Sunday that she had fainted; it was especially cruel since, it was rumoured, for all Mary's care young Putland was dying of consumption, and soon the Governor's daughter might be a widow.

Harriott would have liked to visit her at Government House, but knew that with John in his present mood this was out of the question. Now that they were in Sydney, it was more obvious than ever that her husband was following John Macarthur's glittering star. He was now as dazzled by the man as his younger brother had been from the very start. She longed to remonstrate with John, to have it out with him and beseech him to consider before it was too late, but she knew it would be no use, for by November he had an added grievance.

It had happened when she was out shopping in the market with Eliza one day. The Governor had called on John unannounced at their High Street house with his Surveyor, curtly announcing that part of their garden was needed for Crown purposes. John and Gregory should give up any idea of building extra premises there, he said, and they need not think their lease would be extended after the eleven years, since the Crown would take it over from them. Heated argument had followed, during which John had said something about the laws of England. Governor Bligh had then silenced a shocked John with the words: *'What do I care for them? I will make laws for New South Wales and every son of a bitch shall obey!'*

One oppressively hot morning, Harriott and Eliza, in search of fresher air, took their convict servants with them to buy fruit at the market, then walked down to the Public Wharf. There they could look right across the blue waters of Sydney Cove, where many ships were riding at anchor. From India, China and the South Sea Islands the traders came, and there were others that would soon be making the long voyage back to England. Some of the sealed letters and dispatches these ships were carrying would have troubled Harriott still more had she known their contents. Her husband had written to the Colonial Office that 'the Governor is behaving so very arbitrary that I do not consider either my person or my property safe a single hour; indeed, I think it will not be long before I am sent to goal ... every species of injustice and oppression is exercised here in its full force. ...' Mr D'Arcy Wentworth's letter to Lord Castlereagh concerning his suspension as a surgeon was also awaiting dispatch, '... in an effort to defend my character against the accusations of the Governor ...'; and Mr Macarthur himself was writing, not without relish, that 'life in New South Wales is becoming a perfect hell', and that 'the Corps is rapidly galloping into a state of warfare with the Governor'. A letter of complaint from

111

Gregory Blaxland was on board, too; as were similar missives from many others. Only a dispatch from His Excellency himself, written from 'this sink of iniquity, Sydney', to Sir Joseph Banks, struck a note of optimism: '. . . the Colony is recovered from a deplorable state, indeed, I can give you every assurance of its now raising its head to my utmost expectation . . . The discontented are checked in their machinations whilst the honest settler feels himself secure, and the idler no encouragement.'

'Harriott, look!' cried Eliza, pointing out to the harbour and shading her eyes as she did so. 'There – behind the Governor's ship – isn't that Mr Macarthur's schooner *Parramatta*, the one that's just got back from Tahiti? Gregory told me there's some fuss going on about that ship. Apparently when she sailed from Sydney last June there was an Irish convict on board. They let him escape when they reached Tahiti, so now she's come back the Governor has ordered the ship to be placed under arrest. Mr Macarthur has had to forfeit his bond and has been dispossessed of the vessel. He's furious, as you can imagine, and says the master and crew can no longer look to him for provisions!' Eliza's face had become quite animated. 'Nobody can say that life in Sydney is dull, can they?'

Remembering her sister-in-law's light-hearted comment, Harriott decided a fortnight later that it had been an understatement. Events had moved fast in the interim; after failing to provide food for the crew of his schooner and thus forcing them to come ashore, contrary to orders, John Macarthur had received a letter at his farm in Parramatta from the Judge-Advocate requesting him to show cause for his conduct. When it became known that he had refused to come to Sydney to answer the summons, the Colony held its breath and wondered what would happen next.

They were not left long in suspense. The next day, 15 December, Harriott, watching from the windows of their High Street house in Sydney, saw the light-horseman go trotting self-importantly by on his way to Parramatta. It did not need John's tense face to tell her that he guessed what it meant. In the rider's official bag there was a warrant from the Judge-Advocate to Mr Oakes, the Chief Constable of Parramatta, for the arrest of Mr Macarthur.

Now there was no going back for any of them.

Chapter 18

Gregory and Eliza had already left for Brush Farm: all Harriott wanted was to follow them and get back to Newington and the children, and prepare for Christmas. But John refused to leave Sydney until he knew what was going to happen to Macarthur, so there was nothing for it but to wait with him, however much the atmosphere of the town oppressed her. It was stiflingly hot – even the north-easterly wind blowing in from the sea most afternoons brought little relief with it. At Newington it would be hotter still, she knew, but at least there she would be free of all this suspicion and tension, as if the whole place was simmering in the heat and waiting to blow up in their faces. She longed for the peace of the country, where nature controlled the order of things, and not the schemings of men.

Macarthur arrived in Sydney the next day, having scornfully dismissed the warrant served on him by the diffident Constable of Parramatta. With hat tilted arrogantly and his face proud and confident, he rode defiantly through the dusty Sydney streets to the home of his trading associate, the somewhat embarrassed Surveyor-General Grimes. There a second warrant for his arrest was issued and he was brought before the Sydney magistrates on 17 December. His old enemy Richard Atkins, the Judge-Advocate, was Chairman of the Bench. With slurred speech and exaggerated dignity he committed Macarthur for trial at the next Criminal Court six weeks later, and then granted him bail over Christmas. Macarthur stormed out of the court and went straight back to his farm at Parramatta, leaving Sydney to settle down uneasily, holding its breath. It was almost certain a charge of sedition would be preferred against him. What would be the outcome of this?

Now, with Macarthur gone, John was at last willing to return with Harriott to Newington – and to the children and peace. As they boarded the little Parramatta ferry at Sydney, Harriott felt weak with relief.

John had got their convicts to build a private landing-stage on the river at Newington, so now they were able to disembark at their own place instead of going as far as Parramatta. As the ferry pulled in to the bank Harriott saw her older children standing with the governess, Mrs Flower, and waving. She felt a great upsurge of thankfulness: surely John must see *this* was their life, here in the country on their farm, where they could see their children growing and their land developing while their herds of cattle increased. This was what John and she had come out to do, not to become entangled with all the Sydney merchants and their schemes and intrigues!

Energetically she set about preparing for their first New South Wales Christmas. With her pregnancy now safely established she felt well and happy – happier than she had done for some time – and she busied herself in the house with the children. The summer flies and insects were an abomination; nothing would banish them, but at least the family were becoming inured to them: the children no longer ran constantly to her with swollen, inflamed arms and legs. They were learning to ignore the insects, just as she was learning to ignore the shortages, and to delight instead in the few luxuries they could occasionally buy. Was it really only two years since they had spent their last Christmas surrounded by the snow-covered fields of Kent? She baked a Christmas cake – large and fruit filled – and tried to make mincemeat, but she could not get all the right ingredients, and though John loyally claimed it was as good as that his mother used to make at Fordwich, she saw the fleeting nostalgia in his eyes as he said it.

Even so, it was a good time. John went out of his way to devote himself to his family; he took the boys out with him on their ponies each morning to watch the convicts collecting salt from the pans down by the river – already his salt was considered the best in the Colony – and in the afternoons when it was very hot they sat in the coolest part of the house, and he would take three-year-old Anna on his knee and roar with laughter as young Harriott self-importantly tried to make her younger sister recite her alphabet. But the evenings were the time his wife liked best. Then, when the nursemaids had taken the children off to bed, she sat alone with John at the big table in the living room, and in the light of the green-shaded oil lamp he would help her wrap up the small gifts she had carefully collected for each of their children for Christmas – a ball and toy soldiers for the boys, sweetmeats and scraps of gay material for dolls' clothes for the girls, and an ingeniously carved Aboriginal rattle for the baby, Louisa.

She treasured each moment of those days before Christmas, but sensed they were only a respite: such tranquility could not last for ever. On Christmas Day they went to church in Parramatta. As Eliza put it, 'everybody who is anybody' had left Sydney and come back to their country homes for the holiday – and there amongst the crowded congregation were the Governor and John Macarthur. Macarthur had his wife and some of his children with him, but His Excellency was alone. His daughter had not been seen in Sydney or Parramatta for the past fortnight. He sat in the front pew, an impressive figure in full naval dress, surrounded by his military escort. He drove away quickly afterwards with only the briefest of greetings to those nearest him, his face under his plumed hat set and impassive. It was said that in spite of all the doctors' prophecies consumption was draining away his son-in-law's life. Harriott thought with pity about Mary Putland. Faced with the rapidly mounting opposition to her father, how could she bear the weight of personal tragedy as well?

Macarthur, on the other hand, was in the best of spirits: he had a joke or a cheerful word for everyone, and might not have had a care in the world as he stood outside the church chatting in the bright sunshine. 'I do really believe he's enjoying it all,' thought Harriott with sudden loathing. 'That man revels in a fight – he's utterly devoid of compassion!' And she hated the way admiration and respect glowed on John's and Gregory's faces as they listened to him.

'One must admire the man, whether one likes him or not,' said John later, chuckling. 'Don't you agree, Gregory?' He turned to Harriott. 'Guess what he's been doing during his bail? To his great delight he unearthed some old bill a week ago drawn by Richard Atkins on his brother fourteen years ago. With interest it totalled eight-two pounds, but not surprisingly the Judge-Advocate refused settlement. So what did our friend do but write direct to the Governor about the protested suit pending the recovery of the money?'

'And what was the reply?'

'His Excellency said he could not discuss the matter "at present".' John laughed sarcastically. 'It just shows that he's even more pig-headed than we thought, that he will not acknowledge what a wretched creature Atkins is – the man who is supposed to be the supreme law-giver of the Colony!'

'But it must be difficult for poor old Bounty Bligh when you think of it,' interposed Eliza, yawning. She stretched like a sleek, plump cat after her good Christmas dinner. 'I mean, he can't very well publicly disgrace his miserable drunken Judge-Advocate, can he? After all, unless he gets instructions from London ...' Her voice trailed off. It was too hot to make profound statements, and really, what did it matter? 'Let's leave the two stupid men to fight their own battles, I say,' she finished lightly. 'Why need we take issue with either of them?'

Dear Lord, help me to see it all in Eliza's casually detached

115

way! thought Harriott enviously. Gregory doesn't mind what she says because he knows she never really worries, but John – surely John must see how desperately I care? I *know* that all our futures depend on the outcome of the struggle between Bligh and Macarthur.

With the new year came other distractions. Everyone began discussing the celebrations planned for the end of the month to commemorate the twentieth anniversary of the foundation of the settlement of Sydney. Major Johnston was a veteran of the landing on 26 January 1788 when the Union Jack had been raised for the first time at Sydney Cove, and was arranging a dinner at the army mess in Sydney to celebrate. Both John and Gregory received invitations.

'It should be a damn' good party, John!' Gregory was full of cheerful anticipation. 'Now how about Harriott and Eliza coming down to Sydney for a week as well, and bringing the older children? There's bound to be quite a bit of excitement and jubilation – military bands, parades, flag-waving – it will impress itself on the children's memory far more than Mrs Flower's worthy and exceedingly dull history lessons!'

Eliza was enchanted at the prospect; so were the children. Any pageantry and variety to break the monotony of the scorching summer days was welcome. Cheerfully she brushed aside Harriott's objections.

'It'll be fun – something out of the ordinary – you'll see! Everyone will be in town – and then of course there'll be the Macarthur case coming up next day at the Criminal Court. . . .'

Harriott looked at her sister-in-law's innocently eager face and was silent. That was just the trouble. Too many things were going to happen in Sydney all at once, and she was afraid. John had said feelings there were already tense about the forthcoming trial, and of course Macarthur himself was doing his best to add to the excitement. Failing to get Richard Atkins superceded as Judge-Advocate, he had taken up the attitude of the injured innocent and was busy sending letters in all directions pleading ignorance of the charges to be preferred against him. And now he was having yet another set-to with Governor Bligh on the old question of the lease of some land in Sydney which he maintained was his.

'If Bligh had his way he'd knock down half the houses in town,' John said angrily. 'John Macarthur's piece of land on Church Hill was granted to him by Governor King years ago; now Bligh has got poor old Grimes to write to Macarthur and say he can't build there. Instead he's offered him a wretched plot in that squalid area at the end of Pitt Row, near where the public gallows stood. He won't accept it, you wait and see!'

John was right. When they arrived back in Sydney from Parramatta on 20 January the Blaxlands found they had arrived in the middle of what Eliza called 'first-class entertainment'. Macarthur, who had been in town for some weeks, had hired some of the New South Wales Corps soldiers, when off duty, to erect a fence around his contested piece of land on Church Hill. The first stakes were already in when, to the delight of the Sydney populace, up rode the Superintendent of Public Works, Mr Divine, with a party of constables to put a stop to it. To the accompaniment of catcalls, whistles, cheers and counter-cheers the posts were pulled down, and as the protagonists departed in great dignity, neither side conceding victory, the whole town rocked with laughter.

The anniversary celebrations drew near, and there was a carnival spirit in the air. Perspiring townsfolk and their convict servants put out more and more garlands and flags in the streets and on the fronts of their houses. Few gave a thought to the father and daughter at the top of the hill in Government House. They had returned to Sydney for the official parades, but the Governor's personal standard hanging limply at half-mast in the hot sunshine was silent witness to the fact that they themselves would be in no mood for jubilation: young Lieutenant Putland had died at the beginning of the year.

The principal concern of the male population was that there might not be sufficient to drink in town on the great day. Ironically enough there were several ships full of what they wanted lying at anchor in Sydney Cove. The *City of Edinburgh* with twenty-two thousand gallons of spirits on board was leaking slightly, and the delicious aroma of her precious cargo whetted the appetite cruelly as it wafted gently across the harbour on the warm air and permeated the streets. And although two American ships had been allowed to dispose of their wine, they were prevented by the Governor's embargo from discharging the rum they had on board. When it was eventually brought ashore – sad anticlimax: it was immediately put under lock and key in government stores!

This did little to increase the popularity of His Excellency, and took away any great interest in the news just come from England that Post-Captain William Bligh had now been promoted to Commodore. Yet his promotion may have indirectly done some good; it softened the Governor sufficiently to allow the New South Wales Corps a pipe of wine from the *City of Edinburgh* for their mess dinner on 24 January.

It was, as Gregory had anticipated, a great occasion. 'Memorable' was not the word that all the guests could apply to it: the majority, taking advantage of such excellent hospitality, remembered little of the evening, and it was their irate wives trying to get them into bed when they got home who found it memorable.

But the few who had left the mess with reasonably clear heads had much to remember: the band playing outside on the parade ground as they dined; the martial sight of the regimental colours draped over the doorways; the Commanding Officer's order to the servants that none of his guests' glasses should be allowed to stand empty – as one of the leading liquor traders in the Colony, he could afford it – and, most of all, the interesting, carefully chosen guests. Macarthur himself was noticeable by his absence; he was spending this last evening before his trial in full view of the town, walking up and down in front of the messroom, innocently listening to the martial music. But his son and all his friends were present at the dinner, not only John and Gregory, but the two traders who had stood bail for him, the six officers whom the Governor had assigned to act as judges under the Judge-Advocate in the Criminal Court, and other well-known colleagues.

As faces reddened, tongues loosened, and toasts grew ever more numerous, Major Johnston looked upon all his guests with a benignly alcoholic smile; later seeing them on their way, some maintained, with a knowing wink and a jovial 'Till tomorrow!'

It was unfortunate that the Commanding Officer of the New South Wales Corps had himself imbibed even more liberally than the rest on that historic night, because he fell out of his gig on his way home to Annandale. He badly injured his arm, covered himself with bruises and rendered himself insensible. So he never could confirm or deny the story.

Chapter 19

The next morning promised another very warm day. John and Gregory were up early, but when they reached the courtroom in the Orphan House well before ten it was already crowded, and they were soon uncomfortably hot in their dark town coats put on to observe the formality of the occasion. For several hours the small building in the centre of Sydney had been the focus of attention. Settlers had converged on it from all over the surrounding countryside, and now, sweating and shoving, they jostled for places with Sydney merchants and soldiers in shabby uniforms.

Seats had been kept for more important people near the front of the court. As the two brothers pushed their way through there was a sudden drop in conversation, and soon after they reached their seats the Judge-Advocate walked solemnly in. Behind him came the judges – the six New South Wales Corps officers in full uniform, with scarlet jackets and swords. Finally, to the accompaniment of excited whispers and much craning of necks, in came the prisoner, John Macarthur.

'How grim he looks! He's clearly all set for a damn' good fight,' whispered Gregory with relish, 'and he hasn't the disadvantage of a thick head like most of his judges.'

The truth of his words was quickly evident. Several of the officers who proceeded to take the oath were obviously still suffering from the effects of the previous night's carousing, but the prisoner was completely calm. It was a deceptive calm, however, which within seconds had been replaced by cold fury. In measured, angry tones Macarthur struck out at his opponents, most of all the unprepared and astonished Judge-Advocate. He questioned the legality of the court there assembled, especially the authority of 'Richard Atkins, Esquire, who for years has cherished a rancorous inveteracy against me'. In ringing tones he went on to list objection after objection; and as the Judge-Advocate hastily shifted his seat and vainly called out, 'No court! No court!' there rose from all sides a crescendo of excited cries and murmurs. The prisoner at the bar continued his challenges, and the spectators at the back stood up. Sporadic applause broke out as he finally appealed directly to the officers who formed the court.

'You will now decide, gentlemen, whether Law or Justice

119

shall prevail.... To you has fallen the lot of deciding a point which involves perhaps the happiness or misery of millions yet unborn, and I conjure you, in the name of the Almighty God ... to consider the inestimable value of the precious deposit with which you are entrusted.'

'I will commit you to jail, sir!' cried the Judge-Advocate desperately – but already it was too late. Swayed by Macarthur's impassioned rhetoric, Atkins's judges were no longer behind him, if indeed they had ever been. He had lost the day.

As he fled out into the hot sunshine and hurried up to Government House to give a panic-stricken report of the proceedings, the remaining six judges decided that as they were sworn in they could still act as a court. Hastily they agreed that 'the objections set forth in the prisoner's protest are good and lawful to Richard Atkins sitting on his trial'.

Macarthur was remanded to his former bail, and borne off by a jubilant military escort to the house of an army friend.

It was nearly five o'clock before John got back to his house in the High Street. All afternoon, as Harriott anxiously waited at home for news, messengers had been clattering between the barracks, the courtroom and Government House.

'John!' She ran quickly to him and grasped his arm. 'Oh, I'm glad you're back! Gregory was bringing Lieutenant Lawson home to dinner with them about half an hour ago, and they called in on the way and told me – but what will happen now?'

'Now?' With a sigh of relief he flung his coat down on a chair, and flexed his aching shoulders. 'First of all, I'm ready for some food.' He looked hot and tired, but his face was jubilant. 'It's been a wonderful day, Harriott – a real victory for John Macarthur! You should have heard him – that bastard Atkins won't forget his words in a hurry, and as for the Governor –'

'The Governor?' she broke in quickly. 'Oh, John, how can you call it a victory for anyone with the court broken up in disorder, no real decision on Macarthur, and all these soldiers roaming the streets singing and shouting?' She shivered suddenly, and her voice sounded frightened. 'This is how a revolution can begin –'

'And tomorrow the guillotines will be set up outside Government House, and we'll all don red caps, and you'll get your knitting and chant, "*A bas les aristocrats!*"' John finished for her mockingly. He took her by the arms and gave her a little shake; but his eyes were tender. 'You silly little goose; this is New

South Wales in 1808, not the France of your misbegotten ancestors! Have faith in my judgment, Harriott, and be thankful we have such a leader as Macarthur. By tomorrow all will be peaceably settled, you'll see, and then, God willing, we'll really have some justice in this Colony.'

'Mama, Mama, wake up! It's Anniversary Day, remember? And you promised we could go and see the soldiers parade, remember?'

Small stroking hands and coaxing voices pulled her back to consciousness from an exhausted sleep; and she woke to find John's place empty in the bed beside her, and three pairs of bright eyes watching her. For a moment she stared in bewilderment at young Harriott, Johnnie and George. 'What time is it? Where's Papa?'

'Oh, he went out ages ago with Uncle Gregory,' said her eldest son airily. 'He knew you were tired so told us not to wake you too early. Mama, it *was* exciting! There was a big noise outside in the street when we were having breakfast and we saw Mr Macarthur being led away by two constables to the jail!'

Harriott sat up immediately, fully awake. So they had arrested him, after all! She felt a spurt of relief. Perhaps even now order would be re-established. She must get up at once, pull on some clothes, find out for herself.

Sending the children away with a promise to take them out later, she dressed quickly, drank a glass of milk that a servant brought her, then went hurriedly to find if Eliza knew where John and Gregory had gone.

Eliza was sitting at home calmly writing a letter, and looked up in surprise at her sister-in-law's anxious face. Yes, it was absolutely true, John Macarthur had been carted off to jail on some new order of the Governor's, and the six judges were all shut up in the courtroom again, wondering what to do. She had overheard someone in the street say that the Governor had sent for Major Johnston, but the messenger had returned from Annandale to say the Major was sorry, he was too covered in bruises to make the journey. As she told the story Eliza went off into peals of laughter.

'Oh, Eliza, how can you?' Harriott could hardly control her impatience. 'Don't you realize what all this means? To me it's like a nightmare! All those people outside in their holiday clothes, laughing and waving flags in the sunshine as if they hadn't a care in the world – and others behind closed doors whispering of rebellion!'

She went home and tried to relax, but it was too hot, and

121

she was far too worried. It was a relief when at four o'clock Eliza arrived with her children to accompany Harriott and her children, for a walk into the town.

If anything it was still warmer outside than earlier in the day and dreadfully humid. There wasn't a breath of air. Dark clouds hung motionless over the sea, but over the town there was no sign of any relieving rain to cool the temperature. People were thronging the main streets, laughing, gesticulating, arguing; some stood about in small groups talking to soldiers, but the majority were pouring along the High Street in a relentless wave, to converge with the crowd on the Barrack Square. Harriott and Eliza, borne along in the throng, grasped their excited children by the hands.

Although it seemed that every house in town must be emptying, there was one home in Sydney whose occupants remained firmly indoors, trying to behave as though nothing out of the ordinary was happening. At Government House the new Commodore was dining in private with his widowed daughter and Richard Atkins and a few close friends. Nobody had much appetite. It was a relief to know that Macarthur was safely in jail, but they were uneasy at the rumours of large crowds assembling in the Barrack Square.

As soon as dinner was over Atkins went shambling off to investigate. Governor Bligh would have been even more concerned had he known that Major Johnston had just driven into Sydney after all; but, instead of coming to report to Government House as commanded, was at this very moment conferring with his officers and civilian friends at the barracks. With arm in sling and face still bruised from his accident, the Commander of the New South Wales Corps was being persuaded to assume the illegal title of Lieutenant-Governor. He was also signing a release for his friend, John Macarthur.

A great shout went up from the waiting crowds when they saw Macarthur brought to the barracks and hurried into the mess-room, and they awaited the next move in great suspense. Harriott and Eliza were some distance away, watching and waiting like everyone else, with the children chattering and jumping up and down continually.

After what seemed an eternity a small group of men emerged from the barracks by a side doorway. From the far side of the parade ground it was difficult for a moment to identify them, but the familiar figure in front was undoubtedly that of John Macarthur, and close behind were the scarlet-and-white uniforms of several army officers. Johnston was not among them, but now some civilians were also coming out of the mess-room, their dark coats conspicuous against the military uniforms; and they, too, were clustering purposefully round Macarthur.

'Look, look! There's Papa – Papa and Uncle Gregory!' Johnnie's sharp eyes had been the first to spot them. He pointed excitedly. 'They're all stopping by that big gun – are they going to fire it?'

'No, stupid! Mr Macarthur's got a piece of paper – they're using the gun to write on, that's all,' said his younger cousin, George, delighted for once to be able to correct Johnnie. 'I wonder what they're writing, Mama?'

'I don't expect it's anything special, George,' said Eliza in a tone of conviction that didn't ring quite true. She turned to Harriott. 'What do you think it is?' she asked in a whisper.

Her sister-in-law shook her head. She was pressing her hand against her mouth as if to stop herself from crying out; and her dark eyes as she gazed across the square at her husband were anguished.

In the stiffling heat, with dark clouds now rolling in from the sea, and the crowds watching expectantly, John Macarthur was hastily writing a petition to 'Major Geo. Johnston, Lieut. Governor and Commanding the New South Wales Corps'.

26 January 1808

Sir,

The present alarming state of this colony, in which every man's property, liberty, and life is endangered, induces us most earnestly to implore you instantly to place Governor Bligh under an arrest and to assume the command of the colony. We pledge ourselves, at a moment of less agitation, to come forward to support the measure with our fortunes and our lives.

We are, with great respect, Sir,
Your most obedient servants,
JOHN MACARTHUR

He put the final flourish to his signature, and then, 'Who'll sign after me?' he asked.

John Blaxland stepped forward. 'I will,' he replied quickly.

He wrote his name immediately under Macarthur's, then stood aside so that the others pressing round could add their names as well. There was Simeon Lord the merchant, and after him, not to be outdone, Gregory Blaxland signed in a quick, impetuous hand. As the list of names grew longer, more and more men crowded round to follow their example, all anxious to promise their new allegiance. Only a few who signed lacked the intelligence to realize that the leader to whom they pledged their loyalty was not Major Johnston at all. Their real leader was John Macarthur, the man who watched them all silently, with a triumphant smile.

Across the square, Harriott's face had drained of colour. But Eliza and the children did not notice. They were watching enthralled as Major Johnston came out into the square and, as a great cheer rose up from most of the onlookers, ordered the Corps under arms.

Soon after, at half past six, the band began to play martial music, and the regiment formed up with fixed bayonets on the parade ground in front of them. 'They're going to arrest the Governor!' The words, whispered at first, were tossed from one to another through the crowds, and each time repeated ever more confidently and loudly. 'They're going to arrest the Governor! They're going to arrest the Governor!'

'*Mon Dieu*, no!' breathed Harriott, but nobody heard – the band was loudly playing 'The British Grenadiers'. And the Corps, with Johnston at their head, his sword in his one good hand, marching with happy confidence as if they were providing the carnival the people had been promised – marching to Government House.

Beside the new Lieutenant-Governor with his bandaged arm strode the two Blaxland brothers.

Early next day a weary but exultant John Blaxland let himself into his High Street house. What had happened in the intervening hours was already part of Sydney's history – even now, tired as he was, the significance of the events he had witnessed was only just beginning to sink in. He must tell Harriott: try to tell her in the right order how everything had happened. How they had gone to arrest the Governor and found their way dramatically barred by Mary Putland. She stood, all fire and fury, at the gates of Government House, defying Major Johnston and his soldiers and trying with her parasol to push aside their bayonets. She had shown greater courage than her father; they had to scour the house and outbuildings before they found him, and when he was eventually discovered hiding in a small upstairs room, he was brought down by the lieutenant who arrested him, with his gold epaulettes covered in dust and feathers. Some said he was actually hiding under a bed when they burst into the room, but Bligh's own tale was that he had just changed into his uniform to face his inquisitors and was in the act of bending down to retrieve some private papers. Whatever the truth of the story, John could still laugh grimly – however proudly old Bounty Bligh wore his Camperdown medal for valour in battle, the only decorations he could sport on his naval jacket for confronting the Sydney mob were white ducks' feathers!

It must have been a jolt to his pride, too, when, on coming down to the drawing-room of Government House, he was handed a letter written by Major Johnston, to 'William Bligh, Esq., F.R.S.' – no mention of 'His Excellency', or 'Governor'. It asked Bligh to resign his authority and submit to arrest. Fortunately the old bastard had given in calmly enough – he'd even shaken hands with Johnston later and said he was sorry he had incurred public displeasure – as if that made up for everything!

John pulled off his boots one after the other and let them drop with a thud onto the floor of the quiet house. God, he was tired now, but it had all been worth it! He and Grimes and several others had had to spend hours rummaging through all the upstairs rooms of Government House for Bligh's public and private papers. They'd need all the evidence they could lay their hands on, Macarthur had said, if they were going to present their case later in England. He must explain to Harriott why that had been necessary. After all, everything had otherwise been very gentlemanly – really it had been a damn' good achievement to depose the Governor without firing a single shot! At nine o'clock it was all complete, and Bligh and his daughter had been left at Government House in the care of five sentinels. So much for Harriott's fears of terror and bloodshed!

Sydney had gone berserk after that. Every remaining bottle of rum in town must have been drunk to celebrate. People cheering. John Macarthur carried round the streets in triumph by the soldiers, an effigy of Bligh burnt amidst much rejoicing. Within a few hours coloured paper transparencies of the Governor being dragged out from under the bed, his daughter like an avenging angel beside him, were being hawked in the streets, and people put them in their windows and lit candles behind them. What a night it had been! He would have come back later to fetch Harriott and the children, but felt sure they would be out somewhere with Eliza and her family, joining in the general rejoicing. Besides, it had seemed better to go back to the barracks in case Macarthur or Johnston might need him.

Harriott and the children must be sleeping unusually late. He had thought the sound of his arrival would wake them, but it was only a servant who was peering vacuously downstairs at him.

'Tell my wife I'm home,' he said sharply, 'and bring me some food.'

The fool of a convict girl looked scared, and shook her head stupidly.

'She's not here, sir.' She began to leer at him. 'She's left town. She took the children and went back to Newington on the first ferry this morning.'

Chapter 20

It was the honeymoon period of the rebel regime, but, like many honeymoons, was not entirely free from worry. With a dragoon deferentially behind him Macarthur rode round Sydney like a triumphant king. Johnston, his henchman, wore the mantle of borrowed fame less easily. Weak but well intentioned, he sat in the rebel headquarters with his bruises fading and doing as Macarthur told him – and privately wishing to Heaven a senior army officer would soon arrive from Van Diemen's Land or England to relieve him of his responsibility. On top of everything else he had a bad conscience about the Governor and his daughter. It wasn't the happiest of situations having the man you'd ousted confined barely a stone's throw away on the other side of the Tank Stream, even though there were sentries posted at the gates of Government House!

William Bligh was to remain a virtual prisoner there with Mary Putland for almost twelve months. He could dream of a ship coming to rescue him, or the Hawkesbury settlers who had reason to be grateful to him, or the British Government – but how long would that take, with London still unaware of what had happened to him, and Whitehall seven long months away? All he could do to relieve his anger and frustration was to write furious, impassioned reports and letters, or else stamp up and down within the confines of house and garden. A few close friends were permitted to call on him, but nobody of importance visited him. Apart from that there was nothing to do but wait, and wait, and wait.

For the new leaders, however, time was precious. So much to do, so many changes to make – but where to begin? First of all Bligh's former officials were dismissed and replaced by Macarthur's friends. John Blaxland found himself appointed a magistrate the day after Bligh was deposed; so did seven others. A series of farcical trials were held to 'legalize' the changes. Macarthur himself was acquitted of the charges outstanding against him so that he too could be made a magistrate, as well as Colonial Secretary; and D'Arcy Wentworth was retried and acquitted. Then old grudges had to be paid off: Atkins replaced by Grimes, and poor Gore, the conscientious Provost-Marshal, who had earlier had the unfortunate task of arresting Macarthur, transported, for his pains, to the Newcastle coal mines for seven years.

John remained close at hand in Sydney, in case Macarthur or Johnston wanted him. Gregory went back with Eliza for a few days to Brush Farm, but John contented himself with a hurried note sent out to Newington. Why in God's name Harriott had run out on him he had no idea, but if she chose to be obstinate then he'd show her he, too, had a mind of his own. At this crucial time it was here in Sydney that his duty lay. She was well, he knew, and so were the children; Gregory had seen them, and so had Eliza. He had no worries on that score, and as far as the farm went, his bailiff was perfectly reliable. It wouldn't hurt any of them at Newington to do without him for a week or so. After all, if John Macarthur had temporarily abandoned his sheep for affairs of state, then, as a loyal friend – whatever Harriott might think about it – John Blaxland would damn' well do the same!

So he stayed in Sydney, awaiting developments – an important one being the decision to send a delegate to England 'to state the grievances of the inhabitants'. It was an almost unanimous choice that Macarthur should go.

The meeting, large and noisy, was vociferous in his support. He accepted his election as delegate graciously – even more graciously when somebody suggested a subscription list be got up to cover the expenses of his journey. Owing to the landing of a large quantity of wine that week-end in Sydney Cove, everyone was in an expansive mood: Simeon Lord offered to start the list with five hundred pounds, and John and Gregory, standing near, felt compelled to follow suit and each offered a hundred. In an excess of generosity somebody else suggested that Major Johnston should be presented with a sword worth a hundred guineas for his services, and amid general acclaim that, too, was agreed upon.

In the more sober light of day, however, Johnston soon began to think a fine sword was poor recompense for all the administrative difficulties he was having; indeed, there were moments in the following weeks when he could even envy Bligh his privacy in Government House. Everybody plagued him. The Blaxland brothers were worrying him again about their wretched grants; the rum traders were as discontented as ever; and the small settlers were writing to him that 'the whole Government appears to be put into the hands of J. Macarthur, Esq., who seems a very improper person ... a turbulent and troublesome character ... and we believe him to be the principal agitator and promoter of the present alarming and calamitous state of the Colony.' He could mark time with the settlers – the Nepean and the Hawkesbury were some distance

128

away, and the smallholding owners did not get into town too often – but the two Blaxlands were in Sydney, able to poke and prod at him on his own doorstep!

At the end of February Johnston got his new Colonial Secretary to send the Blaxlands a stalling letter to say that 'their claims to land, men and cows would be favourably considered', but then they grumbled that the letter had been written by Macarthur. No wonder that later he complained that 'the Blaxlands became troublesomely importunate to divert my attention from the most urgent public business to the immediate consideration of their private affairs'. It was a hard life indeed, occupying the exalted seat of Lieutenant-Governor!

If Johnston was beginning to feel disillusioned, so was John Blaxland. Macarthur was still his hero, his hope, his bright star. But could it be that the man was also human; with the failings, the selfishness, the suspicions that mar lesser mortals – not an esteemed leader? Pushing such questions to the back of his mind John rode home to Newington.

The day the Sydney banners had proclaimed as 'Ye glorious and memorable 26 January 1808' had been a landmark for Harriott, too. As soon as she had escaped from Sydney she knew her departure had been inevitable; it was the sight of John standing by the gun in the Barrack Square, waiting to denounce the Governor in full view of everyone, that had finally tipped the scales and given her the strength to act. To walk out on him at that moment was the only way to make him understand he no longer had her support. Her flight back to the farm was her own act of rebellion and, once it was made, she felt a strange satisfaction and peace.

She walked in her garden, waiting each day for him to come, the full-blown roses and midsummer poppies blooming round her and the shadows of the willows by the river dappling her children's sunburnt faces. But the soft compliance that in the past she had always felt at the thought of him had left her now. She still loved him – loved him with an intensity that frightened her – but now a new self-awareness tempered her love. She was nearly thirty; she had six children and soon, God willing, would have another; and she had found herself. John might still dominate her body; but her mind was entirely her own. If her thoughts and opinions did not agree with his, then he must accept that they should differ.

John had grandly talked of freeing the Colony from the Governor's repressions, but what about Macarthur's? Could he not see that almost every rebellion only succeeded in replacing one

129

tyranny with another? Of course she wanted a good future in their new homeland as much as John did; she would not have insisted on giving baby Louisa the second name 'Australia' had she not believed in it. ('What an odd name to choose!' Eliza had said, wrinkling her nose. 'Nobody in England has ever heard of it!') Yes, there was something about this harsh country with its wide sky that bred self-reliance and independence – qualities she wanted to see in her children.

John was swinging down the path towards her at last, coming with long, easy strides. She felt his arms round her and his lips against her hair, and was glad he had not tested her resolution too severely by kissing her on the mouth.

'So Macarthur has spared you at last,' she said evenly as he released her. 'What news from Sydney?'

She saw him straighten. 'Had you stayed longer you might have known,' he replied. 'It's damned hot out here – let's go indoors and drink some tea and I'll tell you.'

She listened quietly, without comment. Only when he mentioned that Macarthur might go to England did she show interest. 'But will he press our claims sufficiently?' she asked, and was surprised when her doubts were reflected in his slow answer.

'I don't know.' He paused, not meeting her eyes. 'It may be that I ought to go myself, Harriott, when *The Brothers* gets back to Sydney. She's due to arrive any day now, if Russell has done his job. Simeon Lord was saying –' He broke off abruptly, seeing the look on her face, and cursed himself for saying more than he had meant.

'What do you mean, that *you* should sail home? Why not Macarthur?'

Skilfully he avoided a direct answer and turned the conversation to the children, but her question hung in the air like a poised sword between them during the days that followed.

It was a bright, windy morning in March when *The Brothers* was sighted off Port Jackson, with dolphins leaping under the bowsprit. As she sailed innocently into Sydney Cove, her bows dipping heavily in the blue waters under the weight of forty thousand sealskins, nobody would have guessed that within a few weeks of her arrival the Blaxlands' ship would have set the whole flimsy structure of the new government by the heels.

As Harriott had guessed, John was less happy in his mind than he had been about supporting Macarthur. He would not admit it to anyone, but he was beginning to have an uneasy suspicion that the volatile, violent leader could not be relied

130

upon. Since Macarthur had interests in the same shipping company in London that shared ownership of *The Brothers* with John, might he not in his present mood try to swindle him out of some of his just profits? Everyone knew that sealskins were now fetching very high prices in London. Far better, then, to detain the vessel for a while in Sydney: not only would it keep an escape route open for John in the next few weeks should he need to leave in a hurry, but it would also give him time to appoint another, and more reliable, master. The earlier antagonism he had felt for Captain Russell was growing. He was almost certain that the man was smuggling goods ashore – oil, turpentine, butter and cheese, and particularly rum – and if he could accomplish that under John's very nose in Sydney, what could he not do with the sealskins in London?

An odd thing, but somehow not surprising to John, was that Macarthur appeared to be backing Russell. He quickly wrote to John and Gregory giving them 'earnest advice' to allow the vessel to proceed without delay to England. But John was not having any interference. Certain now that Macarthur was encouraging Russell, he determined to get the master replaced. After unsuccessfully attempting to bring a rum-smuggling charge against him, John petitioned Johnston for the removal of Russell from the command of *The Brothers*.

Macarthur sat up and took angry notice. Suspicions, fears of persecution – of assassination, even – were closing in on the rebel leader. Increasingly he imagined that everyone was trying to get the better of him, and nobody more than the Blaxlands. He dictated a letter for Johnston to sign saying 'His Honour has no power to interfere', and hoped that would be the end of the matter. But John could be angry, too. Quickly he wrote back asking Johnston to accept his resignation from the position of magistrate, saying he felt compelled to proceed himself to England to protect his property. Macarthur hastily drafted out another letter; in it he agreed that a replacement could be found for John Blaxland on the Bench, but 'the Lieutenant-Governor would not sanction your quitting the Colony'.

Furious, John pushed the paper across to his brother. 'Look at it, Gregory – with that fool Johnston's signature meekly at the bottom! You can be damn' sure that those are no more his words than they are ours: it's Macarthur who is at the root of it, he's using Johnston's name to intimidate us!'

He snatched up his pen and quickly wrote that he intended to go 'unless I am detained in the Colony a prisoner', then sent it off to Johnston's headquarters and sat back to wait for an answer. None came, so he tried another tack and questioned some of Russell's dealings over money. An irate correspondence ensued, and might have gone on for ever had he not asked Simeon Lord's opinion about it.

'You and Gregory should go to the ship and have it out with Russell,' was the merchant's advice. With growing enthusiasm for another's fight he added hopefully, 'I'll come with you if you like. We can say we've come to inspect the accommodation you may desire when you go back to England.'

Captain Russell received the three men on board with polite coolness. A good tot of his own rum inside him, and the knowledge that he had Macarthur's backing, gave him unusual courage when confronted by three such important gentlemen of New South Wales.

'If you want to occupy the master's sleeping room you must pay for the privilege,' he said daringly to John.

As it was neither his ship nor his master, Lord could afford to be truculent. 'You're a thief and a rogue,' he shouted.

Gregory was behaving like an excited dog let off the leash at last. 'I'll thrust your teeth down your throat, Russell!' He turned to the watching seamen. 'Come on, men, help me bind the villain!'

But Macarthur's invisible cloak still gave some protection. 'Who do you think you're talking to?' sneered Russell. 'You're just a cabbage farmer and a dairyman! If I had a billygoat I'd compete with you!'

With one enthusiastic bound Gregory leaped on to the unfortunate master, punching him until he leaned over the taffrail crying for mercy.

'Go to your cabin, then,' Gregory cried triumphantly, 'but if you bring back any firearms we'll hang you from the yardarm straight away!'

On 28 March the unavoidable trial of John and Gregory Blaxland and Simeon Lord for assault on Captain Oliver Russell took place. It would have been a straightforward case had not the bruised and nervous master, after exhaustive questioning, admitted that Mr Macarthur had given him advice – which he had earlier denied on oath – also that the chief officer, whom he had forced to swear to having witnessed the fracas, had not been on the quarterdeck at the time. Now the tables were turned with a vengeance! It was, for Sydney, yet another superbly entertaining instalment in a series of astonishing trials. The court was cleared while excited spectators took bets with one another on the outcome, and when the magistrates returned they informed the unfortunate captain and the even more unfortunate chief officer of *The Brothers* that, as perjury had been proved, they were both sentenced to be transported for seven years.

On the following day, Gregory Blaxland was fined £5 for assault. Simeon Lord was acquitted, and so was John Blaxland.

Chapter 21

'What idiots men are!' said Eliza lightheartedly as she helped Harriott fold some newly washed sheets they had just brought in from the garden. 'That incident on *The Brothers* was a typical example. All the same, I can't help wishing I'd been there to see!'

How lucky she is to be so complacent, thought Harriott enviously. The fuss on the ship, and the legal proceedings that followed – she just didn't know whether to laugh or cry! Eliza might see the funny side of it and not care that Gregory and John could be the laughing-stock of Sydney, but she herself felt near to despair. With each day bringing some new turn of events, what was to be the outcome? Now there was hardly anyone left to give expert legal advice – even the dubious Mr Crossley, Governor Bligh's ex-convict advocate friend, had been sent packing – and the rebel government was twisting and squirming to find a face-saving way out of its many difficulties.

They had quickly realized that the so-called convictions of the master and chief officer of *The Brothers* were illegal. How could anyone be convicted summarily by the same court before which they were alleged to have perjured themselves? Hastily Johnston had to sign a proclamation annulling the men's sentences. Grimes, Atkin's successor, huffily resigned his position as Acting Judge-Advocate and in April sailed off in *Dart*, the first ship to leave for England after the Sydney rebellion. Meanwhile Captain Russell, thanking not only his lucky stars but also Mr Macarthur, went scuttling back to his ship.

John, fuming, again decided to appeal to the law. Unsuccessful at first – one set of magistrates was dismissed, then another – he finally got Russell committed for trial on a charge of perjury at the next Criminal Court. His satisfaction was short-lived; only a Judge-Advocate could subpoena the necessary witnesses, and since Grimes's departure the post was vacant.

'Delays, delays, delays!' stormed John furiously. 'Macarthur's behind it all, that's obvious. He knows damn' well the high prices sealskins are fetching in London now, and is too bloody jealous to want to see me making a good profit. There's gratitude for you! I'm going to issue a public instrument of protest!'

'John, John!' remonstration Harriott. 'You're getting at hot-headed as Gregory! What good can it possibly do you?'

He stood there in the paddock, arms folded, feet apart, his rugged face flushed with anger. 'Do?' he glared at her. 'It will relieve my temper, if it does nothing else. Johnston, Macarthur, Russell, the whole pack of them – they're a lot of bastards, every one!'

Harriott sighed resignedly, and held her tongue. Already there had been too many arguments between them. Little point now in exulting that John was finding out at last that his idols had feet of clay. For months she had prayed he would see what type of man Macarthur really was, but the realization had come too late to be of any use. Shut up in Government House, Governor Bligh could not help, and anyway she knew John's opinion of *him*! She looked at her husband despairingly, hating to see the growing disillusionment in his eyes.

John's anger increased a week later when Macarthur calmly announced that it was impossible, after all, to bring Russell to trial in the Colony 'for want of a sufficient number of dis-interested officers'. He therefore recommended that Johnston should allow the master to return to England with his ship. The only condition was that he should take with him a bond sur-rendering himself to His Majesty's Government on arrival – but since everyone knew this would be worthless outside New South Wales, it was tantamount to saying that he could go free.

The Brothers sailed in early May, with Russell but without John, her part-owner. On board was a dispatch from Johnston to London stating that the Russell case was 'a mask under which a few officers have displayed a vexatious opposition to my Government'. Had he been honest, he could also have written that it marked the end of an era in the history of the Colony. All pretence that there was any harmony amongst the members of the rebel administration was at an end. He had made a final effort, a few days earlier, when he had summoned all military and civil officers who had taken part in the rebellion to meet him in Sydney, because 'he had unquestionable evidence that their growing discontent arose from the confidence he reposed in Mr Macarthur'. But his appeal for loyalty came too late. His government was already falling apart.

Harriott's seventh child and fifth daughter, Elizabeth Maria, was born at Newington in June 1808. It was a cool winter's day when her labour started, and at first she did not trouble to call John. He was somewhere out on the farm seeing to the repair of a fence that had blown down in the strong winds the night before. She sent word by one of the convict servants to the midwife at Parramatta, then calmly carried on preparing food for the evening meal. It was her seven-year-old son who found her an hour later, leaning against the dairy door, holding her stomach and with her face grey-white.

The governess and servants came running, and watched by the scared children they half-supported, half-carried her to her room. When John was fetched hurriedly he took one look at her pain-racked face and closed eyes and rushed out again, sending a couple of men off in a boat to fetch not only the midwife but a doctor.

The next couple of hours, trying to keep the children and himself distracted, were the longest he had known. The women were in and out of the room where Harriott was lying – he knew he could do nothing, but all his thoughts and his very being were there with her in her suffering. Always before she had borne her children so easily; why was she having such difficulty with this one? The more he thought about it the more he realized what a strain the previous months must have been for her. He had been pig-headed, selfish, obstinate – he could see it all now. He had argued with her and sworn at her; so sure that he was right and her views and advice were only those of an ignorant woman. How wrong he had been! All those weeks he had been in Sydney, thinking only of himself, his own position and self-aggrandizement, all that time she had been here at Newington, uncomplainingly caring for the children, the servants, the dairy and the farm. Fool that he was, not to have thought about it! Harriott was worth a million men – she had never let him down, however much she disagreed with him; she had always been loyal. All he had succeeded in doing, for all his boasting, was to get their lives into this mess, and soon he would have to leave her. . . . He buried his head in his hands, and only looked up when the children tugged at his jacket and told him the doctor had come.

He was too distraught at the time to take much notice of the man; getting him to Harriott was all he worried about. Only when he was leaving an hour later did John have a good look at him, and fleetingly wondered why his face was familiar. The name, Dr Redfern, meant nothing to him – it was Harriott who told him a few days later that she, too, had recognized him.

'It was at Sheerness all those years ago when we were on our honeymoon, John, remember? He was one of the officers – a young surgeon – we saw brought ashore from the rebel ships in the Nore Mutiny. They transported him to Norfolk Island and he's been there ever since – until D'Arcy Wentworth sent for him recently after he was reinstated in the hospital here.' She sat in a chair propped up with cushions, nursing her sleeping baby. She was still weak from the difficult childbirth, but her expression was calm and happy. 'What a small world it is, John – to meet again someone we last saw in England, and under such different circumstances! But that poor doctor's memories cannot be as pleasant as ours.'

John, sitting on the bed beside her, drew in his breath. Such a ready-made opportunity might not occur again – he dreaded doing it but he had to tell her. She was getting stronger each day now.

'Harriott, I've got to go back to England,' he said.

For a full minute she said nothing. She remained perfectly still, holding the baby close to her, and gazing at him with wide eyes. Her hair was unbound and fell loosely on to her blue muslin wrap, making her look ridiculously young.

'When?'

The single word, utterly expressionless, dropped between them like a stone. If she had moved, asked why, shown any reaction other than this icy calm, he would have known better how to deal with it.

'I don't know yet – as soon as I can get a passage – surely you can understand, it's better I go instead of Gregory because I'll probably be better at pressing our claims. I'll have to go to the Colonial Office – try and see Castlereagh – really get our grants settled once and for all. . . .' Before her level scrutiny his voice tailed off.

'You said Macarthur was going. After all, you put up money for him, I heard.' Still the expressionless voice, the inscrutable face from which all the light had died.

'Yes.' He shuffled his feet, crossing and uncrossing his legs awkwardly. He had hoped she had not got wind of that long since regretted generosity, especially as Macarthur now showed no hurry to be gone at all. 'But now that he's Colonial Secretary – so many outstanding problems to be dealt with first –'

Impatiently she reached out for the hand-bell on the table beside her, calling the nurse, and when the girl came she handed the sleeping baby over.

'Take her to the nursery,' she said, 'put her in her day crib and stay with her. My husband and I do not wish to be disturbed.'

When the girl had left, Harriott turned back imperiously to John. 'Now: I think it's time you and I had a talk together.' She still remained sitting in the bedside chair, but was leaning forward, her body tense and her whole face alive. She looked like an animal about to spring. 'Ever since we arrived here I've watched you slowly change. I've seen you change from the kind, understanding, intelligent man I was ready to follow across the world to – to one who has been blindly led – made a tool of by all these unscrupulous men. They were glib enough with their promises if someone of your integrity and reputation would back them! Oh, they would give you all the land and cattle and trade in New South Wales if they could add the name of Blaxland to their infamous proclamations!'

'Harriott! You're being unfair –'

'Unfair? It's they who were unfair to you – and you in turn to others! You mock now at the name of Sir Joseph Banks, but have you forgotten what he did for you? And Commodore Bligh – "old Breadfruit Bligh", as all your associates like to call him – think of the welcome he gave us. But, from the start, did you ever really try to help him? I know he didn't give us all the grants we were promised, but it was easy to understand why. He was sent out here to help the little settlers, to prevent any one man from being too rich or powerful, and to parcel out the land more equally and fairly. He was only doing what the British Government had sent him to do, and like any good naval officer he obeyed.'

'But without vision, without foresight!' interrupted John heatedly. 'You can't turn a land like this into another England! Macarthur had the sense to see that – he, and the army –'

'The Rum Corps!' Scornfully she almost spat out the words. 'They're not proper soldiers any more ... twenty years out here as garrison troops!' She shrugged and raised her hands, palms upwards, in the expressive gesture inherited all unconsciously from her French father. Then, suddenly, she leant back, exhausted, against her cushion. 'I knew you'd go, John, I've known for a long time you had no choice, and that it would come to this.' Her voice was low and unutterably sad. 'I think I've always known in my heart that one day you'd go home, and the children and I would stay here ... wondering if we'd ever see you again....'

'Harriott, don't be such a little fool! Of course I'll come back, God willing!' He went to her and put his arms round her, roughly pressing her against him, his head close to hers. 'You'll not be left alone, Harriott – there's Gregory, and Eliza. I know Gregory enjoys going off for days every now and then and poking around in the bush and outback, but he'll be here when you need him, and I'll see all's in order with our affairs before I leave you.'

He was holding her head against his cheek as he talked, stroking her hair, his hand gentle. But she pushed him away determinedly and held him at arm's length, looking him straight in the eyes.

'It's not for that I worry, John. I can look after everything in your absence, as I've already shown you, have no fear of that.' Her chin lifted. 'I'll be – waiting – just like all the other wives whose men leave them. But remember one thing, I bear your name as I've borne your children – proudly – but only come back to us if you can forget the past completely and we can start afresh together here.'

She leant against his shoulder then and let her hair fall forward; he could no longer see her face, but he could feel her tears.

John Blaxland set out for England one sunny day in September as a passenger on the *Rose* under Captain Brooks.

Six weeks earlier, Lieutenant-Colonel Foveaux had arrived in Sydney on the *Sinclair* from England, to take over command of the Colony from a heartily thankful Johnston. It had been uncertain which of two senior officers might arrive first – Foveaux or Paterson, Colonel of the New South Wales Corps. But since hearing news of the rebellion Paterson seemed in no hurry at all to leave his more peaceful task of forming a settlement in Van Diemen's Land. Probably the memory of a duel years before, when his junior officer Macarthur had nearly shot him dead, was sufficient deterrent. So for the time being Foveaux was welcomed instead – and quickly dashed the hopes of the prisoner in Government House by making it clear that it was not Bligh whom he would support.

Seeking relief in his interminable letter-writing, the Commodore sent a desperate appeal to the Governor-General of India, Lord Minto, furiously writing, 'This is not only rebellion but mutiny, of so black a hue as all England must indignantly bring the principal actors to condign punishment.' But unknown to him, Macarthur's star was already on the wane, and Johnston's, too, and soon – they would all be sailing home.

PART III

Men feel very differently towards each other in this
bustling place to what they do in the solitude of New
South Wales.
> – JOHN MACARTHUR, from a letter written in
> London, 1811

Chapter 22

One day in the following April Bess Blaxland was contentedly
making bread in the kitchen of her new Fordwich home when
she was disturbed by the jangle of the doorbell. She looked up,
impatient at the interruption, and wiped her floury hands on
her apron.

'Bennett,' she called into the small outer kitchen where they
did the laundry, 'leave the ironing a moment and see who it
is, will you? I think both the maids are upstairs helping my
mother.'

Really, visitors at such an early hour! It was too bad, particularly with Mother still going on about how difficult it was to
get used to living somewhere smaller after the big Manor
House! For herself, she preferred it. Christopher and his wife
and little son had wanted to be on their own and had moved
to Canterbury after John and Gregory had left England. The
old family home was too big for three women on their own,
and so – with relief on Bess's part and reluctance on her
mother's – they had moved to this more modern house a short
distance away, near Fordwich church. It was easier to manage,
and with two maids and Bennett coming over once a week from
Westbere to help with the laundry, Bess could really manage
quite well, if her routine was undisturbed.

'Ma'am, there's a naval gentleman at the door, who says he's
looking for anyone of the name of Blaxland.' Bennett's expressive face was a mixture of awe and interest.

'A naval gentleman?' Bess clucked her tongue impatiently,
took off her apron and smoothed her hair, and hurried off to see.

A young man was standing in the hall fingering the hilt of his sword and looking round him curiously. In spite of his lieutenant's uniform his sunburnt face had a surprisingly diffident air.

'Miss Blaxland? I have been some time in trying to find you, or a Mr Christopher Blaxland. I was told you lived at the Manor House, but upon inquiry I found its name had been changed to Watergate House now, and –'

'Yes, it's very confusing – we moved from there a year ago, How can I help you?'

He was regarding her strangely, as if to size up her possible reactions. Only then did she see he was holding a letter.

'For me?' He seemed reluctant to part with it so she held out her hand. Really, the young man seemed practically tongue-tied, and with all that baking to finish before midday, it was quite exasperating! 'May I have it?'

He hesitated a moment longer, then almost pushed it at her. 'I think I should tell you before you open it, ma'am,' he blurted out quickly, 'this letter is from your brother, Mr John Blaxland.' He swallowed, then ran his finger round the neck of his uniform jacket as if the braid on it had suddenly become too tight for him. 'I have to inform you that he arrived in this country yesterday on His Majesty's ship *Powerful*, in which he was conveyed as a prisoner.' Ignoring Bess's startled exclamation he went on, 'We sailed up the Channel yesterday and Mr Blaxland was disembarked in the Downs. A Deal boatman brought us ashore. It was my unfortunate duty to have to escort him to Canterbury Prison.'

'John – here? Back in Kent, and a prisoner?' Bess regarded him in utter bewilderment, scarcely noticing that in the doorway behind her, Bennett, listening, had gone first scarlet, then deathly white.

The young naval officer feared no hurricane, but was terrified of female scenes! He looked at the two women, and the older one holding the unopened letter and staring at him, the other an attractive, golden-haired creature who looked as if she had seen a ghost. 'The letter will explain, ma'am,' he said hurriedly, 'and now, if you will excuse me, I have to be on my way to rejoin my ship.' He edged towards the front door, saluted, and without more ado escaped thankfully out into the sunshine of the village street.

'Of course, it was good of you,' murmured Bess automatically, her eyes on the letter. Ignoring Bennett, who followed her dumbly, she returned to the kitchen and, with fingers that trembled slightly, broke open the seal. It was John's writing without a doubt, but untidy and agitated, as if he had written in a great hurry. Frowning, she sat down at the well-scrubbed table, smoothed out the single sheet of paper and began to read.

MY DEAR FAMILY,

You will no doubt be alarmed at the tidings I am forced to send you, but as this may be my sole opportunity to inform you of my arrival I send these hurried lines by Lieutenant Brown who has kindly promised to deliver them to you.

By a grave miscarriage of justice I am returned to this country a prisoner, and grievously sick. Whilst on my way home from New South Wales to substantiate my claims at the Colonial Office in London I was removed from the ship at the Cape (at the instigation of the infamous William Bligh, who unknown to me had sent a letter ahead of me to Lord Caledon, the Governor there, containing false allegations). I and my baggage were taken ashore against my will and I was tried by a Dutch tribunal and placed in a Dutch prison for a month, contrary to the laws of England. I caught jail fever there, and was later put aboard His Majesty's Ship the *Powerful*, commanded by Captain Johnston, and brought back under wretched conditions to England. I verily believe I should have ended my days down in the cockpit there but for the interference of a friend, who obtained one of the officers' cabins in the gun-room for me.

My sole desire now is to be permitted to proceed to London to plead my cause at the Secretary of State's office, but before doing so I am in dire need of clean linen and other necessities. Can you bring them to me? How long I will be detained here I cannot tell. God willing, not long, I trust! But come soon if you can, I do pray!

JOHN

Bess put down the letter and gazed unseeingly at her carefully kneaded dough, which was shrinking in the draught from the open window. Outside in the village street a drift of fallen petals from the cherry trees floated by, and above the uneven rooftops of the cottages the spire of the church pointed as unalterably as ever into the translucent blue of the spring sky.

'He's home again, then, ma'am?'

The soft Kentish voice at her elbow jolted Bess abruptly back into the present. Turning to Bennett she was surprised to see that in contrast to herself the girl was now looking quite composed, her narrowed eyes gleaming, almost triumphant.

'Yes, but–oh, Bennett, in such a manner!' Involuntarily Bess's eyes filled with tears. John here, home again, as she had always hoped. But never like this, in the degraded state of a

143

prisoner! What could have happened? Why? why? why? The last letter that had arrived in Fordwich at the end of 1808 had mentioned briefly that there had been some trouble in the Colony the previous year, and a change in leadership; but no indication of anything serious. Indeed Christopher had laughed when he read it, commenting somewhat acidly that his brothers, playing their schoolboy games the other side of the world, had forgotten what a real war was like. 'Rebellion, indeed!' he said with some sarcasm. 'An odd sort of rebellion without the firing of a single shot! But then, Gregory always was prone to exaggeration.'

Bess had wanted to defend her absent brothers, but discretion got the better of her. Christopher's smugness was partly understandable, after all; he was now a senior militia officer and very full of his own importance. Sometimes, to hear him talk, one would think he was the sole bastion of southern England against the French! The theatre of war had shifted in the last years to Spain, and Britain had suffered heavy losses there. The army had to be reorganized by drafting large numbers of the militia into fighting units; new men had to be found at home to replace them, and as a recruitment officer Christopher was in his element.

As always in moments of stress, Bess's practical nature came quickly to her rescue. Blinking away her tears she pushed back her chair and stood up, ready as she had been for most of the forty-two years of her life to sort out the troubles of her well-loved family. She was needed; she had a purpose in life once more! Thinking of John's urgent appeal she turned back to Bennett, her voice brisk.

'Now, my girl, as you know all about this anyway, I'd better take you with me. We'll keep the news from my mother at present – time enough for her to know later. I'll say I have to go into Canterbury unexpectedly this afternoon to get some provisions, and want you to help me. I don't know anything at all about prison-visiting, and if we can't get hold of Christopher we may have to go on our own, so it's better the two of us should go together. Now, let me see! First, clean linen, then we'll take food and wine, and some medicaments ...' Her face was almost cheerful once again as she started bustling about the kitchen, thoughts racing and hands busy.

They caught the early afternoon stage from Fordwich to Canterbury, and went at once to Christopher's home. But he was down at Shorncliffe Camp for the day, Sarah said, regarding their cloaked figures and their baskets with curiosity. Bess had no wish to enlighten her at that moment, so left her to her speculations. She and Bennett proceeded to make their way along the busy cobbled streets towards the Cathedral, then walked on a further half-mile to the forbidding prison with its high walls.

The sullen jailer at the gate was used to chasing off soliciting women – since they had been taking in French prisoners-of-war, every female in Kent turned up with some trumped-up excuse to visit! – but there was something about the resolute manner and ginger hair of the older of the two women demanding to see the Governor that made him hesitate. She looked as if she could be devilish obstinate, and anyway she seemed a cut above most of the bitches who came sniffing round the prison gates.

Half an hour later, after two interviews and much persuasion, Bess and Bennett were being led along a dark, dank passage, picking their way carefully between stagnant puddles and stinking heaps of refuse that lay all along the worn stone floor. Their guide eventually stopped at a door at the end, which had a small eye-level grating and a chalked name roughly scrawled over it.

'This is it? Blaxland?' he grunted.

Bess nodded dumbly, then stood aside as the warder made great play with his bunch of keys and finally swung open the creaking door. The only light inside came from a high barred window and for a moment the two women could make out only a few dim objects: a chair, a bucket, and a pile of straw against one of the damp stone walls. With a thudding heart Bess saw the recumbent figure of a man, and tiptoed across, signing to Bennett to follow.

She bent forward. 'John!' She hardly spoke above a whisper, 'John, It's Bess! And Bennett has come with me to bring you some things – John, oh, John!'

Looking back afterwards on his homecoming, John was surprised at the inconsequential things he remembered. First, his transfer from the warship to the small boat that brought them ashore. He had been weak after his illness and the long time he had spent cooped up on board – too weak to climb down unaided; so they had rigged up a rope cradle to swing him down into the bobbing craft. Then there had been the surprising gentleness of the Deal boatman's big hands that had hauled him aboard; the familiar rough Kentish voice saying, 'We'll have you ashore in a trice and finding your land legs again, never ye fear!'

He had lain in the bottom of that leaking boat for the next twenty minutes, practically vomiting his heart out. But there

145

had been compensations: when he had looked up at last there was the evening light of an April day gleaming on the white cliffs he remembered so well, with Dover Castle rugged and firm on the horizon to the west; ahead, the shingle beach and the low line of the fishermen's cottages at Deal. Someone – it was probably the young lieutenant – had splashed his face with water. He remembered thinking, inconsequentially, how coldly salt the Channel tasted compared with the sea off the coast of New South Wales. He must have lost consciousness after that, for the next thing he knew he was in a damnably swaying coach with a dull ache in his belly and a throbbing head; his escort, sitting beside him, said they were bound for Canterbury. Between the waves of pain that kept sweeping over him he looked out at the fast-fading light and thought how small everything looked, and how loudly the birds were singing.

At Canterbury he heard the bells of Great Harry Tower, and the sound, once so familiar, must have roused him; that, and the bowl of soup they gave him when he was taken to his cell in the prison. He was too exhausted to make any protest; but the hot, greasy liquid revived him, and he was able to finish the letter he had begun to write on board, and hand it over to the lieutenant before he left. Then, no longer able to think straight, he stretched himself out on the straw and fell into an exhausted sleep.

They kicked him awake unceremoniously at dawn; and he greedily consumed the tea and rough hunks of bread they brought him. From what his jailer said he could count himself lucky to have a cell to himself; most of the other inmates were crowded three and four together, French and English indiscriminately – 'But then you're privileged,' the man said, with a knowing wink and a leer. The day passed monotonously after that; he slept spasmodically, still dog-tired, constantly disturbed by the sound of cries and shouts and heavy footfalls outside.

Then – it must have been late afternoon – the cell door opened and suddenly there was the kind, concerned face of Bess leaning over him. For a moment he did not see anyone else, and in his weakness he broke down in tears.

He forgot what they said at first, but remembered she had touched his sore, cracked lips with her fingers as if to convince herself it was really he. Then she straightened up and looked over her shoulder and there, unbelievably, was Bennett. She was standing behind Bess like some improbable apparition conjured out of the damp, mildewed cell walls. Bennett with her hair as gold as ever beneath her dark hood; Bennett with the unforgettable eyes as blue as the waters of Sydney Cove; Bennett with the slim ankles, the slim wrists. She did not speak: only undid the cover of the basket she was carrying and handed Bess some ointment and bandages; then looked at him with her half-reverent, half-mocking smile. It was a moment out of time, out of eternity; but in that look he knew she was telling him, as clearly as if she had shouted it aloud, that their coming together again was predestined and inevitable, the obvious conclusions for them both.

John's visitor next day aroused very different emotions. Christopher, blustering and pompous, so incensed him at first by his 'what-did-I-tell-you?' attitude that he felt like taking similar action to Gregory's with Captain Russell – and immediately realized he must be recovering even to consider it! He knew he must let Christopher have his say; his brother's influence was his quickest hope of salvation. So he gritted his teeth and listened with as much patience as possible while Christopher straddled the small cell like their headmaster of King's School long ago, waving his podgy hands and balancing his stocky body carefully on his well-padded, immaculately booted legs.

God! He's getting a paunch already, thought John: he may boast how he's galloped round Kent drumming up the Army for the last two and a half years, but he hasn't the muscle and sinew he'd have developed in New South Wales! Again he repented; all men had their different paths in life; even brothers. And for all his bloody bombast, when he'd finished preaching Christopher would do his best to get him out of this abominable place, he was certain. . . .

A week later, the governor of Canterbury prison signed a permit authorizing 'John Blaxland Esquire, late of New South Wales' to proceed to London as soon as he was fit to undertake the journey, there to present his petition at the office of the Secretary of State. If his health did not permit him to travel forthwith, then he was to be placed in the charge and care of his brother (Mr Christopher Blaxland of Canterbury, a well-known and respected gentleman), who would accompany him on the journey when he was fit.

On 20 May 1809 John was granted an interview in Whitehall with Mr Cook. That gentleman rustled his papers, cleared his throat, mumbled in embarrassed fashion and then peered over his spectacles at his anxious questioner. No, he must confess he had no real knowledge of the charges that had been preferred against Mr Blaxland. Reports took so many months to come

147

from New South Wales, as he would appreciate; the events that had taken place in that small and remote colony the preceding year seemed, to say the least of it – um – er – exceedingly confused. Lord Castlereagh and other ministers had so many more important issues at stake nearer at hand, what with the Peninsular campaign, and the French Emperor apparently turning his eyes to Austria again. . . . Mr Cook spread his hands awkwardly, and gave a non-committal, civil-servant smile.

Clearly, not only the case of Mr Blaxland but that of many other gentlemen from New South Wales would have to be gone into more carefully in the following months; but for the present, until all the evidence was collected, there was nothing to do but wait. Meanwhile, however – again the shuffling of papers, the obvious mental consignment of the whole affair to his 'pending' tray in place of that marked 'for action' – Mr Cook could see no objection to Mr Blaxland's being allowed out on parole, as long as he left his address.

John Blaxland took the first available stage from Charing Cross down to Kent. The mayflower was coming into blossom on the hedgerows, the woods as they approached Canterbury were carpeted with bluebells, and the trees were an incredible fresh, new green. He began whistling, quietly at first, then noisily, thinking how wonderful was England in springtime. And, for the present at least, he was free.

Chapter 23

As John travelled back to Kent after his interview in London, two ships were preparing to sail from Portsmouth to New South Wales. They left at midday two days later. On board the larger ship, HMS *Hindostan*, was the 73rd Regiment, going out to replace the 102nd Regiment, the Rum Corps, which had been ordered home. On board the accompanying fifty-gun frigate *Dromedary* was the regimental commander of the 73rd, Lieutenant-Colonel Lachlan Macquarie, the newly appointed Governor of New South Wales.

Neither the Scottish army officer nor his men greatly relished their assignment. Who could possibly wish to be sent to some remote colony when the eyes of all Britain were turning hopefully towards the new Commander-in-Chief, Lord Wellesley, and his fighting forces in Portugal? Macquarie himself was flattered, but not overjoyed, at his questionable posting. The main instructions contained in Lord Castlereagh's official dispatches to the new Governor were, first, to take over from Commodore Bligh – and God knew where the irascible fellow would be by the time they got there! – and, secondly, to restore order in the Colony after its late troubles. Easier said than done! He had also to send Johnston home under close arrest, and to try Macarthur before the Criminal Court in New South Wales. It did not augur a very happy start to the rule of any new military Governor! The whole situation seemed damnably confused, with some of the offenders already home or, rumour had it, on the high seas. Who the devil would still be in the Colony by the time he arrived was anybody's guess! Meanwhile there was nothing to do but to settle down, with his wife, to enjoy the seven months' voyage out by way of Rio de Janeiro and the Cape.

Macquarie might have been less anxious had he known that the two principal rebel leaders were already safely out of the way. In March, two months before the new Governor left England, John Macarthur and Major Johnston, guessing which way the wind was blowing, departed from Sydney to answer charges against them in London. Their going was not without pomp – the New South Wales Corps band on the wharf to play for them, and Lieutenant-Colonel Foveaux to see them off. But, in spite of the military send-off and all the cheers, the occasion somehow lacked lustre: their star was already on the wane, and most of the Colony clearly breathed a sigh of relief at their going. It was not the departing ships that attracted most attention in 1809 it was those arriving in Sydney Cove. Since the rebellion, provisions were getting short, and it was for these that the quayside watchers looked so hopefully whenever a sail was sighted rounding the Heads!

They were in the ambiguous position of having two Lieutenant-Governors by now; Paterson had eventually prised himself away from Van Diemen's Land in January and sailed to Sydney to take command of the New South Wales Corps. But he rapidly departed to the vacant Government House in Parramatta, leaving his second-in-command, Foveaux, to do the practical ruling in Sydney as before. From then on Paterson spent the greater part of 1809 drinking; granting pardons to all and sundry as the spirit moved him; and lavishly distributing land grants.

The only fly in the ointment of this reasonably amicable situation was, as always, the former Governor. Bligh had been under house arrest for a year. He had appealed to everybody, he had written to everybody, and even when Paterson came in answer to his urgent request, still no help was forthcoming. To add insult to injury, Paterson had arrived on HMS *Porpoise*, Bligh's own ship, and had at first flatly refused to allow Bligh to take command of her. It was therefore scarcely surprising that, as she sailed into Sydney Cove, bringing the new Lieutenant-Governor, Paterson, Bligh had sent a message aboard that, by virtue of his naval authority, he intended to have Paterson put under arrest. Poor Paterson had to land privately; but after that initial show of defiance Bligh still could only wait, and wait.

Such a stalemate situation was very embarrassing, and even Paterson stirred himself sufficiently out of his lethargy to realize that the Colony's greatest need was to be rid of Commodore Bligh. What was the use of so many others planning to leave on each departing ship if the cause of the trouble still remained, like an angry caged lion, waiting to pounce and roar? So at his colonel's request Major Johnston, almost a year to the day since he had deposed Bligh, waited upon him at Government House, Sydney, where, the Commodore complained 'The sentinels, constantly heated with liquor, seemed to have been directed to bellow "All's well!" with peculiar tones of hellish composition.'

With what naval expletives Bligh greeted the announcement that he was to be removed to a barrack, then put on a ship to England, was not recorded: sufficient to say that he dramatically veiled the pictures of King George III and his Queen that hung in the drawing room of Government House, so that his 'beloved Majesties' should see nothing of Major Johnston's shameful visit. But for all his protests he was put in the barrack for seven days, with Mary Putland voluntarily leaving Government House and sleeping on a sofa there to keep him company. He raged so violently that finally Paterson reluctantly agreed on a compromise: Bligh should be allowed to embark with his daughter on the *Porpoise*, as long as he would sign a written guarantee that he would proceed immediately to England.

At last he had got what he wanted! All the sailor in William Bligh exulted as he strode freely about his own quarterdeck again. He was so elated that he momentarily turned all the ship's guns on the only other large vessel in Sydney harbour, the *Admiral Gambier*, which was waiting to take his enemies, Johnston and Macarthur, back to England, too. How wonderful, and what glorious retribution it would have been, to have uttered that one small, simple, easy word of command – 'Fire!'

With agonizing self-discipline he refrained, but he still managed to have the laugh on them. The *Admiral Gambier* was soon on her way home as planned; not so the *Porpoise*. A promise to a rebel government was, in the Commodore's estimation, not worth the paper it was written on. So he spent the next twelve months cocking a snook at them all by sailing no farther than Van Diemen's Land. It was very pleasant after all, progressing gently up and down the New South Wales coast, even though some of the ports where he called were damnably difficult about provisioning him. He let Mary go ashore for a few days from time to time, but all offers of hospitality for himself he firmly refused. Nobody could touch him on his own ship, and if he chose to make a bloody nuisance of himself and not leave New South Wales until his official successor came out from England, then he would have the greatest satisfaction in so doing.

Bligh achieved his ambition. Only when he heard that Macquarie had arrived did he set sail again for Sydney. However, after a formal handover to the new Governor, he showed no desire to leave in a hurry. To the embarrassment of his successor he rented a small house in Sydney for four months where he stayed with his daughter, went on an extended farewell tour of his ever-loyal supporters on the Hawkesbury, and finally sailed in the *Hindostan* in May 1810. With him went a number of loyal friends – Palmer, Gore, who had been released from jail by Macquarie, Divine, Oakes, and Fulton, his chaplain – but not Mary, his daughter.

The *Porpoise* set sail for home the same day. It was ironic, as one onlooker remarked, that on board Bligh's own ship was the entire 102nd Regiment, the New South Wales Corps. After twenty years, the sunburnt, shabby, hard-drinking soldiers of the Rum Corps, and the last of the naval Governors whose life they had made so difficult, were sailing away for ever from the blue waters of Sydney Cove.

Harriott had not particularly wanted to go and watch Macquarie's arrival ceremony at the beginning of that year, but Gregory and Eliza persuaded her. 'Come on!' they urged. 'Everybody who's anybody will be there; you must come with us!'

To please them she had done so – one of the rare occasions she had been to Sydney Cove in the fifteen months since John had left. The place brought back too many memories. She stood in the hot sunshine with Eliza and Gregory and other gentlemen waited respectfully with Paterson and Foveaux to welcome the new Governor. As the band played 'God save the King' and the thunder of the ships' guns rolled round the harbour, she marvelled at how quickly men could forget. Only two brief years, and so much had happened! John had gone, Macarthur had gone, Johnston had gone. Many of the army officers they had known had left already, and the whole Corps would soon follow. Commodore Bligh, too, would be leaving, she supposed – thank God he hadn't chosen today of all days to return to Sydney in the *Porpoise*! – and Mary. She had received one letter from her widowed friend, charming and affectionate. Mary had written from Van Diemen's Land, regretting that the uncertainties of the times had prevented their meeting more often, and saying with feeling she could imagine how much Harriott was missing her husband. She had mentioned neither the difficult life she herself had been having at sea, nor the differences that had existed between her father and John. Only at the end had she written a little wistfully that she often looked back on the happier days when they were all newly arrived in Sydney, and life had been less complicated.

Eliza was giving her parasol a little twirl, and rather self-consciously smoothing the tucked bodice of her best dress. 'We'll have to look to our laurels, Harriott, with the arrival of Mrs Macquarie and all these new officers' wives in the Colony. I hope they won't think we're too behind the times and dowdy! Anyway' – she smiled with happy anticipation –

152

'perhaps now we'll have a better social life in Sydney and Par-ramatta. We could all do with some fresh faces and gay parties.'

'Off with the old, on with the new,' commented Harriott wryly, and repented at once when she saw Eliza's hurt look. It was no good being bitter: Eliza was right, they had all to make a new beginning. If John had been here today he would, no doubt, have been an anxious as Gregory to establish good relations with the new Governor. And Gregory did have a par-ticular reason: of the many land grants Colonel Paterson had handed out so liberally in his short term of office, the largest of all, over four thousand acres on South Creek, had come to him.

'We don't want to lose our grant,' said the practical Eliza, 'and past Governors haven't always stood by the decisions of their predecessors. And another thing, that ridiculous pro-clamation Bligh had the impertinence to publish from his ship last year – the one forbidding any ship's captain at his peril to take anyone connected with the rebellion out of the Colony, and specially naming Gregory! We want to make sure *that's* forgotten, now we've a new Governor.'

Harriott was silent. Certainly she remembered. Gregory had roared with laughter at the temerity of 'the man, Bligh' – and had gone off at once for a river trip of several days with friends up an unexplored reach of the Nepean. Although she missed John desperately, Harriott felt very anxious at the time and was immensely thankful he was in England, out of it all. She knew that he had arrived, but it had been a long time before any news of him arrived. There had been a long and cheerful letter, written on the *Rose* on the way to Cape Town; but then it was another six months before she received a disappointingly brief communication from England. Only a few scrawled lines, saying he hadn't written because he had been unwell but was now recovering; that he hoped soon to go to London. Mean-while he sent all his love to her and the children. All rather vague and disquieting. . . .

On the other side of the world it was only two hours past mid-night, and deep snow was lying on the Kentish countryside. John stood before the glowing embers of a fire in the small oak-panelled bar-parlour of the Yew Tree Inn at Westbere. He had ridden over from Fordwich after dining with his mother and Bess, and had spent the evening seeing the New Year in with the villagers. As the black-jacks were continually replenished from the landlord's big barrels, and the tankards filled ever

elder brother come home from overseas as a prisoner, and classed as a rebel, y'know,' he said testily, 'especially with such a well-known name as ours in Kent; and for someone in my position.' To his curious fellow officers in the militia he had had to carry it off by explaining, 'Life in the colonies undoubtedly alters men. Take for instance my elder brother, John – formerly such a stable chap....'

Christopher also had a few well-chosen words to say on the subject of village girls. 'I hear you've been seeing a lot of that former nursemaid of ours. Of course, I realize that Harriott probably asked you to look her up, but some people seem to find Bennett a damned attractive creature, for all her lack of education. Do you think it wise or desirable...?'

Grinning at his solemn-faced brother, John packed his bags, kissed his mother and Bess, promised to keep them informed of any developments, and set off for London. Next day he found a small furnished cottage in Wandsworth, to rent for the coming months. He notified the Secretary of State's office of his change of address, settled in with relief, and sent for Bennett to keep house for him.

By the late summer of 1810 most of those who had played leading roles in what was now being called 'the Rum Rebellion' had come home. Only Bligh and his supporters were still missing. Those who were waiting began to forgather in twos and threes in London – assertive, slightly bewildered men who found the capital a different place from that of their earlier memories, and gazed about them curiously at the many changes. Even their own formal clothes suddenly seemed old-fashioned beside the smart bucks of Regency London, and they found to their chagrin that the rouged and scented Piccadilly ladies expected far more than the tot of rum demanded by the convict girls in their shacks in Sydney. As each successive ship brought back more familiar faces from New South Wales – faces more lined and sunburned than English ones – the new arrivals, with an unexpected rush of comradeship, encountered former acquaintances in the unfamiliar setting of offices of junior Ministers and lawyers in London. Suddenly they found there was a bond between them, these hardened, weather-beaten men with the strong language and free and easy ways; they screwed up their eyes when they were talking, as if they were more used to gazing at distant horizons than at the grey stone buildings and crowded streets of the city. Here, in London, it was galling the way people took so little notice of them; the sight of a military uniform whose wearer had returned from

157

fighting the French obviously made a far greater impression than their own tales of troubles in a remote little colony the other side of the world.

Macarthur and Johnston had been back in England since October 1809, but John was wary about having more contact than necessary with either of his former associates. That he would be called upon to give evidence on Johnston's behalf in any inquiry he knew, but meanwhile he had his own future to think of. His bitter experience of Macarthur's changing loyalties had already disillusioned him – and look at the way the man was behaving now he was back in London! There he was, trying to get the sympathy of influential people – with gifts of emus to Lady Castlereagh and a swan and a goose to Lady Camden, wife of the President of the Council! And pouring his troubles into the ear of the Duke of Northumberland and any other aristocratic friends prepared to listen. John ran into him from time to time on visits to the Colonial Office, and on each occasion Macarthur appeared to be growing ever more extravagant in his anti-Bligh assertions. Indeed, John was really beginning to wonder about the sanity of the man; his latest idea was to rush about London pestering lawyers to help him bring a civil action to serve on the former Governor, for damages of a mere twenty thousand pounds!

An inquiry could not take place until all the key witnesses returned to England, but time was precious if a defence was to be prepared while they were waiting. No criminal court outside New South Wales could try Macarthur, a civilian; but Johnston, as an army officer, could be tried anywhere. It was scarcely to be wondered at that when he received the congratulations of friends on his promotion to lieutenant-colonel, George Johnston's face still wore an anxious frown.

It was on a grey, foggy day towards the end of October that three ships slipped quietly into Spithead with limply hanging flags and dripping sails. As most of England enthusiastically talked of the safe return of the long-awaited explorer, Matthew Flinders, after his imprisonment by the French, Bligh and his supporters stepped ashore at last from the *Hindostan*. It was four and a half years since he had left England with his daughter to take up the post of Governor. Now he returned without her, and with a heavy heart. The tired, shivering men of the New South Wales Corps, peering at the unfamiliar English scene as they waited in the mist to land from the *Porpoise*, found their homeland unwelcoming and unappealing. It was the first time they had come home in twenty years, and already the unaccustomed damp climate of early winter was taking its toll of them.

Now all the witnesses for the defence and prosecution could be assembled; there were only a few more documents and letters and memorials to add to the mountainous pile of evidence already cluttering government desks, only a few more lawyers' meetings, a few more sessions with counsel, and then the official investigation could begin at last.

At the turn of the year a court martial was announced for 7 May 1811, to be held at Chelsea Hospital, London, for the trial of Lieutenant-Colonel George Johnston on a charge of mutiny. The curtain for the final act was about to go up at last.

A cool breeze was ruffling the surface of the Thames and sending scudding clouds to pattern the green lawns and quadrangle of the Royal Hospital as John arrived at Chelsea on the appointed day. He looked at Sir Christopher Wren's imposing building with a quickened beat of the heart. Figures were already making their way towards the impressive entrance flanked by its tall columns, and stopping in small groups to talk and gesticulate under the colonnade that stretched along the entire north side of the building. Even from a distance he could see a variety of attire – dark formal clothes and full-dress uniforms, legal gowns flapping in the breeze, and here and there the scarlet coat and tricorn hat of an old army pensioner.

As he walked towards them past the bronze statue of Charles II in the centre of Figure Court, John was suddenly accosted by an old soldier with one arm, who was watching the proceedings with interest. His scarlet coat cut in the old-fashioned style of Marlborough's time showed he was a regular army veteran and an inmate of the Hospital.

He caught hold of John's sleeve with a shaking hand. 'Beg pardon, sir, but what be all those gentlemen? 'Tis a court martial, ain't it?'

'Yes. Lieutenant-Colonel Johnston of the New South Wales Corps.'

The old man blinked rheumy eyes uncomprehendingly. ''Oo be 'e? Infantry or cavalry?'

John was taken off his guard. 'It's – it's the 102nd Regiment. They've only recently returned from garrison duty in New South Wales.'

'Not chasin' the French? Not fightin'? Is that why 'e's bein' court-martialled?' The pensioner spat disparagingly. 'Garrison duty – that's not proper soldierin'!' There was a world of scorn in his old voice as the breeze tugged at his empty sleeve. 'Me and my pals, now, we've seen bloody battles and real warfarin' – Valenciennes, Tobago, Seringapatam – you name it and we was there!' He sucked his few teeth reminiscently. 'What was that place you said, sir? New South somethin'-or-other? Never 'eard of it. If there'd been a battle there I would 'ave, that's for certain.' He paused, suddenly renewing his interest in the present. 'There was one gentleman, now, come in 'is carriage some ten minutes ago. A fine-lookin' naval gentleman. Now 'e was worth seein', 'e was, with all 'is gold braid and medals. They did tell me it was the famous Captain Bligh of the *Bounty*. Now that was a man! 'E wouldn't run away from the fightin'!'

Smiling to himself, John made his escape and crossed to the main building. As he approached he could read the Latin inscription stretching the length of the colonnade which stated that the Hospital was founded in 1692 for the support and relief of maimed and superannuated soldiers. Its age and size – and the old man's disparaging remarks – made him feel suddenly insignificant.

Following several others bound for the court martial, he walked through the outer entrance into the octagon porch, which was flanked by captured standards and guns.

To the right steps led to the chapel, to the left to the Great Hall of Chelsea Hospital. It was used for the pensioners' meals, as a rule, but today the men would be eating in the Long Wards.

It was an impressive place for a court martial, over a hundred feet long, with oak-panelled walls, high curved windows; and over the dais at the far end a huge mural of Charles II on horseback, surrounded by allegorical figures. Despite its size the hall already seemed crowded. When John was shown to his seat he found himself surrounded by familiar faces, and had a sudden, crazy feeling that this had all happened to him before. Where else had he once sat with all these same men – William Bligh, glowering and resplendent in full naval uniform, his eyes blue and piercing; Macarthur and Johnston; Gore, and the chaplain, Henry Fulton; Surgeon Harris, Palmer the Commissary, and the Superintendent who used to ride round Sydney on the white horse, Mr Divine? Even old Richard Atkins had turned up, like some evil genius out of nowhere, for once surprisingly sober with nothing stronger than a glass of water at his elbow. And Oakes, the constable, carefully avoiding Macarthur's eye as if hoping he would forget that once he had tried to arrest him. Officers and sergeants of the New South Wales Corps were here, too, still in their shabby, sun-bleached uniforms. . . . What else, then, was needed to complete the illusion? It was not Johnston's sword that should be lying on the table in front of them all, but the crystal and china of the Government House dinner service the other side of the world at Sydney – yes, that was it! It had been at Bligh's dinner party given in honour of Harriott, long, long ago. Never before had life, for John, come round in such full circle.

He moved slightly and felt Harriott's newly arrived letter in his pocket. He frowned. God! Why need life be so damnably complicated, why did each of her rare letters make him feel such mixed guilt and affection? The messages from the children, her own loving, anxious questions! Had the inquiry taken place? Would he be able to come back to them soon afterwards? Was he able to press his claims with Lord Liverpool now that Castlereagh was gone? Had he heard that at the last moment Mary Putland had decided not to travel home with her father but instead to stay behind and, after a whirlwind courtship, marry the handsome Colonel of the 73rd Regiment, Francis O'Connell? Harriott was delighted for her friend – though sorry for the poor father who had to come back to England without her. 'So you must not think too hardly of him, poor man!' She ended by saying she hoped her dear husband knew how much they all missed him.

Unconsciously, John pushed the letter deep into his pocket. As he did so, paradoxically it was Bennett's face, not Harriott's, he saw. Bennett, lovely and appealing, clutching his arm, gazing up at him and whispering, 'They'll not keep you, sir? They'll not put you in another horrid dungeon?' And he had kissed her and chaffed her for an anxious, stupid child, and promised he'd be back in Wandsworth soon – and left part of his heart behind in her safe-keeping....

'Silence, silence!' the court ushers were thundering, as into the Great Hall, with due solemnity, came Lieutenant-General Keppel, the President of the Court, followed by Charles Manners-Sutton, the Judge-Advocate-General. Behind them in procession came a long line of generals, colonels and other officers, all assembled to try George Johnston, the polite, ineffectual army officer with the anxious face who now stood facing them.

The court martial lasted thirteen days, and forty-two witnesses were examined before it was over. When the report of the proceedings was published it took up nearly five hundred closely printed pages – John's own evidence covered forty – but it could not convey the tensions and high emotions of this group of men from New South Wales, gathered together for the last time in their lives.

As the fitful English sun shone down from the high windows on to the naked blade of Johnston's sword, those who had taken

161

the leading roles in the mutiny took the stage one after another: Bligh, as autocratic and assured as ever, reminded within the first few minutes of speaking that 'it would preserve the general decorum of the proceedings better' if he would be 'rather more cautious, in his language; Macarthur, stormy-eyed and theatrical, angry at being no more than a witness for the defence, and having to parry awkward questions; and then one after the other, all the other witnesses, included Blaxland, the 'gentleman settler'.

There could have been few courts martial in history in which the central figure was of less importance. At times poor Johnston – 'Jack Bodice's tool' – seemed almost forgotten in the dramatic struggle between Bligh and Macarthur and their arguing counsels.

When sentence was finally passed, on 5 June, by the large number of military judges, Lieutenant-Colonel George Johnston was found guilty of the act of mutiny, as described in the charge, and was therefore sentenced to be cashiered.

It was the most lenient sentence possible – so lenient that a month later the Horse Guards felt compelled to issue a statement that the military court in the Great Hall of Chelsea Hospital had 'been actuated by a consideration of the novel and extraordinary circumstances which, by the evidence on the face of the proceedings, may have appeared to them to have existed during the administration of Governor Bligh'.

Subsequent events provided unspoken comment on the verdict. A month after the court martial Commodore Bligh was gazetted Rear-Admiral of the Blue Squadron, and two years later his loyal friend, Sir Joseph Banks, procured for him an ex-Governor's pension – as he had always been promised.

Johnston was allowed to go back to New South Wales in 1812 as an ordinary settler, but Macarthur had to remain in Europe, an impatient, fretful exile, until Castlereagh's instructions to Macquarie were withdrawn in 1817. Only then, after eight long years, did Macarthur return to the Colony where for a brief few months he had reigned as uncrowned king.

Had Bligh and Johnston still been alive in 1832, they might both have expressed no more surprise than did Harriott Blaxland when John told her that, at last, doctors had had to put John Macarthur under restraint, and pronounce him a lunatic. The old Admiral, who by then was lying at peace in Lambeth Churchyard, might indeed have raised his bushy eyebrows with an 'I-told-you-so!' expression on his face. In his piercing, sea-blue eyes, would there have been a fleeting expression of ironic amusement?

Chapter 25

Four weeks after the verdict, the Judge-Advocate-General was writing to Lord Liverpool concerning the New South Wales rebellion that 'it is not necessary for the public service, nor do the ends of justice require, that the proceedings respecting the affair should be carried any further'. It was finished. There would be no more discussions, no more recriminations. They could all put it behind them for ever and go home.

But where was home? Was it England or New South Wales? John had given his evidence, he had done what they wanted of him. Like everyone else, he had been exonerated for his part in the rebellion, and he was free. Lord Liverpool could no longer refuse to substantiate his claims now that the inquiry was over. All John had to do was badger the Secretary of State's office a little longer for the necessary papers to take back to Governor Macquarie; then he could be off, away, sailing back to New South Wales on the first ship that would give him a passage. Back to Harriott and the children, to Gregory and Eliza....

Why then this feeling of anticlimax? Had he been tense for so long that he'd forgotten how to relax? Bewildered by this unexpected reaction, he returned to Wandsworth where Bennett anxiously awaited him. In all the months that he had rented the little house she had barely been out of it: the town traffic and the noise frightened her, she said; and she seemed as out of her element away from the quiet countryside as a child at a grown-up party. She came running to him now as he walked in, tears of relief in her eyes as she flung her arms round his neck and kissed him, and he realized how much he had come to accept her presence as a necessary part of his life.

'It's all right.' He deliberately spoke briskly, to take the emotion out of his homecoming. 'I told you they weren't trying me. I'm free.'

'Thank God, sir!' She pulled his hand to her lips and began to cover it with feverish kisses.

'You stupid child, what did I tell you? All's well! Now you can go home to Kent, to your own little cottage –'

Her face clouded. 'And you, sir? You'll come home, too?' she asked apprehensively.

Without replying, he took her in his arms and held her close,

163

feeling comfort in her familiar warmth, rocking her as though she were a child. All the years he had known her he could never get her to call him anything other than 'sir'. It had irritated him at first, just as he used to be irritated by her strange, unlikely name, but now he found both her form of address and her name absurdly different and touching.

'Home?' He repeated the word thoughtfully, and above the gold of her hair his eyes were troubled and uncertain. Where was home? For weeks he had pushed the question behind him, but now he was faced with it fair and square. Conscience answered only too clearly – as clearly as Harriott's letter rustling in his pocket had done at the trial – but where did conscience get you? The last years, the last months, had taught him so much. You could do what you thought was right at the time, as he had done in New South Wales, and could end up in prison for your pains. If he had never left England; if he had stayed, been more like Christopher instead of Gregory – he smiled wryly and dismissed the thought – if he had remained in Kent and married a simple Kentish girl, someone like Bennett? Bennett who had given him such passionate love as he had thought never to find again; Bennett who was clinging to him now, young and lovely and appealing. . . .

'But, Bennett, of course I must go back! I've left them so long, Harriott and the children. It's almost three years since I saw them last.'

Her lovely mouth set like a rebellious child's. 'All the more reason for you to stay, then, sir. They've grown used to being without you, all of them. Your brother's there to look after them, you told me so. And anyway, she has the children.'

'You wanted children, Bennett?' he asked gently, remembering the way his own had loved her so devotedly. 'Why did you not marry after I left?'

She pulled away from him a little, looking into his face with a strange, almost triumphant smile. 'No, sir.' She held her head proudly. 'My mother, whom they called the witch, told me I should be barren. "You shall know love," she said, "and you shall give your love freely to the man who is ordained for you, and it shall be shared by none other but be complete in itself."'

'Bennett, don't talk like that – you don't know what you're saying!' Witch's claptrap or not, he knew what she meant, though he would never admit it. Her beauty and her boundless love were complete in themselves, and needed no reproducing. If he would only stay, they were his for ever – that was what she was telling him.

Oh God! What was he to do? He released her and, turning his back on the small room that held all her loveliness, he walked over to the window that overlooked the small patch of a garden where the first June roses were already blooming. Harriott, Harriott. He forced himself to think of her in the New South Wales farm at Newington, surrounded by the children – Johnnie, who was ten now, growing quite responsible, and who 'rode excellently'; George, who surely must become a sailor, because he was 'for ever playing with water'. The girls – Harriott, 'already quite a beauty – she'll break the young men's hearts later on', and the younger ones, already learning to help in the dairy. Even the baby, who had been only a few months old when he'd left – she would be running around now, and talking.

Although he tried in all conscience to imprint their shadowy images upon his mind they would not remain there for more than an instant. Like something one could no longer quite believe in, as fast as he tried to capture them they faded. And standing there behind him, watching him, breathlessly waiting for his reactions, he was only too conscious was Bennett.

He swung round sharply, his voice rough, almost aggressive. 'Come on' – he did not trust himself to look at her – 'let's get packed up and ready to leave. We'll go back to Kent first thing tomorrow.'

By the next afternoon they were there – going straight to Westbere, where John installed Bennett as quietly as possible in her cottage, and booked a room for himself for the night at the Yew Tree Inn. He must have time to think, to be on his own in his own familiar countryside where his roots were, before going to Fordwich or Canterbury to be confronted by a barrage of questions from his mother, Bess or Christopher. With only four miles separating him from his mother's house at Fordwich news of his return would quickly reach the family, but he needed just one evening, one more night and one more day, to try to balance between past and future, try to make some semblance of order from the confusion of his desires and thoughts!

He spent the evening sitting in the bar-parlour of the inn, slowly downing satisfying draughts of local beer and listening to the conversation going on around him. The local farm folk accepted his return as unquestioningly as they accepted the changing English seasons; he was one of them, a man of Kent, able to join in their talk as if he had never been away from them. Talk of fruit trees – whether they were setting well, or whether the recent cold winds had nipped the apple blossom –

165

talk of crops, of lambing and calving, and the rate the hop vines were growing. It had been so for as long as he could remember, and would continue to be so long after he was gone. And between the discussions and the drinking there was always a game of darts to play, or ringing the bull. Old hands liked to challenge newcomers to this, watching to see if their aim was true enough to send the heavy metal ring that hung from the ceiling beam swinging through the air, to land on the hook protruding from the nose of the painted bull's head on the opposite wall.

Then, as the long dusk of the summer evening drew to a close and the nightingales in the nearby woods were starting up their song, Bennett came over from her cottage to help the landlord, just as she had always done, slipping quietly between the laughing, good-humoured men as she tended the oil-lamps and lit the flickering candles. The lighted taper she carried lent her face an ethereal beauty.

'Bennett,' John whispered quickly as she passed close to him, 'I'll not go back to Fordwich until tomorrow night. I'll take you first to Newington.'

Only a flicker of her eyes let him see her pleasure. Many times she had begged him to take her back, but always he had made excuses. To return with her to the place that held so many other memories for him – memories of his two wives, of his children – would, he felt, be too deliberate, too flagrant a test of his emotions. Yet now, finally, he knew it was something he had to do: only by setting Bennett against the background of Newington could he hope to assess the depth of his feelings and find his answer.

It was a warm, perfect English summer day when the coach set them down under the flowering chestnut trees outside the Rose Inn at Sittingbourne. Having learned that his old friend, the landlord, had died during his absence, John took Bennett to lunch there without fear of embarrassment. They ate their meal at a corner table, unrecognized, only her shining eyes and happy laugh making anything appear out of the ordinary.

'Now, how shall we go out to Newington?' he asked her as they finished their meal. 'I don't want to call at the house now that it has new owners, but we can get a chaise to take us to the village –'

'Oh, must we go by coach?' Her blue eyes looked disappointed. 'Couldn't we see if the landlord has any spare horses? It's so long since I last rode with you, and to do so again, to Newington – !'

John did as she bade him: her gay mood was infectious. The

countryside looked green and beautiful, and the whole afternoon lay ahead of them. What more could any man ask of life than to be in Kent at such a time, when the dog-rose was beginning to compete with the glory of the wayfaring shrub and white hawthorn in the hedgerows, and tall, silky wild irises lined the streams where the duck mallard and her new ducklings were swimming?

They set off sedately, he leading on a black mare and she behind on a chestnut. In the distance a cuckoo called and above them skylarks spiralled up into the soft blue sky until they were lost to sight, and only their ceaseless singing still lingering on the air.

For a mile they rode without speaking, enveloped in the deep contentment of the day, and of each other. Nobody else in his life, not even Harriott, made John feel less need for talk or comment; Bennett's thoughts were his thoughts, and when she smilingly pointed out a flower or a bird, he had just noticed it, too. By common consent they turned down a less used bridle track that led round a different way to the village. In the distance he could see the flint tower of Newington church rising above the cherry orchards.

'It's just as it used to be – nothing has changed!' Bennett cried exultantly. 'Look, that meadow full of buttercups – that's where I used to go with your children!'

They dismounted, tethered their horses to a gatepost, and walked towards the golden meadow. He pulled her down amongst the lush green grass and she laughed as a surprised butterfly fluttered up from the buttercups.

'No – wait! What's that tapping?' Her quick eyes darted to a stone where a thrush, completely unconcerned by their presence, was banging a snail's shell to extract his dinner. She laughed delightedly. 'In that country where you were, across the sea – do you see birds doing such wonderful things as that thrush, and are there such flowers? I cannot believe it can be as beautiful as here!'

'No – yes. At least, it's all so different.' He pulled a grass and chewed it reflectively, lying on his back and gazing up at the sky. 'Nothing looks as soft as it does here – it's not so green, but the sky's a deeper blue. Many of the birds sing sweetly, but sometimes the bush is strangely silent, almost frightening. You'd like the flowering trees – the yellow wattles ...'

'But no primroses or snowdrops or buttercups for your children to pick?' She pulled a face, then jumped to her feet, spreading her arms in a wide gesture that embraced all the countryside around her. 'Surely, then, England is the best and most beautiful place to live!'

167

He laughed lazily, and put out a hand to grab her ankle and pull her down beside him again, but she was too quick for him. In a flurry of blue skirts and streaming gold hair she was off, running across to where their horses were waiting, laughing as she called over her shoulder, 'Come on! I want to ride again! I'll race you across the meadow down to that stream over there!'

He got to his feet reluctantly and followed her, smiling at her eagerness. He went to hold the bridle for her, but in one light-footed bound she was up, proudly sitting on her mare, laughing down at him. He mounted his own horse and they started off at once, Bennett taking the lead and keeping a little way ahead of him. He was happy to ride behind her so that he could admire the ease and grace with which she rode, and marvel as he always had at the way all animals responded to her.

'Let's canter!' she called, but then reined in her horse momentarily as from the grass ahead there rose a sudden flash of black and white. 'Look, sir – a magpie!' She turned in the saddle, her face briefly anxious as she shaded her eyes with one hand as she looked round, and let the reins fall slack in the other. 'You remember? "One for sorrow, two for happiness" – quickly, where's the other one? You look, too!'

Suddenly, from behind the hedge on the far side of the meadow, there came the sound of a shot. It was not very loud, but it was unexpected enough to make both horses take fright. John had been holding his reins firmly and was able to control his mare and calm her in a second, but Bennett was taken completely unawares. Her chestnut twitched its ears, reared up, and in a flash had bolted, tearing across the meadow as if all hell were behind them. Bennett, with only one hand on the harness and looking back at him over her shoulder, never had a chance. As they reached the stream the horse shied, reared up again and threw her. It all happened so quickly that John could only watch, horrified; one moment she was sitting proudly erect in the golden summer sunlight, the next she was lying in an incongruously twisted heap with her back against a small boulder at the edge of the stream, her blue skirts wet and bedraggled amongst the tall purple wild irises.

'Dear Christ in heaven!' John was off his horse and over to her in a flash, bending over her in horror as the chestnut mare, calm now, disconsolately regarded them both before beginning to drink the muddy water.

He could see at once that she had probably broken her neck. She could not move herself at all, but was still conscious. She

168

seemed unaware of what had happened as she lay there, not in any apparent pain, looking up at him from puzzled blue eyes as though trying to remember.

'Bennett, Bennett!' He could only repeat her name in a stricken voice, helplessly stroking her forehead and the pale gold hair. Tears began to roll down his agonized face and his shoulders heaved. 'Oh, Christ, why, why?'

'Wait – don't cry – have you seen it, the second one?' Her voice was like that of an anxious child, wanting to give but also to receive comfort.

For a moment he could not think what she was talking about, and then he remembered. He looked up, and as if in answer to her question there suddenly appeared from behind the hedge across the meadow the figure of a young boy – a farm lad, or, more probably, a poacher – who with tousled hair and scared face, seeing what had happened, came running towards them. There was a dead rabbit's head sticking out of the leather pouch at his waist, and he had a gun over his shoulder, but it was not at these that John was staring. His eyes were fixed on the newly killed bird the boy was clutching in his hand, on the blue-black of the long tail feathers, and the contrasting snowy plumage that was already matted with blood.

He cursed the boy in language that would have made the hardiest New South Wales Corps veteran turn pale, and shot him off to fetch help; then he bent down again over the dying girl.

'Bennett, Bennett, listen!' All his heart was in his voice as, cupping her head in his two strong hands, he whispered to her, 'It's all right – I've just seen the second magpie! Remember, two – for happiness – as you said....'

A faint flicker of relief showed in her face, and for a second he thought he felt a slight pressure of her fingers, but then her head fell limp. The only comfort he knew in that instant of agony was that she hadn't seen that the magpie was dead.

He arrived back at Fordwich, at his mother's house, three days later. How he had got through the intervening time, and all that had to be done, he hardly remembered; in the desolation of his grief it had passed like some nightmare. Now there was another grave at Newington among the cherry-trees, and yet another memory.

If his perceptive sister, Bess, sensed anything of the emotional ordeal he had been through, she never hinted at it; for there was a firmness, a composure about her brother now that he had somehow lacked before. It was as if he had been racked

169

with doubt, but now, however much it had cost him, he had found the answer.

'Has any mail come from London for me?' he asked, as soon as he had paid his respects to his mother.

Although the old lady would have given her right hand not to produce it, she reached out at once, opened her writing-bureau and handed him a large, official-looking letter. It carried the impressive red seal of the Secretary of State's office, and as he fingered the seal he could feel his mother's steady eyes fixed on him.

'Go on, John, open it,' she said firmly. Her expression gave no indication of what she knew it would mean to her. All her life there had been farewells, and brave smiles and fluttering kerchiefs as the men in her life left her. It would not do to let her beloved son see that each leave-taking now was a little harder.... 'Without looking inside that envelope I know it means you've got what you came home for – the documents you need to prove your land claims to the New South Wales Governor. There's nothing to prevent your return any longer now, is there? How happy Harriott and the dear children will be to welcome you!'

But try as she would, and berating herself for a stupid old woman, she could not stop the tears that trickled down her cheek as he bent to kiss her.

Chapter 26

Winter was beginning in New South Wales when John Blaxland returned.

Gregory was on the farm when the message came. Without stopping to tell Eliza he raced down to the river and got his convicts to ferry him across to Newington – faster than they had ever rowed before.

Harriott, busy in the house, looked up in surprise at such an early visit. At the sight of Gregory's excited face, her own paled.

'What is it, Gregory?'

'The captain on the river ferry just brought me a message from Sydney – the ship that rounded the Heads at dawn today is from England. While waiting to come in, she sent a semaphore message ashore with the names of the passengers. John's among them, Harriott, John's back at last!'

If he had expected her to faint, or clap her hands with joy, or even to hug him round the neck in her delight, he was disappointed. She just stood there, staring at him as if she could not take in what he had said. For a moment he wondered at her apparent lack of emotion; then he noticed her hands, which where clenching the chair-back so tightly that the knuckles showed white.

'They'll be docking in about two hours, the captain said. Will you come down to Sydney with me to meet him?'

'No, Gregory, no.' Hurriedly she shook her head. 'I'd rather ... no, you go alone. I'll wait here. It will give me time – to prepare.'

In his usual exuberant fashion Gregory went dashing off. Harriott remained where she was, quite still. Her eyes travelled slowly round the familiar room. Outside, in the cool, windy day, she could hear some of her children laughing and shouting. From farther away came the sounds of the farm – Keeper barking at the sheep, the cows mooing as they were brought in for milking, and the voices of the convicts down at the salt-pans by the river. From the dairy she could hear the reassuring clatter of the milk pails, and the butter churns working.

All these things, all her immediate world, for the past three and a half years had been hers to care for without him. She had lived – or existed – through a whole eternity of loneliness, but she had done it. She had won through. Single-handed she had watched over the children, had coped with the farm, the servants and the convicts. She had faced problems of every kind, and frequent shortages. There had been times when drought or floods had made many foodstuffs hard to get; and less fortunate settlers in the colony faced near starvation. She had dealt with bushrangers, and an escaped convict who broke into the house one night and terrified her by trying to get at the chest under the bed that held all their money.

· Yet in spite of everything she had succeeded, a woman on her own. It was she who had kept the farm going, the children well and happy, the servants at peace and their home established through all the various changes and difficulties. Gregory had usually been on call – or Eliza – but however kind their offers of help, at rock-bottom it was she herself who had kept her small world going. Now she could look with pride on all she had to show for it: the prosperous farm, the fine cattle, the new outbuildings that had been put up on her instructions, her well-established and well-stocked vegetable and flower garden. In all the years of waiting, she had not failed.

Why then this ice-cold suspense, this terrible apprehension? That John had come back was the best possible news for them all. Instead of standing like a statue she should be running out to tell the children. Yet she could not bring herself to do so at once; only the sight of him could bring with it the necessary conviction. Throughout the years of separation she had never quite dared to believe in her heart that she would see him again. Of course, she never admitted it. To the children it was always a loyal, 'When Father comes home again we'll do so-and-so, or show him such-and-such.' Even to Gregory and Eliza she had made a point of keeping a permanently serene and confident face. But in the dark stretches of the night when the timber of the house creaked in the wind and she could hear the possums scurrying on the roof, then came the times when she had to press her mouth against her pillow to stop from crying aloud her awful loneliness. Yet even such misery must have a term. Gradually, after the first months, the first year, she had grown accustomed to being on her own.

She was even able to cheer Eliza when Gregory went off for several days on a trek into the interior with young Wentworth, and another time when he accompanied the Governor himself up the Nepean. She arranged for her sister-in-law to join her in small parties to Sydney, or in river picnics with all their children.

*   *   *

172

She saw him coming before he had seen her. She went on to the verandah to wait for him as he walked slowly up from the ferry between the flaking blue-gum trees. A leaner, older John, with a deeper network of lines around his eyes, but a face suntanned from the long sea voyage and a smile that was, for her, as heart stopping as ever.

He saw a more poised woman than the one he had left – as elegant as ever in the way she held herself, but now with an added unconscious assurance, a new belief in herself that gave great attraction to her maturity.

'Harriott?'

'John!'

They embraced shyly, almost formally, and broke away from each other almost at once as if afraid to test too early the strength of their emotions.

'I got the first available passage – I couldn't let you know or send you mail by an earlier ship because I didn't know –'

'I was so thankful when news came that the court martial had taken place and was over –'

They both spoke simultaneously, then stopped, and laughed; then one by one the children, who came spilling out of the house by different doorways, spared their embarrassment, and any further private conversation between them was prevented by excited young cries and exclamations.

John rose to the occasion and within minutes had them all climbing over him like excited puppies.

'Hey, wait a minute! Johnnie – why, no, it's George! I didn't recognize you! Did you look after your mother well, as I told you to? Harriott – my! Are you too grown up a young lady now to kiss your father? So Mrs Macquarie lets you play her harp sometimes, and you can do so tolerably? You'll soon be as beautiful as your mother! And Anna, my little Anna, what a tall girl you are now – yes, you can show me your pressed flowers later. Jane – or is it Louisa? So Keeper had pups, have you kept any to show me? Yes, George, I heard about Uncle Gregory's expedition up the Nepean River – he's promised to tell me all about it.'

On went the excited comments, the gestures, the young laughter. And over the heads of their lively children the eyes of the mother and father met, and looked away; then met again, with no more need for questioning. And, unnoticed by either of them, a pair of magpies rose up from the paddock behind them and flew away, towards where the shadows were lengthening on the distant Blue Mountains.

* * *

173

The Sydney to which John returned was very different from the one he had left. Under Governor Macquarie there had been so many improvements in the past three years that in some quarters it was difficult to recognize the place at all. Even the Blaxlands' old cattleyard had been acquired to make way for a new market place with a bell.

In John's absence the new Governor and his wife had shown great kindness to Harriott and had often included her in their invitations. After all, was she not the wife of one of the earliest and best-known gentlemen settlers, a friend of Mary O'Connell, now happily established as an army officer's wife after all her adventures as the former Governor's daughter? Now Macquarie welcomed Harriott's husband with equal friendliness.

John found it hard at first to get used to some of the changes this Governor had made. It was strange when invited to dinner at Government House to find you might be placed next to a former convict and his wife at table. But one must move with the times, Harriott said, and there was no denying that Macquarie had brought about many improvements. He had reduced the number of licensed houses in Sydney by more than half; all new streets were being made at least fifty feet wide; a new hospital was going up, and many new buildings were nearing completion.

There was so much to see and do in those first weeks after his return that John had little opportunity to think of the immediate past – his clamorous, demanding children made him far more conscious of the future. Their unquestioning acceptance of his presence among them once more; their bright eyes and everlasting chatter; their burning desire to be first to show him anything new – no greater encouragement would any man need to face the years ahead.

Within a few months he was already discussing with Gregory possible improvements at Newington. With their land grants confirmed, and the firm assurance of Government House blessing, what limit to their plans for expansion? First, more salt could be sent to Sydney each week from Newington, they must see to that. And then how about another grain mill, and possibly a lime works? From reports he had had, a coal mine in the vicinity might be a worth-while proposition, and didn't Gregory think that, quite soon, they might consider building a factory to start a cloth industry? With the increased wool from their flocks, within a few years they might work up quite a trade in blankets and tweeds; possibly start exporting....

Harriott, sitting out on the verandah, sewing, listened and smiled as the two brothers talked. To her it was miracle enough

174

that John was home again: now, hearing his eager voice, she felt happier and more relieved than she had ever expected to be again. Contentedly she began to rock to and fro in her chair, and as she did so she felt the first faint flutterings of a new child within her. Her joy was complete. After all the years of watching and waiting, hardly daring to hope, her husband was hers.

Gregory came suddenly striding out to her through the open doors, his face a mixture of amusement and exasperation. 'I don't know what the devil's got into John,' he exclaimed. 'He's got fine plans; but can't you help me make him understand the Colony's not big enough for them? It's pastureland we need – more pastures – before we can get any grandiose schemes going for a vast wool industry!' He turned as his brother joined them on the verandah. 'You've been away – you don't seem to realize, but with these damnable droughts recurring every year or so, the coastal pastures are not sufficient to support our herds.' He thumped on the table, sending one of Harriott's balls of mending yarn spinning. 'Discover more land for sheep and cattle! Then you can talk about your cloth trade, John!'

Harriott was aware that Gregory talked sense. He understood better than John that the Colony as a whole could not expand economically until fresh grazing grounds could be found. And there was only one place left to search for these – across the forbidding Blue Mountains.

Up to now, Gregory had only played with the idea of any major exploration. He had done many short treks with friends into the interior, but none had been for more than a few days. But Eliza had said she often caught him gazing speculatively at the mountains that swept down to within a few miles of their South Creek farm. Could it be that, with John safely back in the Colony, Gregory was seriously thinking of taking up the challenge; and really trying to find a way across those mountains that had defeated so many brave men before him?

One day early in 1813, Harriott, who had gone over to Brush Farm to see Eliza, noticed that her usually cheerful sister-in-law seemed very preoccupied.

'Eliza, is something the matter?'

Eliza put her head down on her arms and began to weep. In response to Harriott's concerned questioning, she confessed that Gregory's restless nature and his 'everlasting dreams of exploration' were beginning to exacerbate her nerves. She went on to tell how, the previous week, she had come upon her husband with Lieutenant Lawson and young William Wentworth, their neighbour, deep in serious conversation over large charts and maps. Afterwards, when she had challenged Gregory

175

outright, he had admitted that the three of them were planning a new attempt to cross the Blue Mountains together. 'They hope to go in May, Gregory says, if the weather's favourable. They're going to try to get across by keeping to the top of the ridges instead of along the river valleys. They think if they can get on to the high backbone of the mountain barrier they'll find a way across it. I think it's madness. How can they possibly do it when so many have tried in vain before them? And all because Gregory met some kangaroo-shooters on the lower mountain ridges who'd got the idea from the Aborigines!'

'But wasn't it Caley's idea? –'

'Oh, I don't care whose idea it was!' Eliza was terribly on edge. 'Certainly Lieutenant Lawson may admire Caley as much as he likes. Caley didn't succeed, did he? So why should Gregory? He'll insist on leading the way and exposing himself to every risk and danger! It's all very well for young William Wentworth, he's only twenty; but Gregory seems to forget that he has a family to consider. What would I do if I lost him! –' She gave way completely then, her voice lost in sobs.

Harriott reached out and clasped her sister-in-law's hands. How strange, she thought, only a short time ago it was I who envied Eliza. I knew then that my marriage was at risk and could do nothing but wait. Now it is the other way round.

'Eliza.' Harriott's voice was low but imperative. Her sister-in-law looked up at once, her eyes still red from weeping. 'Eliza, don't you realize – whatever you do you must not try to stop him! This is something quite outside his love for you and the children, something he's got to do to prove himself – just as John had to go back to England and meet Bennett again before he really could be at peace with himself and me.' She had never spoken so openly to Eliza before, but now she was prepared to admit everything if it would help to take the anguish from the other woman's eyes. 'I believe that something like this – this testing time – must happen at some period in every marriage. And I'm quite certain that you won't keep Gregory or his love by forcing him to give up this idea. Let him go ahead and do it, Eliza. Encourage him and help him in every way you can – he deserves it! If he fails, no failure can be blamed on you. But just think – if he succeeds, you'll be the proudest wife in the Colony!'

Chapter 27

It was in the morning of 11 May.

The two women stood silently together on the balcony of Brush Farm, watching the final preparations for the departure of Gregory and his party to the Blue Mountains. A cool breeze tugged at the border of Eliza's dark shawl and she pulled it close, as if the tighter feel of it round her shoulders would give her comfort. She was glad that Harriott and John were here, and that now Harriott was waiting beside her, an arm linked affectionately in her own to support her in these last testing minutes before the men set off.

Gregory had already said good-bye to the younger children the previous night and had ordered them to stay indoors this morning. He didn't want them running around and getting in the way as last-minute checks were made on stores and ammunition. Only his eldest boy and John's two sons, Johnnie and George, were allowed to help. Their mothers could see the cousins now, excitedly talking together and obviously envying the four chosen convict servants who were being taken on the expedition. Harriott knew it was a great proof of John's faith in his brother that he had brought over one of his own most trusted and responsible servants from Newington to go with them; bad convicts were easy to come by, but a strong and un-questionably loyal man like this one was a rarity; and it was a sacrifice for John to spare him.

An unusually heavy dew had delayed their departure. The ground was wet and slippery; and when a load of provisions fell from one of the horses' backs it took some manoeuvring to get it into position again. Four horses were being made ready and the other three, already loaded, were tossing their heads and stamping their hooves impatiently. One of the servants was sent to unleash the five dogs they were taking with them. The animals had just been given a final feed and now they came rushing out, barking excitedly, full of anticipation. The sudden commotion made the remaining horse rear up unexpectedly, and for a moment it looked as though the heavy box of ammunition being strapped on its back might slide off into the mud.

William Lawson was going round with young Wentworth on a final inspection of firearms. Lawson, at thirty-eight, was a tough, strong bushman with plenty of experience behind him.

The knowledge that he was a surveyor as well as an officer of the New South Wales Corps gave Eliza confidence in him and she said as much to Harriott, quickly adding that she had not, of course, mentioned this to her husband.

Gregory himself was standing by the horses, talking to John. He had pulled out one of the many maps that bulged out his jacket pockets and was spreading it out against the pack of provisions. The men were too far away for Harriott and Eliza to hear what they were saying, but Harriott was suddenly struck by the way each brother instinctively responded to the other's need and how unconsciously they complemented each other. They were bending forward, engrossed in studying the proposed route, but although their faces were hidden by the wide brims of their hats, she knew as clearly as if she could see them what their expressions would be – Gregory's, eager and animated, full of self-confidence yet still looking to his older brother for ultimate approval. And John's, quietly attentive, as he took note of every detail Gregory was telling him, his rapt attention signifying the necessary support and encouragement. John's was the passive role in this adventure; but Gregory knew his brother would be behind him every step of the way.

Now, everything was packed and ready. To the watching women the wait had seemed an eternity. Suddenly it came too soon, the time to say good-bye. Gregory stuffed the map in his pocket, looked round for his wife, and came striding back to the house. He bounded up the verandah steps, swept off his hat with a flourish, and gathered her into his arms.

Eliza clung to him. 'Oh, my dearest heart, take care, take care!' With an effort, remembering her promise to Harriott, she managed to smile, but her eyes kept straying to the mountains over his shoulder, and she was sure he could feel her trembling.

He kissed her again, held her close for the last time, then turned to Harriott. His face was more serious than she had ever seen it before. 'Look after her for me – her and the children.' His voice was low. 'Without you and John, you know, I probably couldn't –' He broke off abruptly, left the sentence unfinished, and laughed gaily instead, as he turned from them and began to go down the steps to join his waiting companions.

'God knows why they're all making such a drama of our departure, do you, Lawson?' Momentarily he seemed to shed his five and thirty years and the strong, broad-shouldered, decisive man in his prime became the eager, devil-may-care Kentish schoolboy who had gone off on escapades into the country with his friends twenty years ago. 'Anyone would think we'd never seen a bloody Aborigine or gone into the interior before. This won't be any different, you'll see!'

For all Gregory's confident words, the three men and their four servants knew perfectly well this expedition would be no schoolboy adventure. They soon had proof of this.

After the first day, having forded the Nepean River and camped overnight at the foot of the first great ridge of the mountains they were made quickly aware of what they were up against. The slippery mud that made the going hard for the heavily laden packhorses gave way to thick, scrubby brushwood, denser than anything they had met before. It was obvious they could not get round it, so they decided to cut their way through with axes. It was back-breaking work hacking out a pathway; and each night their muscles ached so much they fell asleep exhausted. Worse, it made the first five days' going painfully slow. They could only prepare a path a few miles at a time, then had to go back and fetch the horses, camping gear and stores. It meant each section had to be covered three times; and once they only advanced two miles in a whole day.

The sixth day was a Sunday. Gregory decided it should be a rest-day for them all. Not only were his own aching limbs glad of the respite; it gave him time to make up his journal. He was determined to keep as full a record as he possibly could of their whole trek. Wentworth and Lawson also occupied themselves with writing up notes and sketching; but the three convict servants, having fed the animals and prepared the meals for the party, had less to occupy themselves. Now, with time to reflect and talk round the embers of the campfire, the servants began to feel afraid. This wild and unknown country was unlike anything they had ever come across before. After their immense efforts in clearing a way through the brushwood, all they could see on either side were terrifying, deep gullies. And now that they were resting they were suddenly aware of the silence being broken by strange noises. There was a tremendous howling of native dogs, which made their own dogs restless and uneasy. Were natives stalking them, they asked each other in frightened whispers? As darkness fell they heard an emu drumming, and the eerie noise went through their heads all night, shattering the black silence and preventing them from sleeping.

Next morning, two of the convicts said they wanted to give up and go back. It was only John's servant who would listen to Gregory's desperate command that they must push on, and who eventually persuaded the other two men, very reluctantly, to stay.

On Tuesday, 18 May, exactly one week after they had left, the going was so hard they progressed only a mile and a half. Gregory wrote in his journal that night that they were 'very much tired and dispirited'. A new obstacle had presented itself: a shortage of water. The men might voluntarily go on short rations and be ready to endure cracked lips and parched throats as they grimly pressed on, but for the animals on which they depended it was no so easy. The dogs had killed a couple of small kangaroos, which provided meat for them, but fodder was getting short for the horses. The water that they needed so desperately could only be got from the bottom of the deep, rocky gullies. Once it meant a perilous six-hundred foot descent to the bottom of a gully to get it, and then when they had carried up the precious liquid there was not enough for them all that night.

The eighth day was the worst of all. They came up against 'a great perpendicular mass of rock, nearly thirty feet high', which barred their way. Again it meant the agonizing straining of every muscle to manhandle heavy boulders and push them aside in order to make a 'small broken rugged track in the centre', just wide enough for men and horses in single file to pass through.

Unexpectedly, after that, they had their small reward. On reaching the heights the other side they were able to see for the first time the settlements to the east which they had left. They also found a curious cairn of stones. This sign of human presence encouraged and excited them more than anything else they had seen – this, surely, must mean they had penetrated as far west as any European before them?

They toiled on, more cheerful now they had the memory of that mound of stones to inspire them. The brushwood terrain, which had been such an obstacle, was giving way to swamps and coarse rush grass – not the choicest nourishment for horses, but at least one they could exist on. The convict servants benefited less. Overjoyed not to have to scramble down the fearsome gullies to get fresh water, they drank some of the dank swamp water; and one of them developed a high fever as a result. His illness delayed the party, and again the enforced stop made them more conscious of their surroundings. The loneliness and ominous silence began to play on their nerves, and even Gregory commented, 'scarcely any animal to be seen, and very few birds'. Inevitably their thoughts returned to the Aborigines and, as if in answer to their unspoken fears, one night the

180

natives – attracted by their campfires – crept very close. One of the servants, terrified, began to cry out that the natives would spear them all to death. It may well have been their intention, but the five camp dogs, bristling as usual at any sign of danger, earned their supper that night by growling ferociously, and the natives fled.

By the twelfth day the tired little party had reached a point only eighteen miles due west of the Nepean. But, thankfully, they came upon 'two thousand acres of land clear of trees', and a fine stream and wood for their fires. Young Wentworth began whistling with joy, but his two older companions were less sanguine. They guessed that not all their troubles could be behind them, and they were right: progress was stopped once again by 'an impassable barrier of rock, which appeared to divide the interior from the coast as with a stone wall, rising perpendicularly out of the side of the mountain'.

After several attempts to descend the cliffs – Gregory assessed their height as a thousand feet – they had to give up the attempt and instead began to bear to the north, where they found another swamp to camp by. The scenery was now spectacular, but the small party still felt utterly isolated and lonely. It was almost a relief at one time to hear the sound of a native cutting wood somewhere, and, when it was dark, to see the gleam of Aboriginal fires far below in the valley.

On they went, determined as ever, but the strongest of them were beginning to feel the strain. They had become inured to the cuts and sores that the brushwood had inflicted on them earlier as it tore their clothes to ribbons, but now gastric upsets began to plague them. Diarrhoea weakened them, but they forced themselves on; and on the eighteenth day of the expedition came victory – they had reached the end of the Blue Mountain barrier!

Below them, stretching westwards, lay forest land that would provide timber and 'good grass'. It was a sight to give new life to any hard-pressed cattleman. They had found a crossing to land beyond the mountains. Nothing now could daunt them. With renewed energy they cut a path so that their tired horses could descend the steep slopes of the mountain. For much of the way they had to carry the horses' loads on their own backs to minimize the danger of the animals' slipping, but they didn't care – ahead of them lay meadowland with grass almost three feet high! For the explorers it was like a desert mirage to see it – but this was no mirage: this was reality.

Now, at last, they could afford to ease up a little. They made camp on the banks of a pleasant stream and spent all the Sunday resting. After an exhausted sleep they awoke to an unaccustomed frost, and the colder air invigorated them and sharpened their appetites. The dogs had killed a kangaroo, and a lucky shot across the valley brought down another, so there was plenty of meat that day for them all. Then, with a good meal in their stomachs, they prepared for one last effort.

Ahead of them, beyond another wide stretch of well-watered forest land, open meadows, then a river, they could see a high hill 'in the shape of a sugarloaf'. Physically, they were almost at the end of their endurance. They had done what no European had ever done before – crossed the great mountain barrier to the hinterland – but there in front of them was this one last challenge. They had to climb that hill to see what was on the other side and then, only then, would they know if they had achieved what they came for.

It was an easy climb compared with those they had done earlier, but in their weakened state it took their every reserve of strength. Alternately cursing and shouting words of encouragement to one another, they panted and dragged themselves and their tired packhorses up to the summit.

Ahead of them, as far as they could see, there stretched forest and grass land sufficient in extent, as Gregory later wrote, 'to support the stock of the Colony for the next thirty years'!

They gazed long and silently at the view ahead. Then, as the significance of what they looked upon dawned on them, they turned and grinned at one another. They were stinking, tired, filthy; their hair was matted under their sweat-stained hats; between the rents in their tattered clothes congealed blood showed from the torn flesh beneath, and their boots looked as if they would scarcely make the return journey. But in this moment none of them cared. They had discovered their promised land, their future – the opening up of unlimited possibilities for their small Colony.

They had travelled about fifty-six miles in twenty-one days, and had covered much of that distance three times over, in unspeakable circumstances. They had been in fear of their lives many times; but they had achieved what they had set out to do.

Now, at last, they could turn their horses' heads for home.

Old Mrs Blaxland of Fordwich tired very easily now. It was the spring of 1814, and already Bess was wondering anxiously whether her mother would last out the year. She was seventy-five, but since John's return to New South Wales three years before she had aged rapidly; it was as if, with his going, she

182

had found little else to live for. Christopher dutifully brought his small son Mark over from Canterbury to see his mother quite often, but the rather stilted visits gave her little real pleasure. 'The boy's not a patch on John's and Gregory's children, of that I'm sure!' was her frequent comment.

Even the incredible news of the previous year, that Napoleon's huge Grand Army had retreated from Moscow, had failed to rouse her. It was as if she was gradually losing her interest in outside matters and was withdrawing into a smaller, more personal world that demanded less effort and concentration from her.

She spent much of her time now sitting half asleep in her chair by the fire; and it was there that Bess found her one afternoon when she came hurrying in with an unusually animated face to see her.

'Mother, are you awake? Look – a letter! A letter from John, and so interesting I had to bring it to read to you straight away. No, don't rouse yourself unnecessarily; if you are comfortable just stay as you are and let me pull the shawl around your shoulders.'

The old lady had opened her eyes with a start and was staring at Bess uncomprehendingly. 'John? John? Is he here?' She shifted herself in her chair to ease the stiffness in her body.

'No, mother.' Bess was forty-six now, and her face was beginning to look careworn, but her smile was as patient as ever. 'Of course John's not here, but he's written such a long, interesting letter. First of all, he and Harriott have had another son. Let me see, what have they called him?' She rustled the pages impatiently. 'Ah, Edward. Yes, that's it! But apart from that good news, his letter is mostly about Gregory. You remember John wrote six months ago that Gregory and two friends had just returned from a long and arduous trek into the interior and found a way across the mountains. You remember – the Blue Mountains? John told us about them, and how they hemmed in the Colony, and everybody wished they could find a way through so that they had more room for all their sheep and cattle? Well, it seems nobody took much notice of their discovery at first, but now everybody is hailing it! The Governor sent out one of his Land Surveyors – wait, I must see what his name is' – her eyes were not as good as they used to be, and she had to hold the letter farther away – 'yes, here it is – George Evans. He followed Gregory's route and came back very excited at all he saw, and – would you believe it? – he named the farthest point that Gregory and his party reached, "Mount Blaxland"!'

Bess had been reading aloud slowly, but with ever increasing excitement. Now she put down the closely written pages with hands that trembled slightly, but her eyes were shining. 'Just think, Mother – Gregory is famous! John says he's sending a full report to Sir Joseph Banks – how it will please the old man, particularly now he's bedridden! Everyone in the Colony is excited, too, and hailing Gregory and his companions as heroes for their great courage and perseverance.'

'Gregory a hero?' Old Mrs Blaxland's tremulous voice broke in on her daughter's rapid flow of words. 'Gregory a hero, did you say?'

'Yes, Mother, yes! John says his name is on everybody's lips, and the Colony certainly has good cause to be grateful to him –'

'Put another log on the fire, child, there's a chill yet in these spring evenings,' interrupted her mother; but for once Bess was not listening to maternal commands. The full significance of what she had been reading was just beginning to reach her.

'Why, Mother, perhaps future generations will remember him for this, particularly if they've named a mountain –'

'For Gregory?' murmured Mrs Blaxland disbelievingly, then shook her head; she gave her daughter an uncertain little smile. 'Oh no, my dear – not for Gregory. John, maybe, but not Gregory – he was always such a naughty little boy. Of course, I loved him dearly – even more than the rest of you, perhaps, but that was because he was the youngest. But he was such a little handful, never working as he should at school and getting into trouble for playing truant, and stealing off into orchards and scrumping apples. He used to love our good Kentish apples....'

Pride, incredulity and bewilderment in quick succession showed on her face as Bess read out the letter; but the effort of following it all had been too much for her. Now the old eyes were closing, as the present slipped away from her consciousness, and the simpler, more kindly past once more enveloped her with its memories. She was a busy, active mother again, with all her children round her, and the youngest Gregory, with his mischievous, lively little face and his strong white teeth biting on a crunchy, stolen apple as the juice ran down his chin....

Bess sighed softly, then collected the pages of John's letter and crept quietly out of the room. Behind her, in the fading light, old Mrs Blaxland's head fell forward on her chest again.

*   *   *

184

On the other side of the world, at Newington, the youngest Blaxland awoke in his crib, yawned, and stretched his small arms as the sun rose up and shone on the distant Blue Mountains, to welcome a new day.